T0269439

MANDATORY REPORTING

MANDATORY REPORTING

A DUBLIN MYSTERY

JENNY WILSON O'RAGHALLAIGH

Published 2024 by Seventh Street Books®

Inquiries should be addressed to
Start Science Fiction
221 River Street, 9thFloor
Hoboken, New Jersey 07030
PHONE: 212-431-5455
www.seventhstreetbooks.com

10 9 8 7 6 5 4 3 2 1

978-1-64506-087-1 (paperback)
978-1-64506-097-0 (ebook)

Printed in the United States of America

The process of therapy is a mysterious one. How do two strangers connect in a way that generates intimacy between them, despite the imbalance of personal information shared? How is it possible to trust another fallible human with your worst fears, worst thoughts, and worst deeds? I am so grateful to all the people who have engaged in the experiment of therapy with me and taken the leap of faith to count on my discretion and professionalism. None of their stories are in these pages.

J Wilson O'Raghallaigh
Dublin, 2024

Mandatory Reporting: the legislative requirement for selected classes of people to report suspected child abuse and neglect to government authorities.

After Amy died, I waited to see what my mother remembered—every day expecting the axe to fall. She was weeks in a coma, months in rehab. Dad carrying her stuff back and forth in an old duffel bag. Family photos, favorite pieces of clothing, anything to try to reclaim their history together.

By the time she came home for her first visit, I knew I was in the clear. She didn't remember what happened. She didn't remember much at all. Even new memories would slide off her consciousness like it was coated in Teflon. The woman who came home from hospital was like an exact physical replica, but with the slate wiped clean. The woman who used to be my mother was dead, and I was relieved.

I remember the dread and shame, but also the understanding that other people couldn't see it. I mean, between one thing and another there weren't a lot of people looking for those emotions. If they'd seen a change in me, they would have put it down to the grief, the loss, whatever. But I knew they didn't know, and they couldn't find out. Like I said, I was in the clear. So long as I kept my mouth shut. And took whatever this new mom had to dish out.

The guilt I don't have to remember. I keep it with me, down in my gut, wrapped in the trappings of confidence and the disguise of indifference. Nobody needs to know the truth now. I can keep it together. I'm not that kid anymore.

1

I can wait here. I've always been interested in watching people. It used to be a survival strategy, but now it's a pastime. And, I suppose, it'll come in handy this year. This crazy year of being someone different.

My phone has been buzzing since I switched from airplane mode. Little updates, little *Don't worry about us!* reminders from my dad. Ten years since the accident, I've worried about them every day. A few words from three thousand miles away is hardly going to change that. He is probably talking to himself.

Standing alone at Dublin Airport, waiting with a bag at my feet that is very nearly too heavy for me to carry, I refuse to consider that I am in the wrong place at the wrong time. There are plenty of people who haven't been picked up. A Chinese guy with a satchel, a blonde girl with very long legs and a backpack. I'm noticing her, but now really I'm just checking her out.

I like tall women. More space for interest, I suppose. The curves are more subtle on the way up the legs.

"Are you Jonah?"

I turn at my name and look down—another woman, much older, much shorter. Not a huge amount of subtlety to the curves, if you know what I mean. Early fifties, I'm guessing. I was expecting a man.

I smile. "Yes, hi. I'm Jonah." There's a pause. "I guess you aren't Mr. O'Connell?"

"That's right! I'm Margaret." She seems very enthusiastic about it. "Niall has had a stroke. We always took the Rotary students, but Niall said he'd do it this year and now he's gone and had a stroke. A total shock to us all, so we said we'd take you. He said to look for a tall young man with dark hair, and you are definitely that! You're very welcome. I'm delighted." Margaret smiles up at me. "I mean, I was looking forward to the break, but no bother! We've done it before and we'll do it again. Happy to help Niall out."

Although what she said suggests that she isn't that happy, she keeps smiling and I go with it. "Thanks. Thanks so much." Poor Niall O'Connell, who was so friendly on the phone. I remember him making a joke about wearing a carnation to the airport so I could spot him. He must be fairly okay after the stroke if he was able to tell Margaret what to look for. Brain injury, though. You never know.

"No bother! I'm parked outside," she says. I pick up the bag, trying not to show how hard it is to lift, and we walk out of the airport together. There's a bright modern walkway that leads to the parking garage which we bypass and then walk down a little sidewalk, past some dumpsters, and into a small parking lot next to what smells like a gym and swimming pool.

Margaret asks questions the entire time, in the same cheerful tone. Where exactly am I from in America? Have I ever lived abroad before? Will my parents visit me while I'm here? I'm sweating like crazy from the effort of hauling the bag and my hand is screaming in pain. Finally, she pushes a button on her keychain and a Lexus lights up. "Pop it in there!" she says as the trunk glides silently open. I do as she says, while wondering why this woman with what looks like a brand-new Lexus didn't pay for parking. Jesus Christ, my hand hurts. I'm sweaty, I've just gotten off an eight-hour flight so I don't smell great to start with, and now I have to sit in this perfect car. I hope it has an air freshener.

Margaret drives through the city on our way to her home. She points out landmarks and tries to explain the bus, train, tram transport system, but I'm taking nothing in. There is something about her voice that is soothing despite its emphatic nature—it's like the last thing she expects is for me to cut in, which is good because I'm mostly concentrating on not stinking up the car. I notice she has her window slightly open.

Very kindly, when we get to her house, Margaret shows me the little apartment out the back I can stay in "until I find something." There is a shower, thank God. And a bed.

2

Looking out the apartment window, I can see directly into the kitchen window of the main house, where Margaret is with her family. I showered, went to bed for a few hours, got up and showered again, and I'm feeling pretty good, especially since I figured out the complex series of switches, pull cords, buttons, and dials that got the shower working and hot. Twice. I decide to walk over and knock on the back door. Just as I get to the house, Margaret comes swinging out with a trash bag and nearly collides with me.

"Speak of the devil! Here he is." Before I know it, I'm sitting on a barstool at a granite and walnut island in her large, open-plan kitchen/living room with a cup of coffee and a stack of buttered toast. Turns out, Margaret has a daughter, Aoife, who is remarkably attractive. Big eyes, perfect skin, long blonde hair, and possibly the shortest skirt I've ever seen in a kitchen. Certainly, a kitchen with a mother in residence. And the daughter has a boyfriend, Ciarán, who knows she's hot. He is sprawled out on the couch next to her looking at me looking at her. While I've been sitting here, he has put his arm around her and doubled the amount of space he's taking up with manspread. I get it. There is also a series of younger siblings who move so quickly through the house I can't tell how many of them there are. The husband, Mick, isn't home yet from work, they tell me.

"So, here you are, Jonah," says Margaret, "in Ireland for the year! What are your plans? Did Niall tell me you are an engineer?" Margaret is making a complicated vegetable dish which requires a lot of chopping. Next to me on the island is a very high-tech food processor and there is a periodic rumble as she jams things in through the opening at the top and the blades whir. Being in a kitchen with a busy, active mother takes me back. In the past ten years I've spent a lot of time in other people's kitchens, looking for this feeling—cozy and safe, controlled chaos. I've had girlfriends' parents want to keep me after the inevitable breakup, they're so used to me taking up space in their kitchen. I think of Georgia's dad, who saw my transcripts from college and told me he'd like to buy stock. In me.

"Well, yes," I say, and it's true, I am an engineer, just not at the moment. This year, I am completely winging it. The only thing I know for sure is I had to get away from home. Far away. "Although," I say to Margaret, "I'm trying something a little different this year."

I would have liked to stick to the original plan, and this is not it. The truth is, I was months from graduating with a degree in engineering from the University of Virginia with a funded PhD fellowship in robotics at MIT lined up, when out of the blue, my freshman history professor suggested I apply for a Rotary International scholarship to go abroad for a year after graduation. Out of habit, I said no. I'm needed at home—I'm always needed at home. But it gnawed at me. A way out? Too far to come home every weekend, and no one could blame me for taking up the opportunity. A break. I dropped it into conversation with my dad, testing the waters, and he got right on board, insisting I apply. "We'll be fine," he said, and I chose to believe him.

It all fell into place like it was meant to happen. A couple of interviews later I was granted the scholarship for a course of my choice in Ireland. Check. A research team in the department of engineering at Trinity College agreed to take me on. Check. MIT let me defer the doctorate a year, the money was in the bank, and the airplane ticket was bought. Check. Check. Check.

Then, weeks before I was due to leave, I got a call from the engineering department at Trinity to say the professor I was under was going on immediate sabbatical and they'd have to rescind the research year offer. Something serious must have happened, but they didn't tell me what—all very discreet, with more than a faint whiff of scandal. I offered to switch from robotics to mechanical, or even computer engineering, but whatever had happened to make that guy go on leave had tainted every decision he'd made—I was clearly not welcome anywhere in the department.

My first reaction was relief, a lifting of the extra guilt I was carrying at planning an escape. Things could stay the same. My life during the week, my mom's life on the weekends. When I told my dad, though, he balked.

"Oh, you're going," he said, and he seemed so invested, it was like it was his plan from the beginning. "You call them back at Trinity, and they'll figure something out." And he was right, as usual. Graduate admissions clearly wanted to keep my money-up-front foreign student tuition money, so they suggested a couple of one-year master's degree courses that take high achieving graduates from any undergraduate discipline: gender studies or applied psychology. I sure as hell knew I didn't want to do Gender Studies.

"So, you're doing psychology?" Aoife is enjoying the story. Or possibly enjoying the effect her attention on me is having on Ciarán.

"Yep. It's very unexpected." An understatement. I had seriously thought about scrapping the whole enterprise despite my father's enthusiasm. I sent an email updating Professor Crehan, the robotics guy at MIT, and put feelers out about canceling the deferment. He sent a quick response: *Nonsense. Do it. At this unfortunate stage in our development, our well-designed technologies have to interact with erratic and unpredictable humans. The more we understand about psychology, the better. And I'm sorry to say we don't spend enough teaching time in our profession on the eccentricities of our species. You will be a much better asset to the team after the experience. See you next year.* Not my first choice, but now that I'm explaining it in this nice warm kitchen, I've got a little perspective on the whole thing. I look back at Aoife, sitting with her legs crossed, and this isn't so bad. This isn't torture.

Ciarán shifts in his seat. "There's going to be a lot of chat on that course. You must be really in touch with your feminine side." Aoife laughs and leans back into him. Margaret dumps carrots into the big machine and the rumble intensifies. Some of the carrots stick in the tube. Too many in at once. Humans and technology.

"And what's wrong with that, Ciarán?" Margaret's voice is light and cheerful, teasing, as she turns back to the large stove behind her. Things bubble on the surface and there are about seven separate doors on the front of it. She bends down and opens one of the lower doors and there's what looks like a stack of plates inside, presumably warming, but it looks like she is cooking dinnerware. I'm trying to think of a comeback for Ciarán but I'm tired and slow, despite my nap. One of the little kids comes skidding into the kitchen and climbs up on the stool next to me.

"What's for tea?" This must be the Irish version of the universal question of every child in every kitchen.

It happens fast. Margaret turns to answer as the little hand reaches into the tube after the stuck carrots, pushing toward the blades. I'm off my seat, lifting the kid up and back, fingers out of danger, feet dangling, before Margaret can even cry out. Not so slow, after all. There's a moment of silence, then the release.

"Oh, sweet Jesus!" Margaret rounds the island and grabs the kid out of my hands, shock turning to frustration. "What's wrong with you?" She pulls the squirming body in close and strides out of the room as Aoife stands up.

"What happened?" Ciarán is a few beats back.

"Liam nearly cut his arm off." Aoife has swept around the island and taken up her mother's position at the stove, significantly improving the view from my seat. I hope she checks the plates.

"Maybe a finger or two," I say, switching off the food processor.

"You were quick," says Aoife. "Only in the door and a hero. No doubt down in the annals of family lore. The day that nice American student saved Liam."

"My mother's not great in the kitchen so I'm always on the lookout for danger," I say, grinning at her again. "You have to be ready for action in my house."

"Is that right?" says Aoife, smiling. It occurs to me the heat isn't just coming from the stove.

I'm sure Ciarán notices too. Just to piss him off, I turn up the wattage on my attention. Plenty of eye contact. Asking questions, leaning in.

3

I have about a week before classes start and I need to find a place to live. I'm sure if I act helpless enough for long enough, Margaret will let me stay in her cozy little place out back but I'm not sure it's a smart move. I've lived in various suburbs all my life and one perk this year is a chance to live in the city.

There is an email from the psychology course suggesting a get together to meet everyone later in the week. That is different. Engineers don't tend to have pre-course meet ups. Either you talk to the person sitting next to you on the first day of class or you don't. Generally, you don't.

Walking through the iron front gates of Trinity and under the wide arches leading to a massive courtyard, I am surrounded by beautiful gray stone buildings and impossibly short grass carefully cordoned off from tourists. I dodge a man in a long academic robe and cap offering tours, and follow a series of signs for student services. When I finally locate the office through one of the thick wooden doors built into the square, there's a student accommodation woman and a ridiculous number of slightly grubby-looking people with big bags standing in front of her. The line is so long I have to follow it back outside through a side door, and I am standing on cobblestones wondering if this is the most efficient way of managing the situation, when two guys who look a lot alike come up to me.

"Are you looking for somewhere to live?" one of them asks me.

I'm looking at the two of them and I'm thinking *Freaks* but I say, "Yes."

"Right, so," says the other one. "I'm Michael, this is Peter. We have an apartment with two bedrooms up in Christchurch and we are letting out the other room and staying together in the one room. We're brothers, see, and if our parents pay for the apartment but then someone else pays us rent, we have more money for drinking. See? But we don't want any lunatics."

I'm realizing now that they are identical twins, but with differently styled, sandy-colored hair. If you can call their hair "styled."

"I'm not a lunatic," I say. Their logic makes sense. Also, this could possibly get me out of this line.

"What are you studying?" Peter asks.

I would so love to say engineering here. I nearly say it, but I can't.

"Psychology."

"Oh, fuck," Michael says, half-turning to his brother. "Forget it. I can't be arsed talking about my feelings all day." They share a look and I know I'm losing them. I can't believe that I am now the freak. Peter starts looking at the line behind me. It's now or never.

"Listen," I say, "I don't give a shit about your feelings, or anyone's feelings, really. I got a grant and it was the only course open. Basically, I'm screwing around for the year. I'm an engineer and after this I'm going back to engineering. To work on robots, for Christ's sake. No feelings."

"Do you have a girlfriend?" one of them asks me. We all know he is asking if I'm gay, but to his credit, he's trying to be subtle.

"Yes, her name is Georgia." I look directly back at him. "But she's in New York. She's coming over to visit later in the year with her sisters." There are no sisters but that swings it. They give each other a more positive look. It pays to be able to tell a good lie quickly. A skill that has served me well.

"Grand," says Michael. I think it's Michael. "A hundred euro a week, cash, on Mondays. Don't fuck with our food and don't drink our drink. And you have to get out if our parents visit or pretend to be visiting if they turn up unannounced. And if one of them stays over, you sleep somewhere else. Agreed?"

I would do anything right now to be away from this line, even live with these two. It's only a year. "Agreed. What are you studying, by the way?"

"Social work," says Peter. There's a pause. "Just fucking with you. Business. We don't give a shite either." He grins at me. This might turn out okay.

4

I decide to go to this pre-course meetup. I've gotten several emails about it—mostly copied into reply-alls. Probably all women, I think, but a few unclear: Pat, Terry, Frances. Any man in the US named Frances would do everything he can to be called Frank but I'm not sure it's a thing here. My dad knew a guy in the service named Richard Head and it still cracks us up. He loves to tell the story of how the guy introduced himself as "Richard" and said it twice looking straight at you: Richard Head. Richard. What a couple of comedians his parents must have been.

The class is meeting in the Stag's Head and Michael/Peter walk down to show me where it is, although I assure them I can use GPS as well as the next man. A couple days in and the apartment is working out fine. There is probably a bit too much PlayStation for my taste but they're clean enough and they seem happy to show me the ropes. I'm hoping they won't come into the pub with me, but they do. The meetup was at eight and it is near nine now, but the bar isn't crowded and I'm pretty sure I spot the class right away. There's about a dozen earnest-looking women sitting around a few small tables, maybe a few around my age and then some much older. All of them look like they've known each other for years. The three of us are standing at the bar and right then I decide there is no way I'm going over there. Class next week is soon enough. I turn to the boys.

"I'm not going over there."

"Fuck right, you're not," says Peter. "You've got to spend that grant money on my dry throat." He is already trying to catch the bartender's eye.

"Nobody over there is fit enough to stop drinking for," says Michael. "Although that granny might start looking better after a few."

I look and there is a stylish older woman wearing purple Doc Martens looking right at me. I pretend I've dropped something on the floor and bend down to pick up nothing. When I glance again on the way up, she is talking to the woman next to her. All in all, there is a great deal of eye contact in the group. And nodding. Jesus Christ. What am I getting myself into? I'm not sure I've ever been as sincere as they look.

"That's more like it," says Michael and I follow his gaze over to the other end of the bar. Ah yes, I can see what he means.

5

I wake up in an unfamiliar bed but clear headed. Thank God I didn't try to keep up with the twins' drinking. The shoulder next to me is bare and has a small dolphin tattoo rising over the shoulder blade like it's breaching a wave. There's a sheet obscuring the rest of my view but the hourglass of the back, waist, and hip looks promising. I remember a class on design that talked about the right waist-hip ratio being the most attractive thing in the human experience. I'm tempted to place my hand on the lowest point of the curve but I'm not inclined to start a conversation, yet. I didn't drink too much and I'm pretty sure I can clearly remember this girl's face if I concentrate. And her name.

She shifts around and looks me in the eye. "Hi." Her voice is a husky whisper.

"Hi."

"I'm Sailí." She smiles and there is a dimple. I'm a sucker for dimples. No wonder I'm here.

"I know who you are," I say. "I wasn't drunk." I wasn't sober, either, but I remember every move.

"Me neither, I'm a tart. I'll go to bed with anyone."

Not sure how to respond to this, I smile.

"Just messing," she says. "I was a bit merry."

"I know," I say, assuming that means tipsy. "I was the one buying the drinks. And clearly making the most of the fact that we were drinking them."

"That's grand," she says, lying back on the pillow and adjusting the sheet, her heart-shaped face surrounded by loose caramel curls. "I was seriously considering bringing you back here before the second drink. Handsome and charming Americans, that's my weakness. I hope you're rich. The Stag's Head is fierce for attracting rich tourists. I've done some of my best hunting there."

"Well, I hate to let you down." Not rich, but not poor. I'm enjoying this.

"Hmmm . . ." She stretches. I think there are two dimples but the second one is a bit harder to spot. "Well, there's always tomorrow."

Although I'm in a different country, this situation is not all that unfamiliar to me. Light banter while looking for my boxers. I find them and offer to bring Sailí a glass of water. She accepts and while I'm searching for glasses in the kitchen alcove off the living room, I see a French press and some Lavazza so I upgrade my offering and make coffee. There is a reflective surface on the microwave and I bend down to check out the damage. My hair is long enough on top to need a pat down to control it, but my light-blue eyes are clear. Not too bad after the late night. I wash my face at the kitchen sink, rinse out my mouth, and plunge the coffee. Walking back to the bed, I notice stacks of canvas leaning against anything that will hold them up. On the walls are works with intense colors and a lot of straight lines. Everything else is white.

"Well," she says, "this is a treat." While I've been making coffee, I'm pretty sure she has brushed her hair and maybe even put on some make-up—she looks good but I'm missing that messed-up and sleepy vibe. I didn't hear a sound and the room looks exactly as I left it. Also, she has put on a very pale pink nightshirt. Show's over.

"You look nice," I say. "Can I buy you breakfast?" She smiles and I think she has probably brushed her teeth already too. Clearly this situation is not unfamiliar to her either—she is like a one-night-stand superhero.

I'm surprised when Sailí says she has to work and I get the sense she is waiting for me to go, so I drink my coffee and start my exit. I ask for her number and she calls it out to me, but there is no sense of urgency and she doesn't check to see I've got it right. All in all, it was a very pleasant encounter but I'm guessing I won't be seeing Sailí again. I will text her, though, hopefully on the right number. I'm fond of that little dolphin.

I head out into the sunshine and my phone beeps insistently. For some reason a pile of text messages come through from home all at once—probably whatever international plan I have has delayed things. I scan through them and nothing seems too urgent, but the familiar weight crashes back. Dad is trying out a new home care provider to cover the weekends—my shift—and so far, it's going okay. We've tried it before, a series of kind and organized women coming in to cook and keep my mother out of trouble, but no one has lasted. She can be vicious.

6

Turns out "Frances" with an "e" is always a woman. In this situation, so are Pat and Terry. At the edge of Trinity College are some awkwardly shaped buildings and in one of them I am seated in a room, in a circle, with fourteen women on the first day of class. Purple boots is here and I recognize a few more from the pub, but in the small talk I don't mention it. Class has started and we are going around the room saying who we are and how we have ended up on the course, and I am getting the impression that I am the only person here by a bizarre series of random events. Most of the stories involve big life changes and the desire to help other people get through what they've gone through. A couple of them are hoping to change careers and, I swear to God, two have already started crying. One woman, a banker trying to find meaning in her work, started crying before she even spoke, and it made her story a little hard to follow.

When it comes to me, I refuse to wreck the love and gratitude theme so I say something about adding depth to my understanding of other people and everyone nods and nobody says, "What kind of crap is that?" so I'm good. I suppose it is technically true, even if it is for the benefit of the robotics industry.

The good thing about being in a big group, I have learned over time, is that it is possible to say almost nothing. You have to stay awake, look interested, and nod. Day one lesson. My presence is markedly conspicuous, though. First of all, I'm the only male. Secondly, I take up a lot more room than anyone else, my legs stretched out into the circle. And finally, I am way behind everyone else in terms of understanding what the hell is going on. That, however, may not be noticeable since I am very nearly completely silent.

After the introductions, Annemarie the instructor starts talking about the lifelong importance of early psychological development and shows us some footage of experiments they did with toddlers and their mothers in the 1970s on emotional attachment. Everyone seems familiar with this but me. Basically, they separated the kids from their moms and filmed what happened. Sometimes they'd send in a stranger and see how the child reacted. Then the kid-mom reunion. It is surprisingly interesting to watch the old footage—some of the kids completely freaked out and other ones looked okay; they played with the blocks or whatever was there. Some of them got on well with the stranger and some didn't.

Turns out, she explains, the kids who freaked were the normal ones. That, I was not expecting. The little fists pounding on the door, the total rejection of the stranger, the screaming. Then the mother comes in and they wrap their pudgy little arms around her and settle right down. That's the "normal" sequence. The little guys who interact with the stranger or sit there waiting: not so normal. Numb, or desperate. Not really counting on the mother to come back. Ready to go it on their own, I guess. It makes me wonder which one I was, back before the crash. Even though Amy was only eighteen months younger than me, I can remember her as a happy baby in my mother's arms, but maybe that was when she was older. They were always close, that I know, but I can't pull up the memories of myself. There are photos of me as a little kid, holding hands with her, sitting tight on the couch. But those are the moments when everybody takes pictures. It isn't necessarily the truth. By the time Amy died, my mother could barely look at me. The question nearly makes me want to call her and ask what I was like as a baby or a toddler, but I'm not sure that's such a good idea. I know she would tell me the truth, if she could remember it.

After lunch, Annemarie tells us to break into pairs for an exercise. Paired work, a teaching strategy I have learned to dread. There's always someone who doesn't do anything. I look at the woman to my right and she is decidedly looking to her right, so I sweep around to my left and come face to face with purple boots.

"I'm Rose," she says.

"I'm Jonah."

"Like the whale?"

"The dude *in* the whale, actually. The one who gets vomited out." I smile at her, and she smiles back.

Annemarie tells us we're doing "insight dialogue" where one person talks and the other person listens without comment or movement. Then after five minutes the listener has to repeat what they've heard. We aren't even supposed to nod or make the usual mmm-hmmm noises people make when they're listening. When Annemarie tells us the topic for the exercise is "early experiences with our mother," I have a sense of rising dread. I would rather be on fire than starting this assignment, on fire with needles in my eyes. What the fuck am I doing on this course? Who am I kidding?

I keep my shit together and turn to face Rose, who seems okay to go first. Annemarie starts the clock, and Rose begins.

Rose doesn't look at me while she is speaking, so it is easy for me to keep my poker face. Instead, she mostly looks at the floor and sometimes closes her eyes. I can see the dark iron mixed in the light gray and silver of her hair, and her dark eye lashes. She speaks in a low voice, very quickly, about her early days on a farm. I have to lean forward to hear her clearly when she describes her mother. As she talks, I can see a movie version of what she is saying: a table with not enough chairs and children standing at the corners; out in the morning and back in for food; a scramble of arms and legs climbing into beds pushed one against another; and an unknowable force moving around it all, pushing in, pulling out, and rounding up. I'm watching Rose speak as if she is in a trance, like it doesn't even matter that I am here. I am not sure I have ever listened to someone for five minutes without something, even me, interrupting. It is possible that Rose's voice is getting softer, so I lean in more. There is a pause in her rhythm, and I freeze. Before she starts again, the time is up.

Annemarie gives us two minutes to summarize what we've heard. I try to recount Rose's story and I can hold onto the facts of it, but I'm missing the flavor. Instead of repeating what she has said, I have an urge to ask her questions about the house, her mother, and siblings that I have to suppress. I'm aware that my accent is in danger of making her story sound like a Hollywood plotline, just what I was imagining. After my two-minute summary, it is time for feedback and Rose confirms that I got the gist of it.

Suddenly I realize that it is my turn to speak. Annemarie starts the clock again and I begin: my early experiences with my mother.

Or not. I look at Rose looking back at me and I don't even open my mouth. I maintain eye contact and then look away, at my shoes, the wall, anywhere. I close my eyes and after a moment Rose shifts in her seat. I open my eyes and hers are closed. I close my eyes again and instead of going back in time, I see her as she is now, a beautiful woman. They had me young and she's only in her early forties now, although she looks thirty. Tall, athletic frame, with the class of beauty that sets her apart from other women—beauty you cannot pretend is not there, even if you are her son. Probably every boy experiences his mother as beautiful without even thinking about it, but so many people commented on it when I was small, it was like wallpaper in my life. All around. So normal. The weird thing was realizing other moms didn't get that kind of attention. Before they stopped coming over, I remember seeing my friends looking at her, or trying to stop looking at her, for the same reason. When Georgia met her the first time, I could see a little shift happen in her mind, although she never said anything. I saw it because I was watching for it, used to seeing it. Luckily, Georgia is no slouch in the looks department. Other girlfriends found it difficult, for sure. Especially with how she is now.

Annemarie says the time is up. I haven't said a word. It's time for Rose to summarize what I've said.

I look at her and she says, "You didn't say a word, you bastard. How am I supposed to summarize that?"

I catch the twinkle in her eye. "Couldn't you hear me?" I ask. "It was a very moving story." We agree that she got the gist of it.

7

From what the other students say, I discover this course I've gotten myself into is competitive and expensive. A one-year master's degree in applied psychology, covering things from counseling skills to forensic assessments. As a foreign student I pay much more than they do, which might explain my presence in their midst, but because of the scholarship I'm not personally paying for it at all. Like I didn't really compete for it, but I don't say that either. Many of my classmates are planning to go on to train as clinical psychologists, which I gather is a dog-eat-dog PhD process with about a hundred applicants for every space across the country. Several others are trying to transition from generic administrative positions into human resources, and one woman is a prison guard trying to deepen her understanding of criminals. I listen to their plans with my studied nodding, but I can't imagine intentionally moving into a career full of misery. Surely life offers enough without actively looking for it.

Because of all the want-to-be helpers, there is a practical experience element to the course which includes working with practicing psychologists in mental health settings and attending personal therapy; we are required to do both to pass. This is how I find out that I must engage in therapy myself, for real. The surprises keep coming and I have to keep acting like I'm expecting every complication, like everyone else. At the end of the day Annemarie hands out envelopes with our clinic placement information in them, and a list of psychotherapists who offer student rates. She recommends we attend a therapist at least once a week for twenty sessions. That is once a week for five months. Or twice a week for two and a half months. I didn't even realize it was possible to go twice a week until one of the students mentioned she'd been in therapy twice a week for a year. Jesus Christ. Still, if I start right away, I could be finished by Christmas. I figure I can manage anything for two and a half months if I have to. But do I?

I try to catch Annemarie on my way out, making a quick left to tap on her office door.

"Come in!" I hear, and when I enter, she is seated, leaning surprisingly far back in a leather swivel chair. In front of her is a huge desk completely covered in paper. On the floor are high stacks of books and journals, and I'm not sure I've ever seen this much stuff in one room. "Sit down, Jonah," she says when she sees me, but there is nowhere to sit. Two additional chairs are holding folders and who knows what else, and Annemarie makes no move to clear them. I stay standing.

"Annemarie," I say, and as I look at her my confidence wavers. Her hair is cut in a short bob, and she looks too young to have it snow white. Her wide green eyes are looking at me like I had better have something important to say. "I was wondering about the personal therapy and the placement."

"Oh, yes?" Her gaze does not waver and she is not smiling.

"I know it is a requirement of the course, but does that apply to me as well? I'm not sure I'm continuing in psychology."

"Is that right?" she asks. I can tell by her tone of voice that this was a bad plan. I've known a lot of teachers in my life. "Jonah, I have given you a place on this course, but you should know I thought very carefully about it when graduate admissions called me. I reviewed your academic record and considered the whole engineering/robotics angle and decided, yes, I would take a chance. You may have noticed, if you've been paying attention, that there are a few people on the course from nonpsychology backgrounds. It could be good for everyone, shake things up a bit. Add a bit of perspective about how psychology is applied in different settings. Now that you are on this course, it is my expectation that you will complete it in the same manner as every other student—with one hundred percent effort. I will support you however I can, and one way I am doing that is by sending you to an extremely skilled and experienced supervisor." There is a pause. "Jonah, there is no *applied psychology light* course.

If you sincerely think this isn't right for you, go talk to graduate admissions."

And what, go home? Gender studies?

"I'm on board," I say. "Really. I'm sorry I asked." I put on my sincere face, and I see amusement work the corners of her mouth.

"Okay," she says, turning back to the mountain of paper. "Good luck." I won't be trying that again in a hurry. "And Jonah?"

I'm nearly out the door but turn back. "Yes?"

"I know it goes without saying, but I'll say it anyway. This course is competitive. We are at Trinity College, Dublin. I understand you are used to excelling wherever you go—like I said, I've seen your perfect transcripts, and I'm sure you have big plans for the future. I'd like for you to also be successful here." She and I are looking at one another and any outsider might think those were words of encouragement. But she's said the magic word. Transcripts. I know when I hear a threat.

Leaving Annemarie's office, I pass through a hallway, down some steps, through the foyer, and into the fresh damp air of the afternoon, deciding on my way to suck it up and get on with things. I find a dry spot on a bench in a small flower-filled garden and sit in the weak sunlight. The first few numbers on the list lead to voicemails, but I finally set up a meeting with a guy walking distance from the apartment who will see me in two days. He answers his own phone and we set up an early morning time. I tell him I'm interested in twice a week therapy and he says we'll decide that when we've met each other. Whatever.

Since I have the phone out anyway, I call home. The landline. My mom isn't great with cell phones or text messages and it's easier to judge what's going on for her if I can track changes in her tone, anyway.

She answers immediately, and I imagine her sitting in her chair by the kitchen window, right by the phone. The type of phone that is attached to the wall, with one of those curly wires—like she would have used as a little girl. Easy and familiar.

"Hey there, how you doing?" I ask. "It's Jonah."

"I'm good, baby," she says, and I start to relax. A good day. "How are you? Met any nice Irish girls?"

My mother pretty much forgets, or refuses to remember, Georgia. She asks me about my love life as if I am continuously on the make—although maybe she has a point. Georgia was clear with me that I should do my own thing over here, but maybe it shouldn't be this easy.

"Nah. Not really. How's the weather?"

"Really beautiful. The leaves are all starting to change. I keep thinking your father is going to have a heart attack with all the raking. If you or Amy were here, it would be such a help to him." She sighs but it sounds light enough. When she mentions my sister, my chest tightens, but it's a familiar sensation and an old story. I can't do anything about it. Or undo.

As usual, I only respond to the positive stuff. "I'm glad it's so pretty, Mom. I can picture you there at the kitchen table looking out at it. Everything is good here. Is Dad there?"

"He's at work." Another sigh, but nothing else.

"I might call him in a while," I say. "Is anybody with you there?"

"That's a great idea," she says. And hangs up.

I call my dad and have a normal person conversation. He laughs his ass off when I talk about the class, and how I have to do therapy.

"Maybe it's a good thing," he says, sounding almost serious. "God knows everyone tried to get us into therapy years ago. I just didn't expect you to do such a deep dive." He knows this is killing me.

"That's great, Dad. Very helpful." I am also on the edge of serious but my tone is light. "I talked to Mom and she sounded good. Is she there on her own?"

He answers me with the same light tone, even though it's not my place to be checking up on him. I'm the one who isn't there anymore. I'm the one who moved three thousand miles away. "Oh, she's fine. I'm only out for an hour, and I've alarmed the doors. We're keeping the normal schedule by and large. I'm sure she was glad to hear from you. I put a memory board up in the kitchen to remind her where you are, and I've got lovely pictures of Ireland and Trinity College on it."

"She mentioned Ireland, all right," I say. "How's the new home-care woman working out?" Dad left the military when our lives changed and started working for a defense industry contractor. The money more than tripled and we never had to move on assignment again, so Mom didn't have to learn a new place. As time passed, Dad and I could manage her care most of the time between us, with him working early mornings and home by the time she'd be getting restless. But I was the weekend man during college so he could make up his hours at work, focus on special projects, whatever. Now that I've made a break for it, that's not possible. Getting someone in to help was always a mixed blessing in the past. Sure, we'd get a breather, but then something would happen to make it more trouble than it was worth.

"So far, so good," he says. "I've told her to keep her distance, and her English isn't great, so that might help." He's joking, but he isn't. My mother's unpredictability has smoothed out a little in the last couple of years, but it's still there, barely under the surface. Anger, fear, sadness, even happiness, all extreme when they happen, and quick to change. Emotional lability, the neuropsychologist called it. I have a scar on the side of my head from when she threw a cast iron skillet at me when I was fifteen. What was I going to do? Complain? After what I did to her? To Amy?

And then we move on. Not much left to discuss on an issue we've covered a thousand times. He fills me in as much as his security clearance will allow on his latest project at work, and I tell him about the twins. Some sports stuff and then we're done.

I get off the phone, take a deep breath, and call Georgia. She's at NYU for a master's in marketing and design and I can imagine her impeccable body moving from one class to another with ease. Shoulder-length, poker straight dark hair and a slight almond shape to her eyes hints at an Asian heritage. The softest skin I've ever touched. Georgia doesn't answer so I leave a message which borders on the pornographic. Five minutes later I get a response text which I'm going to have to think about later, in the shower.

8

I get back to the apartment and as I'm walking in the outside door, Peter greets me with a big toothy smile on his face and a warning in his eyes.

"Hey Jonah! Didn't expect to see you today! How're things?" Clearly one or both of his parents are here.

"Hey Peter!" I say with the same goofy smile and bizarre loud voice to let him know I get it. "I was in the neighborhood and thought I'd stop by!" His grin goes back to its normal ironic twist. We move into the kitchen where, sure enough, there's a floral-covered, fifty-something woman sitting and drinking tea.

"Ma, this is Jonah. The fellow I was telling you about. Jonah, this is our mother, Moira," Peter says, and I can see Michael behind him with the death stare look on his face. These guys suck at this. Anybody could see from about a mile away that they are up to something, much less their own mother.

"Oh, yes," says the mother, "the laptop man!"

"Oh, did I leave my laptop here? Thank God." I say as I pretend to spot it on the coffee table in the living area, where I had left it only hours ago. "I couldn't find it this morning and I thought maybe I'd left it in the library. Thanks, guys, for helping me out with that spreadsheet." I pick up the laptop and cord and jam them in the bag.

"Oh, that's no problem, no problem at all!" says Michael and he still sounds a bit off. I can see his mother throw a look in his direction.

"The library, did you say?" She looks mock serious. "Do they let students in the library? Gentlemen, are you listening? Students! In the library!" she says, turning to the twins now.

"Very funny. Thanks for that, Jonah. She'll be living off that for weeks." Peter switches on the electric kettle and I lean up against the counter.

"It's lovely to meet you, Jonah. The twins told me all about you and your psychology degree. That's so inspiring, wanting to help other people, dedicating yourself to working with the neediest populations. It's good for the boys to see something of the other side of life—the human side. All they think about is money. How's the course going?"

Those fuckers. I look up at Peter's turned back and I know he is silently laughing.

We pass a few minutes talking about the course, and I tell them about the toddler videos. How those early relationships can supposedly influence us all our lives. After a few minutes the mother asks me if I'd like something to eat. This violates the *don't touch the twins' food* rule. Although, with her here, I'm in the role of guest, so that could be different. Surely it would be rude to decline.

"That'd be great, thanks. I'm starving," I say, smiling at her.

"Michael, bring your friend a sandwich, with some of that lovely ham I brought from home. And the crisps."

Michael carefully does not look at me and gets up to start making a sandwich. He clears his throat very deliberately and suddenly I'm not sure I want him making food for me. "Actually," I say, "I just remembered I'm meeting a friend for dinner. I'll wait."

"Are you sure?" says the mother. "A small one?"

"Oh, yes, I'm sure. Positive. Thanks anyway." Michael sits down. It was a good decision, judging by the look on his face.

"Well," she says, "that is so interesting about the baby's attachment to the mother being so strong and all. Sure, I remember with these two I couldn't for the life of me wean them off the breast and then they cried and cried when we sent them to school, even though they had each other, for God's sake! It nearly broke my heart. Weeks and weeks of it."

There's a little pause while I come to grips with the fact that this woman is telling me about breastfeeding these two dickheads I'm living with. I may be doing a psychology degree but I really do not want to have that picture in my head. On the flip side, there is some pleasure in seeing their faces as it dawns on them what I've just been told.

"Well," I say, standing up. "I'd better head off to meet my friend. It was nice to meet you, Mrs. . . ." I suddenly realize I don't know what the twins' last name is. A fleeting sense of panic but then I remember I'm only a friend from college with a spreadsheet problem. I'm not living here with a couple of guys I barely know.

"Moira." She helps. "My name is Moira."

She tells me to be sure to come down to Tipperary to see the "home place" and I assure her I will, reaching down for the laptop bag. By the time I'm on the street I get a text from Peter: *Well done. Thanks. Text you when she's gone. Not one fucking word about the other stuff or you're out.* Priceless.

9

Two days later and I'm walking down James's Street at 7:30 in the morning on my way to my first meeting with the therapist guy. As I pass by St. James's Gate, home of Guinness, there's a tiny one-man truck going along the sidewalk sweeping up litter—probably not a job with the greatest satisfaction in this city. The day is pretty cloudless, though, and maybe it is good to work outside on a day like today. I'm pretty sure the therapist works at St. Patrick's Hospital, which Michael and Peter described as a "nut house" but I think might otherwise be termed an inpatient mental health facility. When I find the address, however, it doesn't seem to be part of the hospital but rather a large Georgian building on the other side of the street with the typical three stone steps up. I look for the right number and find a burgundy-colored door with a button next to it. I push the button and nothing happens. I can't hear a chime or buzz inside. Nobody comes to the door. I rattle the door and it doesn't budge. There's no knocker or handle, so I tap it with my knuckles and still nothing happens. I look at my phone and it is 7:54. If I'm in the right place, there isn't really time to get a coffee, and if I'm in the wrong place, there isn't really time to get where I need to be. I end up standing there huddled in the doorway and waiting for six minutes to pass, the smell of early morning city in my nostrils. The litter collection guy catches up to me and passes by, taking a good look at me in the doorway and then giving me a little nod. At eight exactly I try the button again and there is an immediate soft click. I push the door, it opens, and I walk in.

I'm not sure what I was expecting. Maybe because of the age of the building I imagined leather and wood, a row of dark bookcases. Some Old Masters on the wall. In fact, the room is bright with the windows on two sides letting in panels of natural light. The only furnishings are two light-gray, upholstered chairs positioned in front of a large fireplace, which has an actual fire burning in it. The door I'm coming in opens directly into the room and standing in front of the fireplace facing me is Dr. William Roberts.

Dr. Roberts walks toward me with his hand out and a smile on his face. "Hello, Jonah. Come in, come in."

I notice right away how tall he is; not many men look me directly in the eye. We shake hands and he motions for me to sit down as he closes the door behind me. "I understand from your call that you are doing the master's in applied psychology at Trinity? A fine institution and a fine course. And they require some personal work, which is why you are here, is that right?" He's athletic-looking, perhaps in his fifties, with very light hair and eyes. I wouldn't say I'm at ease, but there is something appealing about the guy. He's wearing dark brown pants and a fine checked shirt, with a tie. When he sits, he crosses his legs and it makes him look very European. Which of course he is. I noticed his shoes are a little unusual. Matte black leather with a buckle on the side. They look like they might be handmade and I'm a little distracted trying to get a good look at them.

"That's right," I say. "Your name was on a list they gave me and I live near here." Even to my own ears I sound a little lame. Like a kid. I try to square my shoulders a little and make a point of maintining eye contact. I don't understand the rising discomfort in my stomach.

"Ah," he says, "the benefits of proximity."

There's a pause and we sit there looking at each other. Finally, he smiles and says, "Perhaps you could tell me a bit about how you came to be on the psychology course?"

Okay. I open my mouth to tell him but then I close it. How honest should I be? I mean, if I'm a total fraud—which I am—does he have some duty to inform the course? Although on the other hand, Annemarie knows I'm an engineer-turned-psychology student so it probably doesn't matter. But it might matter to him.

All the while this is going through my head he sits, his pale eyes observe me and his long-fingered hands rest on his lap. He looks completely relaxed.

"Or perhaps not," he says, smiling again and opening his hands wide. "Perhaps I'll begin by discussing confidentiality. Sometimes people have questions about that." Dr. Roberts goes on to explain that what we discuss is confidential, that he sometimes writes notes that he stores here in this room under a double-lock system to which no one else has access, and that he does not discuss the people he sees with anyone. Legally, he explains, he is obliged to inform someone if he thinks I am a danger to others or myself, or if I discuss someone who might be a danger to children or other vulnerable people. Mandatory reporting, that is called. He pauses.

"So, if I say I'm going to strangle my girlfriend, you'd have to tell someone?" I ask. What? How have I asked this stupid question? Is Georgia a vulnerable person?

"Are you telling me you are going to strangle your girlfriend?" he asks. His face is neutral but his tone is light.

"No. I'm not. I'm joking around. My girlfriend is fantastic."

"Well then," he says, "let's cross that bridge if we come to it."

There is another long pause while I imagine how I would come to the girlfriend-strangling-bridge situation.

"What do you know about therapy, Jonah?" he asks. "Have you ever done this before? Met with someone?" The fireplace is really nice. I think it's marble, although I'd like to touch it to be sure. The scent of the burning reminds me of Boy Scout camp, but different too. At the thought of camp, the muscles of my gut tighten even more. I don't want to think about camp.

I shake my head, trying to breathe slowly. "When I was a kid, my family thought about going into therapy together—like family therapy—but we didn't. It was a tricky time but we got through it. I don't think it would have helped the situation at the time." This statement is pretty close to true. It is also missing a lot.

"I see," says Roberts, drawing out the sound. "Well, there are many different kinds of psychotherapy. I belong to the psychoanalytic school, what I and many would consider the classical underpinnings of all the talking cures. We discuss whatever you bring to discuss. If you bring nothing, we spend time in silence. I do not give advice. Some people find that difficult; some don't. Most find it difficult at times. I know many therapists, and I can suggest others to you if we are not a good fit. Sometimes proximity is not the best way to choose a therapist."

I beg to differ in my head, but I don't say it. Instead, I try to look pensive. I nod. "Well, Doctor, I clearly don't know what I'm doing here. If you are happy to take me on, or whatever it's called, I'm happy to come along. I'd like to attend twice weekly meetings, if that's at all possible." I try to look sincerely interested in the inner workings of my own mind. "I mean, I don't know what your availability is." There is also something hostile-sounding in my tone of voice, and it surprises me. I try a little smile to warm it up.

Another long pause while we look at each other and I absolutely cannot tell what he is thinking.

When Roberts moves, he moves quickly—suddenly standing and all business. "That is perfect, Jonah. Wednesday and Friday mornings at eight a.m. on the reduced student rate." He reaches out to shake my hand, and then hands me a business card with his fee information on it. "We begin next Wednesday. Unless you give me twenty-four hours' notice, you are responsible for the charge even if you don't turn up. I will still be here. See you Wednesday?"

"Great!" I say, and immediately feel like an asshole. Great? "Thank you." Roberts nods and shows me to the exit which is a different door than the one I came in. He presses a button on the wall, there's a click, and he pulls it open. Outside is a street I've never seen before, and I step out, hearing the door click shut behind me. For a few seconds it's like what those kids probably felt stepping into Narnia. Then I remember he's on a corner and figure out the street I'm on now intersects with James's Street. In one door and out another, I guess so you don't run into the next patient. Directly across from this door is a Starbucks and as I inhale, I get the familiar smell of overcooked coffee. There's something Narnia didn't have. I very nearly have to stop myself from skipping on my way across the street.

10

The weekend arrives and Peter/Michael are going to some event in the Pavilion Bar at Trinity that involves drinking and women, and they invite me to come along. Generally speaking, they are good at the drinking part but a little unlucky in the women department—possibly because of the drinking. The whole way down they are laughing their asses off about rugby players and trying to explain to me the complicated politics of rugby followers, soccer fans, and Gaelic games supporters. I understand sports politics in general, but this particular flavor of it, not at all. They keep saying to me that I'll get it when I meet the crowd. I ask a question about cricket, and they nearly choke with laughter. "No one understands it," Peter says, "and sure, who would want to?"

Down at the "Pav," everyone looks normal to me, rugby players or not. I don't really get the event—something to do with the business crowd they're in classes with, but there is plenty of free beer, and as the night wears on more and more people are arriving. I'm standing outside the venue and the sports grounds are stretched out in front of me. The whole scene is so beautiful. An avenue of trees and benches, willowy girls in high heels moving toward me, the sound of laughter behind me. Beautiful. It is so good to be away from home. The muscles of my shoulders loosen.

"Life is good." Michael has arrived behind me and it's nice he sees what I see.

"I was just thinking something along the same lines."

"Admiring the view?" he asks. I have a look around and I

have to admit, Irish women are not hard on the eye. I hadn't been focused on that, but now I am.

Hours later, alone in my own bed, I wake in a sweat with the smell of wood burning in my nose. I am instantly on alert, but there's nothing there. That hasn't happened in a long time.

11

It's Sunday night before I remember to check the envelope they handed out in class last week. My applied psychology placement is with a primary care psychology service out in a place called Castleknock on Mondays and Thursdays. The twins tell me I can get two buses to get there or cycle through the Phoenix Park. They say it's "a handy enough cycle" but as far as I can tell you'd have to be crazy to ride a bicycle through traffic in this city, even though on every corner there are bikes to rent. And I'm not taking the bus. I decide to get a taxi but then remember I have to pay the twins first thing on Monday and I need my cash for that. I'm not sure if I can use my card in Dublin taxis. Looks like I'm back on the bus.

The bus drops me off around the corner from the placement and I walk the last bit. The primary care service is located in a huge old house set back from the road and surrounded by grass and trees. The twins told me this is a rich neighborhood but, compared to where I'm from, everything seems a bit neglected. The houses are big, though, which means a lot with Dublin property prices the way they are, and I wonder how the neighbors like having a health service next door, even if it is disguised as a big Georgian house.

The front door is propped open with a brick and there is an inner door which has a chair stuck in it to keep it ajar. I negotiate my way in past the chair and nobody is there. I walk through the clearly marked reception and waiting area, eventually finding a kitchen, where I spot a surprisingly small woman wearing an apron and a net over her hair.

"Excuse me," I say, and she jumps about a mile in the air. When she has recovered enough to speak, she tells me to go away and come back at nine thirty when the place opens. Instead, I sit in the waiting area. Waiting.

By nine o'clock people start arriving and the receptionist takes me to the kitchen/staff room to wait for Teresa, my supervisor. I notice that everyone comes in and goes immediately to the electric kettle or the toaster. It's like now that they have arrived at work, it is time for breakfast. I accept a kind offer of toast and tea and start being introduced around to everyone. I gather from what they all say that students come and go quite regularly in the service, so they are used to new faces. When I say I'm working with Teresa as my supervisor people nod and say that I'll like her. Some undercurrent in the way they say it makes me think there's a joke I'm not privy to, like I've missed something. Annemarie had described her as "skilled and experienced" and I start to wonder what that might be code for.

Just before ten o'clock Teresa walks in and introduces herself. Now I get it.

One thing I am used to is attractive women. I know that the first meeting with an amazing-looking woman requires a careful balance of nonchalance and warmth that demonstrates you are not intimidated by her beauty: as attentive to her as you are to everyone else. Highly attractive women are used to men who are over-solicitous, just as they are used to men who react to them with brusque indifference as a way of coping. In this moment of our first meeting, I am alert to my potential missteps. I am also aware of every eye in the room catching my reaction.

"Hello," I say in response to her greeting, and shake her hand. I am standing now, and really hoping there is no butter on my fingers, or crumbs on my chinos. "Your colleagues here have kindly given me some toast and tea. I'm still a bit confused by the Irish obsession with toast, but I've decided to go with it."

"A wise move." She nods sagely. "Keeping the natives calm. I'll settle in upstairs and you come on up in a minute or two. Welcome to the team." She turns to leave and I am very careful not to watch her walk away. This is going to be an interesting placement.

I finish the toast, clean my hands, and walk up the stairs. Inside the building is like a house, too, and the stairway has a beautiful sweep to it with a solid, dark banister. The ceilings are high and there is complicated plasterwork around the light fixtures. At the top of the stairs is a huge bathroom with a shower and to the right is a door slightly ajar with the word "Psychology" on it. I push it open further and step in.

Teresa is sitting at a desk against the side wall of the room. She has her legs tucked under her chair and she is leaning forward over the desk, concentrating. I try not to notice the curve of her back or the way the buttons lined up on the front of her blouse are hanging on for dear life. Around the room are small chairs, bins of toys, and bookshelves. The bottom rows of shelves are full of children's books and the top rows are jammed with what look like professional books and journals. The room is big, but there is a lot of stuff in it. When she hears the squeak of the door, she turns to greet me and invites me to sit down.

"Let's figure out this placement, Jonah," she says. "What do you want to learn?"

Suddenly, the whole thing becomes real to me. I have no idea what I'm doing here, and I have no interest in meeting with real people with actual problems requiring them to come to a mental health service. I wouldn't mind sitting in this room talking to this incredible-looking woman, but that's about the limit of my commitment to this service. Right then and there, I decide to be honest. Mostly honest.

"To be completely honest with you, I am not really that interested in learning. Not this, anyway." Teresa raises a gorgeous eyebrow and I tell her the whole story about the scholarship, the engineering, and the pretty pervasive lack of empathy I feel toward the problems of others. Luckily, she meets this information with a guffaw.

"Thank God." She laughs. "To be completely honest with *you*, students at your level are pretty near useless to me because they can't see clients on their own and I end up having to do a ton of training and supervision for pretty much no reward. Your little confession is music to my ears. It'll be nice to have a break from the early-twenties-earnest-caregivers I usually get who want to talk to me about how they are feeling all the time." She rolls her eyes at this last comment and I start to relax.

Between the two of us we work out that I can spend two days a week here doing what Teresa calls "shit jobs" like photocopying, carrying things, and organizing materials, as well as helping with research statistics and maybe work with the administrative staff on some automated appointment system. She will pass my placement, despite the fact that I am not interested in learning clinical skills, and in exchange I will not discuss my emotions with her. Everyone wins. To start with, she hands me a laptop and about two hundred questionnaires to input and analyze statistically. I don't know the statistical package they use in the social sciences, but that's the type of thing I eat for breakfast. That and about a pound of toast, apparently.

12

Her briefing includes a quick rundown of the team. In addition to Teresa, there are three other psychologists: Anna, a staff grade psychologist who is on sick leave; Patrick, who is in clinical training and about six months from qualifying as an independent clinician; and Róisín, an assistant psychologist. The psychology "department" consists of Teresa's room, a smaller second room Patrick and Anna share, and a desk in the hallway. All patient files, she tells me, are kept in locked filing cabinets in either her room or Anna's room.

"Don't you have digitized files?" I ask, and realize after I've said it that it has more than a little potential to sound condescending.

"The Health Service Executive is working on it, Jonah! Someday we'll be in the same century as the rest of the world, but not today." Teresa rolls her eyes dramatically enough that I'm not embarrassed at my question. I collect up my materials and leave her in peace.

The assistant psychologist, Róisín, is camped out at the desk in the hall in a very proprietary manner: one chair and the entire top of the desk covered in well-organized materials; she is making it extremely clear there is no room for anyone else. I take my questionnaires downstairs to the kitchen area and set up at a small table near the window. Opening the laptop, I see the double passwords carefully written out on a Post-it note affixed to the keyboard. Perfect.

I pull out my phone and take a quick YouTube crash course on setting up a spreadsheet in this program. Easy. Each variable has to be named and the parameters quantified. Fill in the data cells well now, and I can worry about the actual statistics later.

I open the first booklet and have a look at all the questions. The form is a behavioral checklist with questions like: *Is your child able to follow one-step commands never, occasionally, most of the time, always?* Or: *Is your child able to get to sleep on his/her own never, occasionally, most of the time, always?* Each question has an answer, and the answers add up to larger numeric scores. I glance over the form in front of me and it looks like this particular eight-year-old kid is a real pain in the ass. Follows instructions: *never.* Sleeps through the night: *never.* Completes schoolwork: *never.* Has conflict with peers: *always.* Each incriminating word is carefully circled in purple ink. At the back of the form there's a space for *Other physical/medical problems,* and the mom or whoever has written in very deliberate purple script: *Stomachache every day—no cause found (allergies?) and migraine.* Next to *Other emotional problems* is written: *Hates school, bullied, no friends.* It occurs to me this kid isn't a pain in the ass—this kid is miserable. Or both: a miserable pain in the ass. I move the form from the top and put it a few down in the pile. I think I'll start with somebody a bit less depressing.

"I saw that." I look up and there is a guy standing at the toaster—of course. "Aren't they meant to be in order?" He's smiling.

"I have no idea," I respond. "I was trying to start with one that isn't so miserable." I leave out the pain-in-the-ass part.

"Good luck with that." He turns around to put some bread in the toaster. "It's not like we get the happy, well-adjusted kids here. I'm Patrick," he says, his back still toward me. Short, carrying a few extra pounds, and wearing a crumpled-looking shirt. "I'm the psychologist in clinical training. I guess you are the new master's student. Welcome."

Patrick turns back around to look at me. "Did you meet Teresa yet?" His face is completely composed and I look back at him without blinking.

"I did," I say, and in that moment something passes between us about how hot she is, and we both grin.

A bit more small talk and Patrick wanders off, promising to help me settle in as much as he can, and I go back to the laptop. Pretty much the entire day is spent organizing the program, and by four in the afternoon I have the variable headings in and I'm ready to start entering in the data from each booklet. However, it turns out that four o'clock seems to be the end of the day in the service. By four fifteen, the lady with the hairnet is back and I take the opportunity to apologize for earlier.

"You gave me the fright of my life," she says, and I apologize again, more earnestly. "Hmm," she says, turning to the dishwasher. "Mind you don't do it again."

I assure her I won't, quickly stash the laptop and paperwork in Patrick's filing cabinet, and flee.

13

In Tuesday's class we have a guest speaker on something called "Gestalt therapy" all day. Apparently, we get introduced to different therapy "schools" throughout the course. Fantastic.

Gestalt therapy, she explains, is about "the whole" of experience: relationships, thoughts, emotions, and "the body," whatever that means. The speaker, Tracey, sits across from one of my classmates and asks her to talk about someone she met on her first day of placement. Meredith starts talking about a depressed man she observed in the clinic where she is on placement. Pretty soon, Tracey and Meredith are in a long conversation about how it feels to be in a room with a depressed person. *Tedious* would be my guess, and then Meredith starts to cry. Tracey stops talking and waits. Meredith keeps crying. I am not sure what is going on, but the silence in the room stretches on and on, and nobody is doing anything about Meredith crying. I want to get some tissues or open a window, or something, when I see purple boots, Rose, staring right at me. She holds my gaze and I sit still. After a while, Meredith stops crying. Tracey says something long and complicated about how Meredith's crying affected her and where she felt the emotion "in the body." Then the exercise is over. Our turn. What a load of bullshit.

Tracey asks us to break into pairs and talk about one of two things: a person we met on our first day of placement or how it felt to be in the room when Meredith was crying. I'm hoping for Rose, but she pairs up with someone else. It's like picking teams as a kid except I'm picked last, by a very thin girl with an English accent, Nancy.

Nancy and I start talking about our placements and she eagerly brings up a woman she met with her supervisor. Nancy describes the woman in a lot of detail: how she looked, her situation at work, her family, and the woman's constant symptom of nausea. She said the woman's hands were shaking and she had a really hard time even looking at Nancy and her supervisor—and she described the nausea so clearly that Nancy herself felt a bit nauseous.

I ask what was causing the woman's nausea and that's it, Nancy says, there is no "real" cause they can find. The woman has been checked out by all kinds of doctors and she's on medication for persistent nausea and she's changed her diet and she's been checked for allergies and there's nothing wrong with her and nothing's helping, which is why she ended up in the psychology department of the hospital, where Nancy's supervisor works. She can barely eat and Nancy describes the woman's extreme thinness—how her skin was almost see-through, with a layer of soft hair. While she is saying this, I am alert to Nancy's own thinness and desperately trying not to look at her arms.

"How did *you* end up nauseous?" I ask and Nancy says she has no clue. She says during the assessment the woman described that sensation of saliva that builds up in your mouth right before you vomit and suddenly her own stomach gave a little warning lurch.

"Jesus Christ," I say, "what if you had thrown up?"

"That would have been a disaster. Can you imagine?" Nancy giggles at the idea.

I glance up and see Tracey the lecturer looking over at us with curiosity. So I get serious quick and ask what Nancy's supervisor is going to do with the nauseous woman, but before she can answer, Tracey tells everyone to switch over to the other person in the pair. I explain to Nancy that I didn't meet any clients so don't have anything to share and she reminds me that I can speak about how I felt when Meredith was crying, instead. Great.

I'm trying to think of what to say when Nancy starts laughing again. "Don't do that. Don't try to construct an answer. Tell me, what did you feel?"

"Uncomfortable?" I say.

"What does that mean?" asks Nancy. That is the type of question I am going to have to get used to, I think.

"Um . . . the absence of comfort?" She looks at me sideways. "I guess I wanted to get her a Kleenex or something. I mean, I'd hate to be sitting there crying in front of everyone." I'm suddenly trying to remember if Nancy had been one of the crying people on day one of the course. I don't think so.

"So, you felt some empathy for her. Did you feel anything in your body?" she says. I'm not sure it was empathy I was feeling for Meredith. More like irritation.

"No." I say, and we look at each other. "I'm pretty sure I didn't." First of all, I don't know what the fuck this is about and secondly, I'm not too interested in getting into it.

Nancy leans in and whispers, "Well, you're good at looking comfortable when you're not. I was watching you when she was crying and you looked like you were really listening and feeling what she was going through. You looked so kind and understanding."

That must have been after I got the signal from Rose to sit still. I'm glad to know it wasn't obvious to everyone. I nod at Nancy and put on a super caring face. She laughs, so clearly I'm better at it when I'm not trying too hard.

14

The class decides to go out for drinks at the end of the day and I follow along with them to Mulligan's, a small, old pub, a couple of streets toward the Liffey. We're in luck and there's space for everyone to sit. I try to buy a round of drinks but they tease me about being the only male on the course and insist that I have to wait a few rounds before buying. A few rounds in and I'll forget my own name, much less that it is my round. I've found with the twins that I can't keep up with the sheer bulk of drinking pints, so I've switched to Jameson to save my bladder. I'm sitting with my back to the corner, a bit jammed in on both sides, so it's just as well. To the right of me is a building discussion about Gestalt therapy and "working with the body," which is way over my head. My new best friend skinny Nancy is next to me on the left, talking with the woman on her other side, so I have a look around. The pub is dimly lit, full of dark wood and upholstered tall and short stools. There are benches along the outside wall and the typical round tables holding our drinks. There's no smoking in the pub (or any pub these days) but it's almost like smoke is rising from the maroon linoleum or the upholstery to add to the ambiance. And the smell of beer is everywhere. There's a definite lack of the "olde-worlde" stuff that is strategically placed around other pubs I've been in, so it's a bit more run down, but also more comfortable.

The women I'm with are really a mixed crowd. Nice, but serious. Even as they describe how sad or confused or worried they are about the people they're meeting, I can see that they really want to be doing what these psychologist surpervisors are doing—figuring out what is wrong and helping people to fix it, or manage it, or whatever. I'm remembering the nauseous woman from the story earlier when suddenly Nancy turns to me.

"So, Jonah, do you have some nice cheerleader at home in America waiting for you?" This catches me completely by surprise.

"Not one," I say, "the whole squad. They're all sitting around with their pom-poms making up cheers for me. It's quite difficult to come up with a rhyme to 'Jonah.' I expect it to take them the full year."

Immediately a few of them pipe up: "Show ya," "Throw ya," "Phone a," "Doughnut." This is a topic that has attracted a crowd.

"Okay, okay," I say. "It's not that hard—although 'Doughnut' is a bit of a stretch. Nobody is 'waiting' for anyone but certainly I have a continuing friendship with a woman who is most assuredly not a cheerleader."

"Oh, a *continuing friendship*. Is that what they call it?" Nancy asks and they all crack up. Maybe I sound like an asshole, but that's what we agreed. The thought of Georgia passes through my mind, and followed closely behind it, Sailí the one night stand. I don't want to think about this.

"What I don't understand," I say, "is what are all of you doing here together when you could be checking out the hot Irish men over there who keep looking over here." That statement provides enough of a distraction to get them off the subject of me and onto the subject of their own relationships. For all her tiny stature, Nancy turns out to be quite the drinker. A few hours roll by and I'm nice and relaxed with the class for the first time. They finally allow me to buy some drinks and when I'm at the bar waiting to place an order, I look down at the woman standing in front of me and recognize the small dolphin on her shoulder, leaping out of the loose-fitting sweater she has on.

"Hey, are you following me?" I lean down and whisper in her ear. She doesn't jump but I feel her body shift a little. She throws a glance back.

"*You* are the one standing behind *me*," she says.

"That's a good point," I say, slowed down by my few whiskeys. "Can I buy you a drink?"

She turns around and suddenly we are very close together, face to face. My body starts to react of its own accord. "Didn't you just see me order, you lou-la?" I don't know what that insult means but the inviting look on her face and the warmth of her body are so pleasant she can call me anything. I have a quick flashback of a different position I saw her in, and I am leaning in for sure now. "Anyway, I'm not really drinking. I'm collecting my mother." I pause. I'm sure I just heard her say the word "mother." In that moment she turns, pays the bartender, and collects a soft drink. Sailí swings back around, gracefully sidesteps me, and heads over to where my class is. My class. Neatly, she purloins a short stool from another table and scoots in next to Rose. The two of them look over at me, clearly having a laugh at my expense. Jesus Christ.

15

The next morning I wake up in my own bed, alone. I'd given Sailí and Rose a wide berth, carefully evaded skinny Nancy's drunken advances, and walked home. Just as well as it is day one of Dr. Roberts. Not wanting to stand out on the street again, I arrive at the door at seven fifty-nine. My watch hits eight and I ring the doorbell. Instantly I hear the click and the door opens at my push. Roberts is standing by the fireplace again.

"Hello, Jonah." He gestures toward one of the chairs. "So we begin."

I close the door and take the seat across from him. He is wearing the same shoes and pants, but his shirt is a much darker shade. He sits.

"Often, Jonah, I won't ask questions. This is your space to fill. Today, however, I must ask a few items for my records and maybe a bit about your childhood. I hope that is agreeable to you?"

The whole situation is surreal and disagreeable but I nod. Roberts goes on to ask about my next of kin, and I give him my father's details. He asks for my current doctor's name, and I give him my family doctor from home but he also suggests I link in with the student general practitioner service at Trinity so I have someone local, and I agree to do that. He gets my address and checks my phone number. He has an old-fashioned clipboard and his script is tight and neat on the page. I can see that he writes down only what is necessary and as soon as he has these details, he puts the clipboard down on the wooden floor, resting his hands lightly on his thighs.

"So," he says, "why don't you begin by describing your family? Tell me what comes to mind."

This is what I should have expected him to ask me, but I just haven't put any thought into it and I'm not prepared. I look into the fireplace and then back at Roberts. His pale eyes are fixed on me, but it doesn't feel like he is pushing for anything. He looks a little curious, that's all, nothing that should be calling up these stirrings of dread. How did I not see this coming?

"That's a little tricky." I notice my mouth is dry. "My family has changed a lot."

"I see," says Roberts, but doesn't drop it. "Tell me what you can."

It's a good way to start, because I honestly don't know how much I can say. I begin with the bare facts, as the rest of the world knows them: "We started out as four but my younger sister, Amy, died in a car accident when I was twelve. She was eleven. My mother was driving and it was a single car accident. Nobody knows what caused it, but the road was wet and they were on an incline, so it could have been anything that led to the car hitting a temporary barrier and flipping."

It could have been anything, but I know what it was, though I don't share that with Roberts. I'm telling him the story as I always tell it, but sweat is breaking out on my forehead and my palms are damp. I keep talking like nothing is happening but he's watching me too closely. I try to take deeper breaths discreetly.

"We do know my sister died instantly and my mother had an injury that landed her in hospital for nearly a year between recovery and rehab. We know, as well, that they were coming home from a ballet exam that had been a complete disaster." I stop there, but the memory comes anyway—three weeks later we got the report from the ballet academy examiner. My dad opened it on autopilot when he was home from the hospital to give me breakfast. A list of criticisms from the last time his daughter danced.

"What were your mother's injuries?" Roberts cuts in and I'm nearly surprised to hear his voice. I look over and he meets my eye. Same open curiosity.

"She did okay," I say. "I mean, she recovered well. She was in a coma for a while but she made progress quickly once she was conscious. She needed time. If you saw her now, you wouldn't even know she had been in an accident." I stop and Roberts doesn't say anything. I stare into the fire. Eventually, I say it: "She had a brain injury."

Those words. I must have said them a thousand times. To friends, to neighbors, to people at the cash register in Walmart during one of her meltdowns.

There's another long pause and Roberts says, "Your family has changed a lot." For some reason, I am suddenly pissed off. My shoulders stiffen and about a dozen sharp retorts spring to mind. It takes all my energy to sit there, not moving or saying anything. I glance back at Roberts and he holds my gaze. I can tell he knows I'm angry and that slows down my reaction. What the fuck do I care what this asshole thinks? Any response from me now is a win for him. I hold myself completely still and silent. Then Roberts speaks.

"Can you describe what your mother was like before the accident?"

A thousand things crowd into my mind, and my throat closes. I don't think I could speak if I wanted to. Roberts looks at me with a neutral expression, even though I'm sure he sees my reaction. Suddenly the smoke from the fireplace fills my nose and my lungs are fighting for each breath, a band of muscle across my chest tightens and my heart beats faster and faster. My peripheral vision begins to darken and I lean forward on the chair, closing my eyes and concentrating on slowing down my breathing. There is something familiar about this that is just out of reach. I'm not looking for it.

Eventually, I begin to calm down, but I'm still not talking. How did we get here so fast? When I open my eyes, my vision is clear and Roberts is still there, his body relaxed, his hands resting lightly in his lap. Nobody says a word.

After an interminable amount of silence, Roberts says, "That's our time," and stands up. I stand up, too, trusting that my legs will hold me despite their weakness, and I put a bit of effort into my posture so I end up about an inch taller than him. I'm not sure he notices as he ushers me out the second door but it helps me feel stronger, better, more myself. At the Starbucks, they ask if I want to join the loyalty program and I don't. Why the fuck would I come back?

16

The twins think it is hilarious that Sailí has turned out to be purple boots Rose's daughter.

"I told you she was the finest granny there," says Michael. "The apple doesn't fall far from the tree, and all that!"

They claim that unless I did something really, truly embarrassing with Sailí in the privacy of her apartment, I have nothing to worry about. So long as I didn't "let us all down," whatever that means. I don't ask them a lot of questions on this; I think it is better that I don't know.

Having seen her in the pub, however, I'm reminded that I said I'd call her, and now that she is linked to my classmate, I should probably get on that. Or maybe *because* she is linked to my classmate, I should leave well enough alone. Sailí is, however, a very attractive woman, which luckily tips the balance of my decision-making. I send a quick text and get nothing back. Perhaps this decision is being made elsewhere. I can wait.

Back in the clinic, no one seems to mind my workstation set up in the kitchen. People talk to me when they come in for tea and/or toast and I am slowly getting to know the place. In addition to psychology, there are also speech and language therapists, social workers, psychiatrists, and a couple of family doctors. The idea is that people can come and access whatever services they need. According to Patrick, there's a good deal of "aggro" at the team meetings on Wednesdays, but everyone is nice to me and I get on with the questionnaires. Now that I have all the variables loaded up, I start entering the data. It turns out I need to calculate what are called "standard scores" from the totals on the sheets and, for that,

Patrick tells me I need the conversion tables in the manual. This gets me back up in Teresa's office between her therapy appointments. I explain to her what I need and she looks for the manual in her office, in the hallway at the psychology desk, and eventually finds it in the second office. I very happily follow her from room to room "looking" and feel a bit let down when it is finally located. She shows me how to use the tables at the back to calculate the scores and then surprises me with a question: "Are you okay, Jonah?" She is looking at me closely.

"I'm good." I wonder why she is asking. What can she see?

"You look a little tired. I hope I'm not neglecting you, it's a busy time. With Anna still away from work, I'm flat out."

"No, no, I'm fine. Just out late, I guess. I hope Anna is okay. Did you say she is sick?" The truth is, I didn't sleep well again last night, but I don't want to think about it. I woke up thinking of camp, and Roberts, my throat tight with woodsmoke. I don't know Anna and I don't really care how she is, but I'd like to get off the subject of me.

"Oh, she's fine. I mean, she's doing okay." Teresa smiles tightly and then redirects back to me. "Well, I hope you are taking care of yourself, and you aren't too overwhelmed with your college assignments, because I actually have another request." I think I see a bit of color rising on her cheeks. Is she annoyed?

I raise my eyebrows and try to look well rested and enthusiastic.

"Listen, Jonah, I know we agreed that you wouldn't have to work with real humans here at the clinic but it would be helpful if you would join me in a group I'm running over the next six weeks, for children of separated or separating parents." She's kidding when she says "real humans" but gets serious quickly and explains that she needs two people to run the group for safety and logistical reasons and she wants the same two people for all the sessions because changing the facilitators throws the kids off and the intervention can fall apart. Anna is still out, and both Róisín and Patrick will be taking time off at one point or another over the six weeks, so I am the logical choice. She explains to me how much she needs my help while she stands there wearing a very tight pair of cigarette pants and what looks like a silk blouse with the top two buttons missing. She has her light brown hair swept up in a complicated topknot with long soft strands framing her face and she smells unbelievably good. I say something about being delighted with the prospect of getting some real experience and about how pleased I am to be of help to her.

"Thank you," she says and I catch a quick expression that might have been either relief or possibly amusement on her face. "The hard part will be getting the small tables off of speech and language, upstairs." I start to laugh and then realize that she is not laughing. Teresa gives me the dates of the group and sends me on my way to negotiate for the tables with an ominous sounding, "Good luck."

The speech and language department is one floor up and every office door is closed. I don't want to interrupt any sessions so I stand there for a minute trying to figure out what my next move is.

"Can I help you?" I nearly startle but not quite. On the steps I came up is a large woman wearing a dress that is at least two sizes too small, with all the challenges to aesthetics that brings. Her hair is the closest thing to a sixties' beehive I have ever seen in person, and she is wearing a surprising amount of eyeliner. It's like she has just stepped off the set of *Hairspray*. I haven't met her yet, so I introduce myself and segue into why I've come upstairs: the small tables. Before I can even give her the dates when we need them, she starts shaking her head: "Oh, no, I'm sorry! That is impossible, I'm afraid." Even her cloud of dark hair is too big for the dress she's wearing, and I have only ever seen that much makeup on a drag queen. "First of all, those tables belong to speech and language. Secondly, we can't be carrying them up and down the stairs whenever psychology wants them. Health and safety! And thirdly, the last time Teresa had someone bringing them up and down these stairs for weeks on end they were damaged *and* there was damage done to the walls. You'll have to tell her no. And fourthly, Teresa knows good and well that she can't have our tables. I've told her before, and I even wrote a memo about it—tell her she can't send you up to do her dirty work!"

"I heard you!" Teresa's voice comes up the stairs. "No need to pass on the message, Jonah." There is playfulness in her tone, but the woman in front of me is not in that zone.

The speech and language woman and I stand staring at each other. I'm tempted to shout "Okay" back down to Teresa but somehow, I don't think that's appropriate. Instead, I say, gambling on the officiousness of her manner, "I wonder could I possibly see the tables in question?" She heaves a sigh and her chest expands significantly. I'm a little worried about the fabric.

"Well, of course you can. I'm not unreasonable. Follow me." I follow her down the hall to the last room, studiously averting my eyes from the back view of the dress. She opens the door and there are three standard-looking small round tables with four little stools at each one. I take a quick photo.

"I wonder could you tell me where you purchased these tables?" I ask.

"IKEA."

The universal language of furniture. I thank the insane speech and language therapist and walk down to Teresa's office door, where she is standing, her eyebrows arched.

"Shall we go to IKEA?" I ask. "It's my impression the little tables are unavailable from our colleagues." I have the sense that the speech and language ogre is listening from the top of the stairs.

"Jonah, you're a genius." She is standing there with one hand on her hip and the other resting on the door handle, and she is clearly trying to hold in her laughter. I'm guessing Teresa is in her early thirties, but in this moment, she looks like a troublemaking school girl. Not really a genius for making an obvious suggestion, but I'm so glad she thinks so. For a second, I imagine us driving off to IKEA together, but she shakes her head and says, "I'll pick them up this weekend. Not to worry! We clearly need a set for ourselves." I nearly ask her for her phone number to text the photo of the tables but something stops me. How many men have asked her for her phone number, I wonder? Any excuse. Teresa points up the stairs toward speech and language and mouths "Lunatic!" then hands me a second manual—the group intervention—along with a copy of a little workbook the kids use. I hold out my phone with the photo of the tables on it and she takes a quick picture of my picture. No numbers exchanged.

On my way down the stairs, I wonder if a psychologist calling you a lunatic has special weight. Back in my kitchen corner, I have a look at the workbook and there is something about it that unnerves me a bit—the simple line drawings and child friendly language makes the whole issue so poignant. I mean, "separated parents" are so commonplace as to be almost not an issue, but when I'm looking at the little pages about "mommy" and "daddy" from a kid's point of view, there's a lot to take in. What the hell do I know about navigating this? I'm hardly a good example. Sure, my parents are still together, but at what cost?

"Are you doing the group?" Patrick has walked in while I'm looking through the workbook. He must see something in my face because he goes straight to reassurance. "It's fine! She asked me to do it but I'm on study leave for thesis work next month. Don't worry. It's very straightforward, and Teresa knows what she is doing. It'll be good experience."

For what, I think, *robots?*

"Any interest in a pint after work?" Patrick asks, and I stop thinking about the kids immediately. It sounds good.

After work we catch the bus and make a slow, traffic-heavy trip into a damp and glistening city center.

"What's it like, working with kids?" I ask Patrick. We are side by side in a double seat, and it's a little too close for comfort. I'm reminded of going to the movies on various military bases in my early childhood, GIs sitting with at least two empty seats between them, talking across the gap.

"It'll be fine," he says, "but to be honest, I'm probably not a great person to ask." He admits in a low tone that he had completed a child placement before, and it hadn't ended well. "I barely passed the placement, the supervisor was such a wagon, and that's why I have to do another child placement instead of the usual specialist placement at the end of training. If there's any trouble in Castleknock, I'm cooked."

"Well, that's not very comforting." I lean back in the seat and cross my arms, trying to imagine how it went wrong for him. I had only been contemplating how weird it would be, not considering that I might fail. But then again, he's on a clinical training doctorate so the standards are pretty high, I imagine.

He glances over and laughs. "It'll be fine with Teresa," he says, "she never fails anyone. Too nice. Believe me, I'm counting on it, and so are the clinical placement coordinators."

We end up in Bowe's, a pub on Fleet Street, near Trinity. I text the twins where I am and they head in to join us. With a few pints under his belt, Patrick admits he has been trying to hook up with Róisín, the assistant psychologist who works with us, but he's not getting any traction.

"I don't know," I say, picturing her in the hallway at work, "she's a little uptight." I try to explain to the twins what her desk looks like—all the right angles. "A girl like that is not going to cross any boundaries and start going out with a guy from work, if you know what I mean." I'm also wondering why he is thinking about crossing boundaries himself, considering what he said on the bus.

Patrick shakes his head and starts extolling her virtues to the twins. "She's smart, she's funny, she's hot."

"She's a little short." It's out before I realize I've said it. He looks at me like I've punched him.

"She isn't short," he says. He isn't the tallest guy. If I didn't have a couple of drinks in me, I'd let it go. But I do have a couple of drinks in me. This is a bad plan he has. It's my duty to discourage him.

"Look," I say, "everything else is a matter of opinion: looks, brains, sense of humor. Short is a reality. That girl is short, and it's too bad because she had potential."

The twins start to laugh when Patrick looks shocked. "He's an arsehole," Michael says, "but he does get the top-drawer stuff. Any minute now some supermodel is going to come in here and sit on his lap, it's that easy. You should see the last woman he was with—both she and her granny were fine creatures."

"It's her mother, for Christ's sake," I correct him, laughing.

"What the fuck?" Patrick asks, totally lost.

To distract him, I bring up Teresa. "Speaking of fine creatures, what is the story with Teresa?"

"Who?" says Michael, and I'm so glad to get to speak about her.

I try to describe her without sounding like a complete idiot but I don't succeed. The twins are openly laughing at me, but Patrick is nodding his head while he scrolls on his phone. He shows the screen and there she is, thanks to Google images. There's the obligatory LinkedIn photo and a couple of speaking engagement type pictures, and then there's one from a conference dinner or something where she is wearing a figure-hugging floor-length dress with a slit up the side that manages to look classy and also unbelievably sexy.

"Holy fuck," says Peter. "The Holy Grail of bosses."

"I absolutely fucking dare you to try it on with her," says Michael, nodding enthusiastically.

"I think she's married to some bigwig doctor," says Patrick. He is looking for more information online but he isn't finding any. Her Facebook page is completely private.

Married? That's interesting. I haven't noticed a ring.

"No bother to this man," says Michael, with the certainty of a fresh convert. He looks me square in the eye. "Go for it."

"Well," I say, leaning in and lowering my voice, "she did very nearly agree to go to IKEA with me today." I don't mention chickening out of asking for her phone number.

"What did I say?" says Michael. "There are beds in IKEA. Loads of them. And couches."

From there the conversation begins to spiral elsewhere and I'm stumbling home hours later before I notice a text message on my phone from Sailí. Finally.

17

The first week of twice a week "therapy," and I am already dreading the session. Since Wednesday I've been mulling over what Roberts asked, and now I'm wondering if he was asking what my mother was like before the accident in general, not *just* before. Not when she was collecting me early from camp, her awkward meeting with the leader while I sat outside in the specimen room, fuming. Not during the long ride home in the car, with me sullen in the seat next to her, my clothes and my scout pack in the back seat stinking of campfires and boy sweat, her fury mounting as she listed one camp infraction after another. Smoking. Stealing from the canteen. Sneaking off. Her frustration with me. Her fear that middle school in the autumn would turn out just as difficult as elementary school had. Her confusion about *what was wrong with me?*

I remember so clearly, the car pulling up fast enough to the house to make the gravel spit, my unexpected trip home delaying Amy's departure for the ballet exam. As we hit the driveway, Amy bounded off the porch toward us, her hair slicked up in a bun and a little pink bag clutched in her hand, fully ballerina, but terrified of being late.

"Get out," my mom hissed. "We'll deal with this later." She quickly hit the button on my seatbelt and glared at me. "Hurry."

Amy jumped in as soon as my slow, resentful feet hit the ground, and Mom started moving. I reached to open the back door but stumbled and the door slammed shut with the momentum. The scout pack stayed in the car.

Roberts wasn't asking about any of that. How could he? I was so pissed off after the last appointment I had planned to phone the other therapists on the list to see if they had availability, but I hadn't gotten around to it and now I think it probably doesn't matter. It's not like the next therapist isn't going to ask about my mother, for Christ's sake. Clearly, moms are on the agenda in any therapy. I ring the bell and hear the click of Roberts' door unlocking. Inside, I freeze: the second chair, "my" chair, has somehow become a couch. Dr. Roberts is standing in his normal spot, smiling. I look around for the missing chair, which is completely gone. Roberts says to me in a normal-sounding voice, "Jonah, welcome. Why don't you try the couch?"

Right away I want to joke about how much he reminds me of a Bond villain, but I don't. Instead, I try to look casual as I move over to sit. Roberts lowers himself into his chair and I realize it is repositioned so that if I am lying on the couch, he is sitting parallel to me, but a bit further back. I'm not sure what to do so I ask: "Am I supposed to lie down here? I think I saw this in a movie once." Roberts meets my uncertainty with a level gaze and makes a gesture with his hand that encourages reclining, so I shift around and lean back. The good news is that the couch is long enough to accommodate my height and my head is supported by the raised end so I'm quite comfortable, physically. The bad news is that the rising dread is back, and I want to walk the hell out of here. Running would be preferable.

Roberts clears his throat and says, "So we begin."

From where I am lying, I can still stare at the fire, which I do as I wait for him to say whatever he is going to say next. After a minute or two, or maybe eternity, I look around over my right shoulder and see him there, sitting, looking back at me, his hands resting on his lap and his legs stretched out and crossed at the ankle. He's got the same stupid shoes on. If I'm waiting for him to say something, it looks like I'm going to be waiting a long time. I turn back to the fire and eventually start ruminating about the last appointment.

"You said my family had changed a lot," I say. No response from Roberts. "Possibly you were repeating what I said? Is that how this works?" Silence. "I mean, you didn't really respond to what I was saying." I sound like I'm whining—asking for something. I don't like it. "And then out of the blue you ask me about my mother? I mean, really?" There is a short pause.

"You didn't get the response from me you wanted," Roberts says.

"Yep," I say, "that's what I just said."

"What do you want?" Roberts sounds curious.

We sit there in silence. I'm giving the guy nothing. What could I say here? I want to go back in time? I want to stop thinking? It was so obvious after my mom came home from the rehab hospital that things would never be the same. Before that, it all felt temporary—like she was on assignment somewhere. I knew Amy was gone, dead, but on some strange level I nearly expected her to come home at the same time. For things to go back to normal. I can remember all the work Dad put into the house before Mom's first home visit, cleaning and organizing. The occupational therapist had said not to change anything or redecorate in case it interfered with her memory, so we basically painted the entire house the exact same colors. Stuff had gotten moved around by various cleaners or neighbors who helped out, and he had to figure out what it looked like on the day of the accident to put it back. I remember Dad pulling up photos on his phone so he could reconfigure everything—and there was Amy, alive. He basically had to look past her to see which way the couch was angled.

At first, Mom came home for day visits, then weekends, then home for good. I remember the first day she came in through the door and she looked so natural, it was like she had just come home from the grocery store and I thought for sure I was in trouble. That when she saw me in this setting, she would remember what happened, but she didn't.

She was still doing physical therapy and occupational therapy, but basically her body was fully healed. No scarring on her face, and her hair covered any evidence of surgery. She looked great, as usual. She walked in and I half expected her to go straight to the kitchen to start dinner, or wipe down the counters, or fold laundry. Instead, she sat on the couch and picked up the remote. I remember Dad catching my eye and giving me a little shrug. We sat down and watched the first soap opera I'd ever seen. Just the three of us.

All of this goes through my head while I'm lying on Roberts' couch and not a word of it comes out. I come back to myself there, staring at the fire, and I'm suddenly dying to know what time it is. Or, more precisely, how much time I have left before Starbucks.

My annoyance at him is gone but I'm impatient to be out of here. I scan the part of the room I can see, but there are no clocks. The weight of my watch is reassuring but I'm sure it's frowned upon to check the time in therapy. A second later, I look at my watch anyway, and only eleven minutes have passed. Thirty-nine to go. It is so quiet in here I can hear the traffic outside. I strain and try to hear Roberts doing something, anything, but I can't even tell if he is breathing. I imagine him dead behind me and I'm sitting here, reclining, forever. I absolutely refuse to look at my watch again.

I remember waiting that day, the day of the accident, for the car to come back. Wanting to get my pack out and empty it, preserve the contraband, before I got into any more trouble. My dad came home early from work, there was no sign of them at dinner time, so we assumed they'd stopped off somewhere, either to celebrate or to comfort after the exam. No answer on Mom's phone. Back then, Dad didn't cook, so he took me out to Denny's and gave me his version of the "What's wrong with Jonah?" talk over chicken-fried steaks. All the while I was waiting to get home, to get that bag.

Just as we were ordering dessert, his phone rang, and that was the end of normal.

Suddenly, I'm back on this dumb couch in a different time and place.

I'm so sick of the silence I say something: "I'm thinking about my mother." That should interest him.

There is no response and I imagine he's asleep. I can't stop myself from twisting around to look and there he is, looking directly back at me, fully awake. I lie back down, but I'm not relaxed.

"She was the same in a lot of ways when she came home from rehab. She looked exactly the same, she smelled the same, she laughed the same."

There's a pause and then Roberts takes the bait. "A lot about her was the same after the accident."

"Yeah," I say. And it's there, waiting to be said: *a lot was different.* So obvious I don't even need to say it.

It was like she was there, but she wasn't. Most of the time, perfectly happy to sit or lie on the couch watching television, which is where she still is, when she isn't in the kitchen chair, looking out the window into the backyard. Her appetite for soap operas is insatiable, and if you flick around the channels, you can still find episodes pretty easily during the afternoon; my dad has a back catalogue for the rest of the time. Despite her memory problems, she seems to keep up to speed on parts of the story and the "previously on . . ." introductions probably help, along with the repeat viewing. Or maybe she doesn't care what's happened before. It doesn't matter. Just beautiful people moving around on the screen.

"That's our time." It takes me a second to react to Roberts' voice and then I sit up, swinging my legs down, remembering where I am. Who I am, now.

Moments later, I'm walking out onto the sidewalk with the second door closing behind me. I look at my watch and sure enough, it's exactly fifty minutes after I walked in. The guy can read time.

18

I've replied to Sailí and we've traded a few text messages. She isn't a quick responder and when they come, they're brief. Maybe she's trying to keep it casual? Good. We've organized to meet for a drink later tonight in Mary's Bar, off Grafton Street, and I'm looking forward to it. I decide to walk down into the city center to get my hair cut, even though it might make me look too eager. The time for playing hard to get is probably over. Passing by the apartment, I consider grabbing the group materials to look over for next week but decide against it. I could call home, but it's four o'clock in the morning there. The same goes for Georgia, too, so that's out; she wouldn't thank me for interrupting her sleep. The thought of Georgia asleep in a bed in an apartment I've never seen gives me a little pang of longing for her. There's a definite pang below the belt, too, but for the first time I notice I'm really missing her. She isn't a deep-conversations-about-our-lives person—she has a natural instinct for what is called for in any particular situation, and she has an aversion to theatrics. I try to imagine what Georgia would talk about on Roberts' couch and I have no idea. I can easily imagine her long, beautiful frame lying on that couch, but I cannot for the life of me predict what she would say.

My mind is still half on my mother, so I immediately think of when Georgia met her for the first time. Social occasions can be tricky because Mom tends to say whatever she thinks. There isn't an editor on duty; that part of the frontal lobe of her brain is not functioning as it should. I remember coming in the front door with Georgia and heading to the living room. I was so sure Mom would be watching television it was disorienting to find her in the kitchen.

When we walked through the old-fashioned swing doors, she took one look at us and said, "Holy shit, Jonah, you two would make good-looking babies." Georgia didn't even blink. Just smiled and reached out to shake her hand.

It was the same when Mom would comment on her clothes or her hair, or casually say she was spending too much time at the house. She would come out with stuff and Georgia would agree with her and that was that—no drama and not one mention of it later, no matter how insulting or crazy it was in the moment. She wasn't the first girl I'd brought home for my on-duty weekends, but she was the one that took it the best. I remember one girl, Shannon, who was reduced to tears by my mother's "a little pudgier than the others, Jonah!" comment that my father heartlessly laughed over for months afterward. It got to the point that I'd be looking at any girl I was going out with trying to predict what my mother would say, as if knowing would prepare them. As if warning them about their most-likely-to-be-mentioned faults was going to help.

I spend the day getting my hair cut in Temple Bar and reading about child development in the library, punctuated by snacks and coffee. By four o'clock, I'm bored and wired, and text Sailí to meet me early for food if she can. I'm sitting outside at the Bailey looking at a menu when she walks up.

Okay, so I have a type, if incredibly good-looking is a type. Maybe it's everyone's type. What I don't like is the waifish, anxious look. The not-sure-about-herself look. I want somebody who doesn't look fragile, and Sailí could be a poster girl for health, lean and strong. She's wearing a tight dress with leggings, low heel loafers, and a fitted leather jacket. Her hair is pulled back in a thick braid, with a few little errant curls bouncing around the edge of her face. "You look good," I say, and she looks me right in the eye. Blue on blue.

"Thank you." The way Sailí meets my gaze tempts me to close the menu and march her straight home. She catches the look on my face and laughs, revealing the dimples and cutting the tension. "I'm starving." Sailí's laugh is a beautiful thing and I catch myself wanting more of it.

We eat well and linger over coffee, the sky darkening, and the outdoor lights and heaters creating a warm glow around us. Turns out, Sailí is an artist; a print maker who specializes in lithography, which explains all the material in her apartment. The process of making prints sounds labor intensive and she describes it with passion. She explains a commission she's working on for a large office building—some of the prints are enormous so she needs extra studio space. And time, lots of time. After several requests, she reluctantly shows me photographs of her work on her phone and it appeals to me—a lot of right angles and straight lines. In fact, they look exactly like something that an engineer would have on the wall. But before I can say that, Sailí changes the subject and asks me about how I'm doing on the course.

I try to describe the class, but I'm worried I sound judgmental or condescending. Or like a cliché: man hates emotion. Or worse, disrespectful of something that's meaningful to her mother. I tell Sailí this and she laughs. "I literally cannot think of anything worse than sitting in a circle watching someone cry," she says, "unless maybe showing your creative work to a bunch of pretentious art students." She's right, that sounds worse.

"But your mom? She likes it?" I don't understand how anyone could like it, but most of these people worked hard to get on the course. Annemarie is a freaking tiger. They must be invested.

"I don't know," says Sailí, her eyes cutting to the middle distance. "She's glad she's on the course, I know that. She was ready for a change."

"What did she do before?"

"I guess I could describe it as administration? She basically worked for the church. I don't know why she stayed there so long. She's a complicated lady, with a complicated history. But I admire and love her and we get on, thank God. And this is something she really wanted to do so I'm glad it happened for her, even if I don't get it." Complicated mother? I know this lane. She hasn't mentioned her father, and I don't ask.

We finish at the Bailey and walk over to Mary's Bar, crossing a crowded, raucous Grafton Street. I have an urge to put my arm around her but resist. My desire for her is a low throb that's building.

In the impossibly small bar, we get a couple of high seats against the wall. A few drinks later we give in to the rising tide and head back to her place. Sailí meets me move for move and I am so pleased to see that little dolphin again, I kiss it.

19

Back at the clinic, I am getting into the rhythm of the place as I turn up and head for the toaster. Teresa has me bring in the boxed tables from her BMW, and we build and stack them in her office. Today she is wearing what looks like a one-piece jumpsuit of some kind with a wide belt that accentuates the narrowness of her waist and the curves above and below. She has on high wedge-heeled boots so her natural height is accentuated and the whole package makes her look like she is flying out to Paris rather than screening kids for the group.

In order to be brought onto the program, the kid has to come with both parents' agreement and preferably, in this first meeting, both parents are present. Teresa gets the names for the group from other clinicians or by referral from the local GPs. Today, my job is to sit quietly in the corner next to Teresa's desk and look wise, or empathetic, or at least not obviously bored. Teresa explains that both the kids and the parents need to see us to "demystify the process" and so we can answer questions. What is important, she explains, is that we gain credibility with the children by being kind and open to both parents. If the kid gets any sense of judgement, or taking sides, we are scuppered before we even leave port.

The other part of my job today is going up and down the stairs with the little duos or trios of parents and kids. Teresa gives me a sheet with the names on it and the appointment times. At ten, we are ready to start, and I head down. The only people in the waiting room are a woman and a kid so I smile and ask the woman if her name is Beverly. She nods, and I bring them upstairs, trying to look friendly, open, and nonjudgemental all at once. I'm lucky I don't trip.

Both Beverly and her son are extremely quiet. Teresa explains the six-week program to them and shows the little boy the workbook. He holds it limply in his hands and looks around the room at all the toys. "You can go and have a look at the stuff if you want," she says to him, but he doesn't move from the chair. Beverly watches and doesn't comment. Teresa is observing both the boy and the mom, and she says gently, "It is really hard to be here today." Beverly shifts her attention back to Teresa and something important passes between the two women. Beverly's eyes well up, and I can see her desire not to show it to the kid. The moment passes and she takes a breath and stands up, suddenly all business, thanking Teresa for her time and for the opportunity for her son to get some support. I walk them back downstairs and out through the security door. When they are gone, my breath lets out, long and slow, releasing the tension.

We go through a few cycles of this, parents and kids, and break for lunch. Teresa is walking to a nearby deli, so I tag along. We start discussing the content of the group—what topics and material are being covered over the six weeks.

"Did you see the part about the photographs?" she asks, and luckily, I had eventually taken time over the weekend to have a look. On the first day of the group the theme is "change," and at one point the facilitators show photos of themselves from childhood, adolescence, and adulthood to demonstrate how people change over time.

"Yeah, I wanted to ask you about that," I say. "Is that just about you?"

"What?" She looks puzzled. "Is what just about me?"

"I mean," I say, "you are going to show photos of yourself, right? Is there any need for me to do that, or are you covering it?"

Teresa cracks up. "Oh, yeah, you are doing it. Absolutely, you are doing it. At least three photos of you over time, printed out if at all possible, so they can pass them around. One of them must be a baby photo. And if you're married, bring a photo of you on your wedding day."

"I'm not married!" I say, and even to my ears I sound ridiculously emphatic on the point. She lets out another hoot of laughter.

"My apologies for even suggesting it. I thought all you Americans married at twenty-two. You are not married. Duly noted." There is really no response to her comment that doesn't make me sound like an even bigger idiot. I stay quiet. Another possibility occurs to me—was she trying to find out if I was attached? Hardly. I take quick note of her left hand. No ring. I knew it.

We go back in the staff kitchen with our sandwiches where we pass a half hour getting caught up on everyone's weekend exploits. Now that I'm aware of Patrick's infatuation, I notice him pandering to the assistant psychologist and reconfirm my opinion that's going nowhere, fast.

After lunch, Teresa returns to her office and I head into the waiting room for our next set of parents and kid. Nobody's there, and as I retrace my steps to the hall there's an insistent buzzing at the inner door. I turn and see a man caught between the two doors, leaning on the button. Before I can reach him, the receptionist releases the lock from some mechanism at her desk and he charges in, banging the door into the wall, loudly. He's not a tall guy, but he is wide across the shoulders and his chest is huge. His white button-up shirt must be tailor-made because there is no way he can wear anything off the rack. He also looks like he is about to explode—red-faced with his fists clenched, one of them holding what looks like our appointment letter. He turns to the receptionist. "Excuse me, I got this letter from here with an appointment I don't want, and I shouldn't have to be at. Can I talk to the person who sent it to me? A Dr. Teresa somebody." His voice is a tightly controlled rumble.

The receptionist glances over at me and I step forward. "Can I help you?"

He turns and assesses my height, weight, and fitness in an instant, dismissing me outright with a sharp little snort through his nostrils.

"I don't know, can you?" He steps toward me and I remain where I am. No fucking way am I stepping backward, even though the guy could break me like a twig.

I force my face into something resembling friendliness and explain that I'm working with Teresa, and we are meeting with families about the group program for kids of parents who are separating. He listens to what I have to say, and there is a long pause, both of us standing uncomfortably close to each other. I note with some satisfaction that he has to look up to meet my eye.

Eventually, he breaks the silence. "My son's mother is bringing him to see you people," he says, "not me. Is there some reason why *I* have to be here? Why *I* have to take off work to come to this little meeting about a problem that isn't a problem, and meet with a doctor who isn't a doctor?"

"Can I clarify?" Teresa's voice sounds from behind me, and I realize the receptionist has summoned her. The guy glances over at her coming down the stairs and sees what everyone sees. He shifts his position so he is lining up with her as she enters into the reception area and I step back, because he has already moved.

Teresa has a warm and convincing smile, and puts out her hand. "I'm Teresa. Are you Gary?"

Gary instinctively extends his hand and shakes hers, wrapping his massive fingers around her slender ones. A little prickle of alarm works its way up my spine.

"It's good to meet you," she says, and looks like she means it. "It is completely up to you if you want to join us for the meeting. I just wanted to make sure that you knew you could come along, if you think it is important to know about the group, or if you had any questions. I'm sorry if that wasn't clear in the letter. Some parents want to come, some don't. It is up to you."

I see Gary bristle at the implication that he doesn't think his son's experience is important. I would like him to step back a little from Teresa, but he doesn't. "As far as I am concerned, this is all mumbo jumbo," he says, waving his hand to take in the whole building. "Seán is fine, he understands that what is happening is between his mother and me, and that it has nothing to do with him. There is nothing wrong with my son, despite what his mother says."

As if on cue, another buzz sounds and we all turn to look as the door opens behind him and a woman and kid walk in. The boy glances around, and then immediately looks at the floor. The woman takes in the scene and does not react, keeping her eyes on Gary. His temperature is rising, and he works to drop his shoulders and step back to give us all a little more space. "Speak of the devil," he says. "Well, Seán!" His tone is light, and his son looks back up at him.

"Hi, Da." I see the kid's eyes move between Gary, Teresa, and me. His mother is behind him, her face completely still.

"Hi, son," says Gary, keeping the bonhomie in his voice, "I was just working things out here. I've had a quick chat, and now I'm going back to work and your mother and you are going to take a turn talking to Dr. Barbie and Ken here." He smiles and looks around like he's made the best joke ever. "I'll see you later, little fella."

Seán quietly says, "Bye, Da," and Gary passes by him and the woman he hasn't acknowledged, and steps out through the door.

"Okay!" says Teresa, like nothing has happened. "Let's go up! My office is right upstairs." She turns and Seán and his mom follow her.

I wait a moment and turn back to the receptionist. "Thanks for calling for backup," I whisper.

"No problem, Ken," she whispers back. "That is priceless."

I race up the stairs, getting to Teresa's doorway just as the mom steps through. I follow her in and Teresa waits until the door is firmly closed behind me before she starts the introductions. From then on, the meeting goes much as the others have gone. Tríona, Seán's mom, doesn't reference the dad and only asks questions about logistics. When Teresa shows her the little workbook, Tríona asks if the kids are meant to bring it home with them and Teresa says they can, but most of them leave it in the center between sessions and take it home at the end. Tríona takes out her agenda book and checks the dates of the course with her own schedule. I can see her examining the pages carefully and then she slowly writes in the times of the course in clear purple numbers. The purple ink brings me back to that first questionnaire I dealt with—the pain in the ass/miserable kid and all I can clearly remember is "stomachache every day" and "no friends." I look at Seán, sitting silently, staring at the floor. Jesus, no wonder.

At the end of their appointment, I show Tríona and Seán out, and there is nobody waiting for us yet, so I go back up to Teresa. She's leaning way back in her chair and has slipped off her shoes and put her feet up on one of the new little chairs, and she is breathing deeply. If I wasn't sure she had heard me come up the stairs I would have happily stood there admiring the scene for a minute, but I barrel in and heave a sigh: "That was something," I say.

"Yes, that was something," says Teresa, pulling her legs down slowly. I'm half-expecting a little "glad that's over" banter from her but instead, she is looking at me steadily. "It would be good to talk that through," she says, "but we could be interrupted at any point by our next family, and I want a little time and space around it."

I'm getting a strong vibe that I have missed something or made a mistake. Something about her assessing look and deliberate speech is setting off my alarm bells. I want to ask her about it, but she has clearly laid down an intention to talk about it at some other time. "Okay," I say, "let me know when works for you."

"Okay," she responds, and the phone rings, signaling our next family.

20

The next day in class, we have a new model of psychotherapy being presented, something called cognitive behavior therapy. And, for a pleasant change, there is another man in the room. Abel, the instructor, describes his work as a clinical psychologist in a matter-of-fact, clear way. He's a skinny guy who clearly used to have more hair than he does now; he keeps running his fingers through a new cut that reminds me of the grass on a putting green, the hair is so short. Cognitive behavior therapy, he explains, is about showing people how their thoughts and beliefs affect the way they feel and behave and helping them to change that. "It's pretty straightforward," he says, and puts up a little diagram of *environment, thoughts, behavior, physical reactions,* and *mood* bubbles with arrows connecting them all to each other.

"You see," he says, "if one of these is very negative, it can pull the whole system down." He draws a little descending spiral. "On the other hand, if you can help people to think in a less distorted way, to challenge their habitual negative thought patterns, you can influence the whole system in a positive way." He retraces the spiral upward.

"What about people's feelings?" Skinny Nancy's voice comes from my left. "Don't you need to let people talk about their feelings?" It's like she is making a point rather than asking a question, but Abel takes it in his stride.

"You do," he says. "Feelings can inform our thinking—if I'm worried in general, I'm more likely to think of things as being threatening. But also, thoughts inform feelings: if I have a thought like 'she doesn't like this lecture,' then obviously I'll feel more anxious about delivering it, and I might even feel angry that I'm being judged so harshly." There is a moment when everyone is silent and I'm wondering if he's pissed off, and he lets out a guffaw: "That, my friends, is simply an example. Although our psychodynamic colleagues might think I *did* let something slip there. Notice how when you all were probably wondering if I was annoyed, everyone was tense and nobody said a word? There's another good example of how thinking informs physical reactions, mood, *and* behavior." He ends with a big ta-da flourish and we all laugh.

Abel goes on to describe how this might turn up in clinic, when people are chronically anxious or depressed and their thoughts take on a whole change in tone: negative about themselves, the future, and other people. It can be hard for people to realize how their thinking is skewed by their mood, but if you can teach them skills to notice and challenge their thoughts, to see reality in a less biased way, it can help control or manage mood.

"But what if what they are thinking is terrible, and correct?" This question comes from Rose, and there is no humor in her tone. "What if their lives really are awful? What if the people around them are as bad as they think?"

"Good question," says Abel, and his tone has also shifted. There is something deeper and more resonant about it, and he is holding her gaze steadily. "Then, you have to catch people's thoughts about themselves, about their own ability to cope with things, or who they are deep down. Cognitive behavior therapy is not about trying to look on the bright side of things, like positive thinking or affirmations. This is about using thoughts as a window into deeper beliefs, and helping people to have the tools to challenge what frightens or saddens them. A person facing a termination from work who is thinking, *I'm going to have to figure something out here, fast,* is in a completely different space than someone thinking, *I knew they'd fire me eventually because I can't do anything*, right? Even though to the outside eye, those two people might be in the exact same spot." We all nod obediently. Rose still looks unsettled, but she doesn't say any more.

To illustrate, he asks for an example of something that happened to one of us in the past week that rates about a two on a scale of distress from zero to ten. I sit back in my chair because volunteers are easy to come by in this group and I can normally wait it out.

Turns out he wasn't looking for a volunteer. "What about you?" he asks, pointing at me. "Tell me something that happened."

I freeze. "I'm not sure I hit a two this week," I say, hoping he'll move on. No such luck.

"Okay," he says, "I'll take a one, or even a zero-point-five. Take a minute to think about it." Clearly this guy has dealt with reluctant participants before. I have the choice of coming up with something quick or sitting there like a rube looking like I'm trying to think of something for an indeterminately long period of time.

"Got one," I say immediately, and I see triumph in his face, but it is good-natured.

I describe the experience I had with Gary in the reception area of the Castleknock center, when he was standing too close to me, complaining about his appointment letter and how he didn't want to be there. I describe how angry he looked, and how I felt like he was trying to intimidate me. "I'd say I hit a zero-point-five on that one," I say, smiling. Easily, this is the most I have spoken in class, and they are all looking at me very intently.

"Ok," says Abel, "what mood were you experiencing?"

"Frustration?"

"Did you think he'd hit you?" asks Abel.

"Maybe," I say. I'm picturing when he was close to Teresa. What did I feel?

"He's a big guy, you said. Could there have been fear?"

"Certainly not," I say, but I'm goofing around a little. There are a few laughs in the class.

"Right," says Abel, "any sensations in your body? Do you think you might have felt anything?"

"I was probably slightly tense," I say.

"So far," Abel lists off, "we've got environment: a new role, the clinic reception with the receptionist watching; mood: frustration and certainly not fear; behavior: standing there not stepping back; and physical reactions: tension. Is that right?"

"Sounds right."

"Okay," says Abel, pushing the nonexistent extra hair back. "What about thoughts?"

"This guy's an asshole?" I say.

"What else?" says Abel.

"Screw you, buddy?" I say.

"Anything else?" says Abel.

"Why the hell is he being such an asshole?" I say.

"I'm getting the theme," says Abel, and laughs. "We could go a bit deeper, look at the thoughts that link these ones to how you think about yourself, but let's take that: *this guy's an asshole.* How true is that statement, do you think? Objectively? On a scale of zero to a hundred percent?"

"A hundred percent true," I say, grateful that he has decided to stay light.

"What's your evidence?" asks Abel.

I think about it. "He stood too close to me, the universal language of male intimidation. He didn't want to come to the appointment. He didn't get why it was important. He looked like he wanted to hit me. He called Teresa and me Ken and Barbie."

"Ah, but that was after!" says Abel. "We're talking about that moment when you were instantly thinking, *this guy's an asshole.* I'll take the first two as evidence. And maybe him looking like he wanted to hit you, although that's a bit shaky because it's an interpretation by you when you were already keyed up. The Ken and Barbie thing is pretty witty, in fact. I know what Teresa looks like and you'd make a good Ken. Now, any objective evidence against the thought this guy was an asshole?"

I can tell Abel is having fun, but I'm okay with it. "He didn't hit me?" I say.

"Ok," he says. "Anything else?" There's a pause and Abel looks around. "Anyone else have any ideas about evidence against Jonah's thought: *this guy is an asshole*?"

"He turned up to the clinic even though he clearly didn't want to?" says skinny Nancy.

"He was relatively polite to the receptionist, even though he was upset. He said '*Excuse me*'," says another classmate. "Also, he had his letter with him and he knew it was Dr. Teresa somebody." Following this there is a short debate about whether Irish people using "excuse me" instead of "sorry" to get someone's attention is polite instead of passively aggressive, and a general consensus forms that in this context it was marginally acceptable as polite. I am completely lost.

"He wasn't mean to the child, and he didn't give out in front of him. He acted like a good father," says Rose.

"That last one was after, but it's a good one," acknowledges Abel. "Now, Jonah. There are a few bits of evidence on both sides from the top of our heads. Do you still want to stick with one hundred percent true the guy is an asshole?"

"Maybe I'll come down to ninety percent," I say.

"Now," says Abel. "If you weren't one hundred percent convinced this guy was a complete asshole in that moment, do you think you would have acted differently?"

"I don't know," I say, "maybe I would have stepped back and given him a little space?"

"Interesting," Abel says, and looks around at us. "Get it?" he asks, and there are nods. Somehow, I feel like a complete idiot and really good at the same time. Maybe only ninety percent idiot.

21

Wednesday already and I am outside Roberts' office at seven fifty-nine, wondering what new furniture surprise he has in store for me. I wait a minute, buzz, and am let in to the same couch scenario as last Friday, determined not to talk about my mother. Roberts and I take our positions, and he says nothing at all.

"I've been missing my girlfriend," I say, and begin to describe Georgia to him. She's an interesting person, very reserved and extremely self-sufficient. I've had girlfriends before who tracked my movements and wanted to talk a lot, wanted to know when I'd be back from whatever lab or class I was in, but Georgia never does any of that. I started seeing her soon after she had been through a big stalking ordeal and knowing her now as I do, I can't imagine what it must have been like for her to have somebody constantly on her tail, making demands.

"I was imagining her in here," I say, and I bet he loves the fact that I'm thinking about his office when I leave. Very psychological, I'm sure. "I can picture exactly what she would look like on this couch, but I have no idea what she would say."

"What she would say about you?" he asks.

"What she would say about anything, really." I think about it a minute. "Or what she would say about me. I thought about her when I left last time. I think I'm missing her."

There's a pause and I continue, "We agreed we could both see other people while I'm in Ireland, and it was no big deal. I'm seeing someone, I guess, but I don't know if she is." Luckily, I've never had a problem with jealousy, not with any of my girlfriends—it's a wasted emotion. If somebody wants to be with someone else, fine. Go for it. I mean, I'm not interested in knowing any details about Georgia's other opportunities but it's not up to me to prescribe what happens. If we ride out the time apart, good. If not, well, it wasn't meant to be.

"No big deal," says Roberts and I'm not sure if maybe he is being sarcastic, so I turn around to look and his face is completely neutral. I settle back on the couch and stare at the fire. This is so fucked up.

"Anyway," I say, "the point is, I'm missing her."

I lapse into silence and my thoughts wander. First, about how I don't want to be lying here on this stupid couch, talking about nothing and then, about that guy from class, Abel, and how his clients probably don't have to babble into thin air like I do. In fact, he seemed completely antibabble. Then I wonder about the women on my course, and what their therapy experiences must be like. It hasn't come up in class and I'm not really hanging around with them to hear about stuff informally. Nobody mentioned it in the pub. I wonder, is anyone else seeing Roberts? Suddenly I'm picturing Rose's purple boots on the couch and I let out a laugh into the silence.

"Sorry," I say, "I was picturing one of my classmate's purple boots propped up on your couch here. I was wondering if any of them are coming to see you too. I mean, you were on the college list that they gave us." There is a pause.

"You are imagining Georgia in here, and you are wondering if your classmates are in here. Whose space is this? I wonder what Jonah would say, if he were here." Roberts says this in the same, neutral tone of voice as always, but it's different to me. Like an accusation.

"What is that supposed to mean?" I say, and I resist the urge to turn around and look at him again. When I did it the last time it felt childish, like I had to reassure myself. Right now, I don't care enough to look. Fuck him. There's no immediate answer and then there's no delayed answer. The only sound is our breathing until Roberts calls time.

One hundred percent asshole I think as I step into the sunshine. I mean, what am I supposed to do? What does he want from me? Fear? Anger? My darkest thoughts? As if I want some guy sitting back there, judging me. I have to ride it out. Sit there in silence if I have to.

I'm not in the mood for class, but by the time I have walked down to Trinity in the pale light of a Dublin autumn morning, coffee in hand, I've shaken off the frustration. It doesn't matter. Everything is fine. It's moments like this I want to call home, just when everyone is asleep. I get to class early and fire off a few emails on the laptop, including one asking my dad to send on some photos. I don't like asking him to go into those early albums, but I don't have much choice.

I send a long note to Georgia about how much I hate therapy and I'm sure she'll have a good laugh at that: the picture of me on the couch. I also mention how I miss her.

22

Thursday morning, Teresa and I have our list of families for the day and the group is starting next Monday, so we have to get organized. My dad has come through with the scanned photos and I'm standing outside her office, looking at them on my phone, when she opens the door and nearly walks into me. Today she is in a long skirt with a tight, scoop-necked top. Her hair is pulled back from her face and curling down her back loosely. Unbelievable.

"Oh, hi!" she says, and I show her my phone. There's me as a baby looking surprisingly fat. She laughs out loud. "What a dote!" I have no idea what that means but it sounds good coming from her.

I scroll through and then there's me on my first day of school, then me as an Eagle Scout, and finally me graduating from college with Georgia—both of us in our caps and gowns.

"Those are perfect," says Teresa. "Is that your girlfriend?" I nod and she comments, "She is really beautiful."

"Yes," I say. "Only the best makes the cut." Teresa laughs again and I agree to print them out for the group. We schedule the day and add in a meeting time to discuss whatever trouble I'm in with her from Monday, but she doesn't call it that. *Extra supervision* goes into her planner.

The day goes well and by midafternoon, counting Monday's families, we have ten potential attendees on board. Everyone has asked their questions and been oriented to what we cover, and agreed to bring the children. Despite this, Teresa tells me at our meeting that we will be lucky to have seven or eight kids turn up. Stuff gets in the way, she explains, real stuff like illness or a breakdown in logistics between the parents, and other stuff like fear and avoidance, or intentional sabotaging of one parent by another.

"You have to remember, Jonah," she says, "we are asking these parents to let their children come in here and talk about all the stuff that is going on in their little hearts and minds, and also all the stuff that is going on in their families and homes. These parents are largely mortified that they have to come here in the first place.

"Which brings us to that moment down in reception yesterday with Seán's dad," she continues. "Explain to me what happened from your perspective." Teresa is sitting at her desk, but she has turned the chair so she is facing me, to the side of her desk. She is leaning back and has her legs crossed, her hands resting in her lap. Her body looks relaxed but she is observing me with an intensity that is different from our casual conversation.

"Okay," I say, "here's what happened." I explain to her what happened in detail, everything I remember in sequence. Then I rehash what happened in class yesterday with Abel, and how the class challenged my thoughts about Gary. Finally, I bring up what she said about parents being embarrassed, or "mortified," and bring that in as a way of maybe explaining why Gary was so combative in the first place. I'm trying to demonstrate learning to her and I'm comfortable about the picture I'm painting. Teresa is listening and nodding but doesn't say anything until I'm finished.

"What else?" she says.

There's a pause when I'm trying to figure this out. I don't get there, and I have to ask, "What do you mean?"

"Well," Teresa says, "what about *you* in the story? I'm really glad to hear you've been reflecting on this, and working out what happened, and coming up with theories about why Gary was throwing shapes, but what about you? Maybe Gary has lots of inner struggles or whatever reasons for being difficult, or maybe he is an asshole, but what interests me, and what is important for our work, is understanding what happened for you. How did you end up in a spot where you were too close up against a dad in the reception area of a health service?" She is smiling gently as she says this and her hands are open in front of her so there isn't an "in trouble" vibe going on, but I am not off the hook.

"I don't know," I say, truthfully.

"Have a think about it," says Teresa. "I'm not asking you to tell me your life story here, Jonah, but this stuff is important. Every move we make, every word we say inside these walls is important. Each member of each family has an impact on every other person in that family, and if Gary has an experience, that has an impact on Seán. We can make mistakes, but we have to pay attention to them. I know you have to do personal therapy as part of the course, maybe consider mentioning what you experienced with Gary in there. It's up to you, though."

I'm listening to what she is saying but I'm getting annoyed too. I know a few things about how one moment in a family affects everything else, one impulsive move. I know about unintended consequences. The thing with Gary was, like, thirty seconds long. Who the fuck cares? I'm over it.

"Look at you, getting annoyed," she says, grinning. This breaks the tension.

"I know!" I say, admitting it. "I mean, I'm thinking, *who cares?* But at the same time, I know it is important."

"It is important," she says. "This is our work. Troubled people, people in distress, families falling apart, and in the middle of that, children." We're somber enough for a moment and then she says, smiling again, "I mean, it's *my* work, but for you maybe it's like a little engineer's holiday before you go back to bridges or skyscrapers or whatever."

"I think if this was a holiday for me, we'd be in our bathing suits," I say, laughing, and then I immediately imagine it and have to look away from her. When I look back there's something in her expression that makes me wonder if maybe she was imagining it too.

"Coffee?" she says, and we start down to the kitchen. All normal. On the way down the stairs, we meet Patrick, who mimes a drink motion to me after Teresa has passed by. I give him an enthusiastic nod. Thank God. In the kitchen, I text the twins and receive an immediate thumbs up emoji. Light at the end of the tunnel.

Later in Bowe's after a couple of drinks, I'm tempted to talk the whole thing over with Patrick to see what he thinks about the Teresa/Gary debacle, but I don't want a big deal with the twins. The phone vibrates in my pocket and it's Georgia on FaceTime, so I accept before I remember where I am.

"Hi!" I say.

"Hi!" says Georgia, and there she is in her upswept ponytail and her fresh gym face, and my heart literally gives a little leap.

Suddenly the phone is out of my hand. "Well, hellloooooo . . ." says Michael, and he and Peter have their faces jammed together looking at her. Patrick can't get near it, but he's trying.

"Hello, twins!" she chirps.

"We're here in the library working away with Jonah on reducing emotional suffering in the world!" says Michael. "You know, we aren't meant to take calls in the library as it disturbs the other students."

"My work has definitely been disturbed," says Peter. "There's going to be a hell of a lot more suffering on account of that." He pauses to take a drink of his pint and I hear Georgia's peal of laughter.

"When are you coming to Ireland?" says Michael. "With your sisters?"

"Sisters?" she asks, and I reach out and swipe back the phone too late. They heard her puzzlement.

"You bastard!" says Michael and I duck out the door, past the nest of smokers, and lean against the wall outside. There is noise and low light, but it is still so good to see her face.

"Hey baby," I say, and her eyes soften.

"Sorry to call when you are out having fun," she says, "but you sounded a little sad in your email."

"Just missing you," I say, "and it turns out I really don't like therapy."

"Big surprise there, Mr. Tough Guy. Mr. No Emotions."

It surprises me that she says that. "Do you really think that?"

"I miss you too," she says. "Everyone in New York City is outraged or depressed or manic. I could use a little steady at the moment." Steady. Is that what I am? Is she like that too?

We talk a bit more but it's hard to hear so we don't stay on for long. She tells me work is going fine but doesn't say a word about her social life and I don't ask. I can see the apartment behind her and there are no obvious signs of male habitation, but I don't know what I'd be likely to see if there were—hiking boots? A tuxedo jacket draped over the back of the couch? We sign off and I head back through the smokers, and into the pub. There's a bigger group of guys sitting with Patrick and the twins when I sit down, and I recognize some of them from my excursion to the Pav. Things go from bad to worse then and eventually I'm stumbling home, later and drunker than I expected, the twins reluctantly in tow.

23

I get up and shower, but on my way to therapy I still smell like the night before. I'm glad I'm not driving for obvious reasons, but I probably shouldn't even be walking. I still get to Roberts' door by seven fifty-nine, and it opens at my push at eight. Lying down on the couch, I'm relieved to no longer have to stand upright, but it does bring a slight queasiness to the fore. Probably, I should be embarrassed about stinking of alcohol, but I can't honestly work up the interest. I'm sure it's not the first time Roberts has had a drunk man on his couch. I begin immediately.

"My supervisor at the clinic said I should bring up something in here. I honestly am exhausted and hungover, and I'm pissed off about being here but here I am, so why not?" No response, as usual, so I launch into the Gary story, and I'm bored and irritable about it. This story about nothing that I've now repeated too many times. In this version of my story, Gary is probably more of an asshole than he was in real life, and I have to catch myself from justifying squaring up to the guy. I go back a bit and try to even out the picture of Gary, and then I bring up Teresa and how she thought maybe I was the asshole in the story.

"I think maybe she doesn't get it," I say, and immediately I'm stepping into those asshole shoes. "I mean, when a guy gets into your space like that, you can't step back. You have to hold your own position, and then you work it out from there. I mean, the guy was huge, not tall, but a big guy, and I didn't want him assuming I was intimidated. He's probably used to people backing down when he pulls that muscle man bullshit; his nervous wife and his little kid, he probably uses it to get his own way all the time. What, exactly, was I supposed to do?" Even as I say it, I'm embarrassed by the immaturity. I keep going, anyway. "The thing is, you have to understand how Teresa looks to get what happened, how Gary reacted. She is probably used to situations like that defusing because she is a woman, and a super-hot woman. She totally doesn't get what it was like before she got there. When she came down the stairs, the guy changed, just by looking at her. Any guy would."

Roberts' voice cuts in. "Any guy would change?"

"Oh, hell yeah." I'm on a roll. "You should see her. She is unbelievable, and I am used to hot women. And she is nice, and she is really smart. Even when she was chastising me, I felt like . . ." I stop here. In my head, that sentence finishes "fucking her," but I haven't said it. I'm a little surprised that I even thought it. Is that really what I felt? Is that who I am?

"Felt like . . ." says Roberts.

"I don't know," I say, and then silence. We both know what I felt like, but I haven't said it. "I made a joke at the end of the meeting, about hanging out together in our bathing suits. She said something about being on holiday and I said that if it was my holiday, we'd be in bathing suits, and I think she thought about it. I felt something. She wasn't mad, anyway," I say.

"Your supervisor wanted you to bring this to me?" Roberts says. "And any guy would change for her."

"Yes." I'm losing patience with this. "I just said both those things, for Christ's sake. I get it, I get what you are saying. I brought this stupid story about Gary to you because Teresa told me to. Whatever." There's silence and the fight goes out of me. I don't give enough of a shit to put this much energy into it. "I'm telling you, Roberts, this woman is so beautiful she should be a Victoria's Secret model, and it's no surprise Gary would change when he saw that. I mean, situations change depending on the circumstances, right?"

"Like the way your mother's accident changed things?" Roberts asks.

"What?" I'm up and heading for the door before I even think about leaving. I know where the release button is, but I've moved too fast for my current state and a wave of dizziness and nausea hits me. My knees buckle and I have to sit down, sliding to the floor with my back against the exit door. Roberts doesn't move. My stomach is in turmoil and my head is pounding. I wasn't expecting this. There is smoke in the room. I can smell it. I'm nauseous, but also something lower down twists in my gut. My mother's accident? *Her* accident?

"It wasn't her accident, Roberts," I say. "It was mine. It was my fault." For a second, my abdomen is silent, no sensation. I'm even holding my breath. Did I say it out loud? I am watching his profile and slowly he turns to face me.

"It was your fault?" It's a question, not a reassurance. He's heard it, and he wants more.

But I can't. The nausea hits me again and I stand, pivot, and hit the button to release the door just as the bile rises. I make it through the open door and vomit on the street, my entire insides pouring into the gutter. When the heaving is over, I turn back to the door, half expecting to see Roberts there, waiting for me. It's closed.

Back at the apartment, the guys are still crashed out and I go back to bed. It feels like moments later when I wake up to an insistent buzzing sound. I wander into the living room and realize someone is at the front gate of the apartment buzzing us to get in. The buzzing stops and I am standing there in my boxers trying to regain my orientation when there is a knock at the door, and I recognize the "Helloooo . . . ?" coming through. Shit, it's the twins' mother. I run into their room, trying not to breathe the foul air, and punch the closest one in the shoulder.

"It's your mother," I hiss, and they fly into action faster than I would have thought possible for two drunk PlayStation junkies. Peter runs into my room, pushes my stuff under the bed, stows my laptop in a drawer, and jumps under the covers while Michael hands me a duvet and pushes me toward the couch. "You've just crashed for the night!" he hisses back at me. "Lie down there now and play along or you're out on your ear."

"You guys should really consider becoming firefighters," I say, and he gives me a death stare.

Michael takes a breath, lowers his shoulders into what is meant to look like sleepy mode, and opens the door. In walks his mother, holding a huge box of doughnuts. Immediately, she is my favorite woman of all time.

"Gentlemen!" she says, "grab your laundry, you're coming

home with me—oh, hello, Jonah!" As she walks into the room her smile fades. "Jesus! What is that smell? Do you have a dead body in here?" She crosses the room and opens the windows. "How can you live like this?" She marches into the kitchen and surveys the damage, ranting all the while, "I will never get used to how disgusting men are. You boys are lucky your father and I didn't live together before we were married or you'd have had *no hope* of being conceived, do you hear me? *No hope.* And believe me, after we did get married it was one disgusting revelation after another. You owe your lives to three Baileys and a cold night, do you hear me?"

"Yes, yes! We've heard it before," says Michael. The shower starts up, no doubt with Peter in it. "Sorry we are so disgusting, Ma." As if to further emphasize his disgusting nature Michael jams a full doughnut into his mouth.

His mother slaps her hand across her eyes. "Oh, God! What have I created?" She looks pretty happy, though, bustling from room to room with a large black garbage bag.

By the time both twins are washed, their mother has convinced me to come home with them for the weekend. I have casual plans with Sailí but something about the invitation appeals to me, so I send her an apologetic text and jump aboard. There's an awkward moment when Moira offers to swing by my place so I can pick up a few things, but I assure her I'm fine with what I've got and the twins chime in with offers to loan me a pair of jeans or a sweater. Before we go, I sneak into "Peter's room" and throw a couple pair of my own underwear into my laptop bag along with my toothbrush—a man has to have standards, even if he is disgusting at heart. We head outside with the remaining doughnuts and a massive bag of laundry and get into the biggest Land Rover I've ever seen. Despite my desire to look at the scenery on the way across Ireland, the plush leather seats, leg room, and soft vibration of the engine lull me into a stupor and I pass out while Moira is still negotiating the city traffic.

24

The closing of the driver's side door wakes me and I sit up. Both twins are still comatose, their mouths open. Moira is up ahead walking fast into a white bungalow with red window frames and a red door, which she speeds through and doesn't close behind her. The house looks like a postcard. I unfold myself from the car and am immediately hit with a potent farmyard smell, and a cold mist. In a field next to the house are sheep with huge blue dots on their sides, and there are cows bunched together in another field. I can see layers of green hills in the distance, bordered by the hedged fields every American imagines cover all of Ireland. I make my way up the driveway and through the front door, which leads into a wide foyer. I don't see anyone, so I meander in the only open door off the foyer, which lands me into the kitchen. Turning left, I run smack into a huge man who is clearly making his way in the opposite direction. He's moving so fast I literally bounce off him and stumble backward into the doorframe, cracking my skull against the wood.

"Janie Mac!" he bellows. "Who the hell are you? And are you all right?"

Before I can answer, Moira's voice comes from behind one of the closed doors. "What did you do out there? That's Jonah! He's friendly with the boys so I brought him home. What happened? I'm in the toilet! Leave him alone!"

I smile at the giant and he grabs my head in his huge hands, rubbing all over. "Oh, Christ, that's going to be a nasty bump. Sit down, here!" He shuffles me over to the table and pushes me into one of the chairs. "Wait there!" He grabs the freezer door and opens it, shouting out to Moira, "He's grand, he's grand. He only got a little bump to the head. Anyway, don't we have enough boys around here without you picking up any old child along the side of the road to bring home?" He produces an ice pack and winks at me. There's a flush with a lot of shouting, but I can't make out what she's saying. The giant comes over and puts the ice pack on my head. I reach up to hold it and he bats away my hand. Instead, he puts one of his huge hands on my forehead and uses the other to press the ice pack against the back of my head, like I'm about nine years old.

In comes Moira in a flurry and takes in the scene. "My God! I leave you alone for one minute and you've gone and broken our guest." To me: "Jonah, this is Dave, my husband, and he doesn't normally bash people around the second he meets them."

"Hi Dave." I can't move my head to look at him because it is in the vise grip of his hands. "It's nice to meet you."

"Probably not yet," says Dave, "but it's likely to get better." He tips my head up and grins at me. "I'll hold this here for a few minutes. You'll be grand." The man's body is right up next to me, and I can smell the outdoors on his rough sweater. Even though the situation is odd, and I haven't had this much physical contact with another man in a very long time, there is something comforting about it. Anyway, I have no choice but to sit here and wait.

"The boys are all a bit under the weather," says Moira. "I'm going to give them a feed and then they can relax in front of the television."

"Under the weather, is it?" says Dave. "I bet I can guess what's caused it." I'm conscious that I probably still smell like the night before, but he doesn't sound annoyed. "The feed sounds good, but there'll be no relaxing until that hedge is in. The fresh air will do them good."

As if on cue, the twins come barging in from the car. Michael laughs when he sees me and his father in our strange embrace. "Fantastic," he says, taking a quick photo with his phone. "What a lovely scene."

"I was just telling your mother how great it is that you boys'll be helping me put that hedge in this afternoon. And tomorrow, probably." The twins open their mouths to protest, but a quick glance at their father stops them in their tracks. "We've got the grant for putting in a hedge, which is all well and good, but then the hedge must be planted!" They shrug and take up positions around the table. Moira is busy at the counter and after a couple of minutes Dave releases me so he can make tea. I touch the back of my head and sure enough, beneath the layer of cold, there's a tender bruise rising up.

Before long, we are eating around the table, with Moira dumping extra helpings on everyone's plates. "The full Irish, this is called, Jonah," she says, "a staple of the Irish mammy's menu."

"The best cure for a hangover, they say," adds Dave, and the twins look sheepish.

"What about your own mother?" asks Moira. "Is she missing you terribly? Do you talk to her much? Have you brothers and sisters around to keep her company?"

The old tension rises and I'm inclined to avoid the familiar route of this conversation. "No, no brothers or sisters, I'm afraid. I talk to her on the phone, but I'm sure she misses me sometimes."

"Oh, I'm sure she misses you the whole time," says Moira. "I miss these twins something awful, and they're only up in Dublin!"

"I didn't know you were an only child," says Peter. "No wonder you are such a spoiled brat."

"I'll have you know," I say, nodding sagely, "according to my recently acquired in-depth expert psychological knowledge, only children are smarter and achieve more than children with siblings. Especially twins." I'm not sure if this last part is true.

There's a pause and Dave says, "That explains a lot."

After lunch, Dave takes us outside. Moira tries to get me to hang back, but I insist on helping out, and she suits me up with rubber boots, waterproof pants, and a jacket from a mountain of work clothes in a little room off the kitchen by the back door. I'm not sure what I expected when Dave said "hedge," but it wasn't these bundles of sticks with roots.

Basically, Dave has dug a straight trench across a field and we have to go along, planting these little sticks in the loose dirt every few inches or so. As a suburban kid, the work has a childhood field trip quality, and I ask Michael to take a photo of me that I can send to my dad. He pulls out his phone and soon I'm hamming it up, looking out into the distance, thoughtfully leaning on my shovel while the twins crack up. Dave laughs along for a few moments but then shouts to give up the photo shoot and get back to work. I forward the best of the pictures to my dad and Georgia, along with a caption: *Going native*.

I'm surprised at how long it takes to plant the sticks. We are out there for the rest of the afternoon, until Dave calls it quits until tomorrow. When we go in, there is more food and then showers, television, and more food again. The boys suggest maybe going into town for a pint, but Moira says firmly, "Not a hope, no chance," and they slump down into the couches again like teenagers. She shows me where I'm sleeping and between the hangover, the multiple meals, and the outside work, I'm sure I'll fall asleep instantly. Moira clearly wants to fuss over me before leaving and she checks the bump on my head, hands over more towels, and offers the house phone for me to call home if I need to.

"Did you send your mother the photo of you as an Irish farmer?" she asks. "What did she say?"

"She isn't great with technology," I say. "I sent it to my dad, and he'll show it to her when he gets a chance."

"I'm the same," she says, but she isn't. "Will you call her now, do you think?"

What I think is that in order to get her to leave the room, the easiest thing is to agree to call my mother, so I tell her I will. There must be some international motherhood alliance that requires her to pester me into making contact with home. I tell her I'll use my own phone, and she wishes me a good night and leaves. The bed is a wonder to behold, with layers of feather-filled cotton duvets and the fluffiest pillows I have ever seen outside of an advertisement. I sit on the edge of it and sink down about a foot. Because I said I would, I call home.

It rings a few times before she answers. She must have been in the living room. We have an extension near the couch, but she rarely remembers to use it. "Hello?"

"Hi Mom," I say. "What's happening?"

"Hi baby," she says, and her warm voice triggers a pang in my chest. "I'm watching my shows." I can picture her walk back to the living room, the sound of her soap opera filtering through, the long cord stretched behind her. "That woman is here that your father insists on having. She's spying on me constantly. You should see her, Jonah. She's like a creepy little troll. How are you?"

"I'm good," I say, praying that the home care woman either

can't hear her or can't understand her. Did she have these thoughts before her accident and not say them? The only person I can remember her lashing out at in my childhood was me, and I deserved it. "Did you eat anything?" There's a pause, and I regret the question. Sometimes she can forget to eat, but then she can get annoyed at being asked. "Anyway," I go on without waiting for her answer, "Dad'll be home soon."

"That's good," she says, and her voice is still low and smooth. "Where are you? College?"

"I'm in Ireland still," I say, conscious that if she is in the living room, she doesn't have the memory board there. "And I'm staying with a family for the weekend. I was helping on the farm today and I sent Dad a picture to show you."

"Okay, that's good," she says, but her attention is fading. "I'm going to go, now. Bye!" And she's gone. I'm grateful for the warning, because I remember the days when she would hang up midsentence if she got bored.

A text has come in from Dad while I was talking to her: *Great photo. Thanks. Find any potatoes?*

I text back: *Very funny. They love that joke here. Talked to Mom. TV, possibly no food. Mean home help comment.*

Him again: *Okay. Thanks.*

Nothing else comes through, so I climb into the bed, which is as comfortable as it looks, but I don't have much time to appreciate it before I'm asleep.

Sometime later I wake, covered in sweat, my chest heaving. I have a pillow in my hands, but what I see is my scout pack, delivered to the house days after the accident by the insurance company, still stinking of smoke. I can picture the contents all around me, dumped out on my bedroom floor. But not the thing I'm looking for. I am still searching.

A sound from outside the bedroom door breaks the spell and I am back at the twins' house, surrounded by soft white bedding. I release the pillow and my fingers ache as I straighten them. Silence again, and then a gentle padding of feet down the hall. Somebody checking on me. Perhaps I shouted in my sleep, or cried. Moira is the type of mother who would hear that and come running, no matter how old her kids are. Fully awake, I am still awash with fear and dread, the weight of guilt mixing with the down comforters. I push the bedclothes off and lie there, letting my sweat dry and my breathing slow. Fucking Roberts.

Pretty much all of Saturday passes with a steady rotation of eating, working with Dave on the hedge, and sitting in front of the television. At around nine in the evening, Peter brings up the option of going into town and this time Moira agrees. She drops us into Tipperary town and we head straight for McDaid's, where we drink too much, and I am informed about the early days of the twins from an assortment of their friends and not-so-innocent bystanders. The picture I'm getting fits very much with my own experience of them, and I let it drop casually that their mother mentioned they were very difficult to wean from the breast. Which is good, I suggest, seeing as they are so far away from access to any other breasts. I'm rewarded for my comments with a punch on the arm hard enough to make my eyes water and the sharing of my Irish farmer photos, which Michael somehow gets to broadcast on the flat screen in the pub. By the time Moira collects us at eleven thirty, we are drunk but not sloppy, and my sides are sore from laughing. In the car on the way back the twins fill their mother in on whatever gossip they've collected, and I realize I didn't see one woman in the bar. I check my phone and there's a happy face emoji from Georgia acknowledging my photo, but nothing else.

On Sunday when I wake, my entire body is sore and I am ridiculously grateful that we don't work on the hedge. Moira drives us back to Dublin early enough for me to text Sailí to meet me for dinner, and they drop me off on Westmoreland Street on their way back to the apartment. Sailí comes in, and we have a laugh over steak and fries in Hellfire before a quiet drink below ground in the Mint. For a minute, it is unclear how the night is going to end, but Sailí clears up the uncertainty with a chaste kiss on my cheek and a friendly but definite "Good night!" Perhaps she is tired, or perhaps this is the price of blowing her off on Friday. Either way, she has probably done me a favor because I am completely exhausted when I come through the apartment door. On the floor in the hallway is a plastic bag with a stack of clothes in it and a handwritten note that says "JONAH" in block capitals.

"What's this?" I call out to the PlayStation twins.

"Ma left it for you. I think it's your laundry." Sure enough, I recognize the T-shirt under the note and flip through, noticing she has gone so far as to iron my boxers. I hadn't even seen her collect up my dirty clothes on Friday. The last I remember they were being kicked under the bed.

"This is awesome," I say. "Start the weekend with doughnuts and end it with clean laundry. I've got to get myself one of these Irish mothers."

"Hands off, she's ours," comes the reply. "Anyway, she doesn't like you."

"I know," I say. "Too handsome."

I get only a rude noise and hand gestures in response.

25

Monday morning, I'm prepping for the group with Teresa. Today she is wearing tight black pants and an oversized fluffy sweater that's a great color for her light blue eyes. The legs of her pants are pushed into high leather boots and her hair is up in a ponytail. The whole effect is like sexy après ski but she is all business as she moves the little tables around and sets up the materials for the group. I give her my photos and she lifts down a high box and pulls a couple of pictures out of it. There she is as a baby, at her first communion, graduating with her doctorate, and as a bride. The wedding photo shows her standing with an older man at the door of a church that looks like it comes right out of a fairy tale. There is a light dusting of snow caught in the carved masonry on either side of the door and in the intricate metalwork on the door itself. She is wearing a dress fitted to her form from a high neck to a mermaid tale bottom, the sleeves tight lace down to her fingertips and she is holding red roses. The effect is stunning.

"Wow," I say, and I mean it.

"I got lucky with the snow," she says, "although the heat was broken in the church and everyone froze. Also, the groom was late because of the ice and we couldn't get through to him, so the whole church was full of really cold people who were certain I was being stood up and were being polite until I finally called it a day. When he eventually arrived, they went from pitying to furious in about a nanosecond and the bar tab later was twice what we had budgeted for. I'm still convinced they were ordering drinks just to put it to us."

"Nobody would stand that bride up." I shake my head. "They

should have known he was on his way even if he had to crawl." It occurs to me after I've said this that I'm walking a fine line. A bit of pink has bloomed on Teresa's cheeks. I hope I haven't embarrassed her, or myself.

I can't follow her expression because she has turned to put the box away. "Well, it meant I had a lot of time to take nice pictures with my father at the church door, anyway! He was delighted I was finally getting married—and maybe a bit proud I kept my maiden name. My mother thought I was mad, but I think he was secretly pleased." As she is turning back, she stops and takes a final photo out of the box—a more recent Teresa laughing her head off with a redhead. "Oh, yeah, that's good," she says. "I keep forgetting how much time has passed since the wedding. I can't claim that as up-to-date anymore!"

"Who's this?" I ask, smiling at their total abandon, the two women clearly lost in a moment of hilarity.

"That's Anna, from the center here. The other full-time psychologist. I forgot she's been out since you started. She's the best. She's the one who picked the workbooks we use. They're great. Even if the language is a little American." Teresa gestures over to the tables, drawing my attention away from the deepening pink of her cheeks and the color rising from her neckline.

On the first small table is a stack of the little workbooks: *When Mom and Dad Separate*. Each table has tons of markers, crayons, and colored pencils, as well as regular pencils and erasers. The theme for the first day: *change is a part of life*. I tense up a little at the thought of the kids coming in later. Even though I've met them all in screenings, this is so far from anything else I've ever done.

"What's the craziest thing that could happen in this group?" I ask Teresa.

"Nervous?" she asks, laughing. "Of course you are, it's new. It'll be fine—children are surprisingly fun and easy to be around. There might be a few who don't want to talk, and there might be a few who talk too much, same as any group of adults. And don't forget, you are on snack duty, so before the group starts set up a tray with juices and treats from downstairs we can have at some point during the program. I won't schedule it; we'll play it by ear. You watch out for anybody who needs extra support or help. If nobody does, just sit back. Okay?"

"Okay," I say, but I'm still wondering.

At quarter past two the first participants start showing up. They've clearly been picked up from school and they're all in their little uniforms. I'm pleasantly surprised at how comfortable they seem, greeting me with a cheerful "Hi!" when I let them through the front door, and then following little footprint stickers up the stairs and into Teresa's room.

By two thirty we have eight participants and I'm turning to go up the stairs when little Seán comes running up to the outside door, making it nine. We head up together and find Teresa and the other kids sitting in a loose circle tossing a cushion back and forth, saying each person's name. Before I can fold my frame into one of the miniature chairs, the cushion comes quick and hits me in the chest as Teresa says, "Jonah." Everyone laughs, including me.

After the cushion game we do another short game making "terrible" drawings and then Teresa works with the kids on "group rules" like letting everyone talk, being respectful to one another, and not telling other people's secrets. One of the kids points out that hitting me in the chest with the pillow before I was ready was against the rules and Teresa solemnly agrees, and apologizes. My impulse is to blow it off, but I understand the intent and see the faces watching me carefully as I gently accept her apology and we move on to the workbooks.

The first activity is about changes in nature, like acorn to sapling to tree or caterpillar to chrysalis to butterfly, and they are asked to draw some kind of change they have seen. Again, I am surprised at how easily they take instruction and how quickly the work begins. One little girl is working so hard on her picture that her curls are bouncing around furiously and I think about how funny her teacher must find watching that all day. While they work, Teresa moves around the tables with gentle comments. She catches my eye and looks quickly down at a table of two boys, so I move over to the tiny chair next to them. The work at this table has slowed a bit, and I realize why as one boy stashes a little toy into his pocket. I'm like a bouncer as they glance up with guilty looks, and I resist the urge to ask about the toy or tell them what a complete fraud I am. Instead, I ask about one of the pictures and the little guy next to it explains proudly that the first part of the picture is spaghetti, his favorite food, and the second part of the picture is his poo. Impulsively, I let out a bark of laughter and his partner in crime finds this completely hilarious. Before long the entire group has erupted in giggles and boy number one is clearly thrilled with himself. Teresa goes with the flow and the children take some time to explain their pictures. Little Seán is all smiles until we get to him and then he clams up completely. His page is almost completely blank with only a simple line down the middle of it, dividing it into two parts. What amazes me is how quickly he goes from hearty laughter to this closed up, silent child who would clearly like to disappear. Teresa allows a few moments for him to speak up, and when he doesn't share, she moves on.

Soon we pull out the photos, and the children all crowd around to see as Teresa lays out her abbreviated life story. When the wedding picture comes out there is a gasp from the girls in unison at the sight of Teresa in her dress.

Little Miss Curly Head looks up very seriously and says with great reverence, "You look like a real princess," and there is universal agreement.

"Is that your husband? He is very old," another girl says, and Teresa shakes her head.

"No, that was my father," she says. "We were so happy on that day, but he was very sick. He died soon after this day in the photograph." Teresa says this in a gentle but matter-of-fact way. "Things change all the time. That is the way things work, and we have to adjust." Following this, there is a flurry of questions from the children: What did he die of? How long after the wedding did he die? Was she sad every day that he died? Where is the dress in the photograph? Was she happy to get married? Was she in love? Did she go to the funeral?

Teresa answers each question with short but honest-sounding responses, and I am amazed at how engaged the children are in the story. When there is a pause, Teresa says, "Jonah has some photos too," and suddenly all the faces turn my way. I lay out the pictures and brace myself for the questions: baby, first day at school, Eagle Scout, college.

First there is silence as they all have a good look, then the poo jokester points at the first day photo and says, "Look at his ears!" Of course, we all look, and another eruption of laughter sweeps over the group. I am so surprised at the open ridicule and sheer joy of the children I catch myself laughing along until I see Teresa holding steady, and I quickly pull myself back together.

Somehow, she is able to not laugh but also not look annoyed as their giggles peter out and one of the girls, who had been laughing along uncontrollably only moments before, says crossly, "Remember the group rules! That is not respectful to Jonah about his ears. Sorry." She looks at me sincerely and there is a chorus of "Sorrys" from the whole group. I accept graciously, again, and Teresa gives me the signal for snack time.

After snack, we finish the group with another picture exercise and the children all happily skip down the stairs to their waiting parents and the journey home. Teresa and I clean up the chairs and tables and put the workbooks away carefully. She has her back to me at the high bookshelf, putting her photos back in the box, when I hear a sound and realize she is trying to laugh quietly. "What?" I say, and she dissolves in giggles.

"Oh, my God, that was funny! Your ears! I wish you could have seen your own face!" She is having trouble catching her breath because she is laughing so hard. She sits down on one of the mini chairs.

"There is nothing wrong with my ears," I say, smiling, and this only serves to increase her incapacity. She now has her head in her hands and her shoulders are shaking. "Now I know why you put in the princess shot," I say, and she nods through the spasms of laughter.

"They don't take any prisoners," she finally manages to say, and we head downstairs.

In the kitchen we find the other parts of the psychology team, Patrick and Róisín. After we get our tea in hand, Teresa invites us up to her office and begins to describe the first session of the group—what was covered, how the children responded, and group dynamics. As she talks, I begin to see the complexity of the program, and of the role she is playing here as supervisor, trying to inform, support, and elicit critical thinking. She covers the group and describes the children's comments about her photos and my photos in the context of their own experiences. Then she shows their drawings and we talk about them in detail. In her reflection, the spaghetti-to-poo picture becomes an interesting mix of a kid goofing around trying to be funny, and a visual representation of the complexity of the child's experience in the whirls and twists of the spaghetti followed by his own ability to metabolize and become dominant over what he is experiencing in the picture of the poo. She holds up Seán's picture with the faint line running down the middle. "What about this? What do you see?" she asks.

There is a pause. "Anxiety?" asks Patrick. "I mean, maybe he froze and couldn't draw any more because of his fear of what's happening, or what you or the other children might think?"

"Sure," says Teresa, "very plausible hypothesis. What else?" Another pause.

"Attention problems?" Patrick again. "Maybe he couldn't stay on the task and was easily distracted by the other children, or the environment. Where was the poo kid sitting?" Patrick acts like he's sweating this.

"Same table. Very good." Teresa responds, "Anything else?" We all stare at the line.

"Maybe he couldn't think of anything to draw?" says Róisín, the assistant psychologist, glancing around at everyone. "Or his motor skills are poor?"

"Also very possible," says Teresa. "He *did* draw something, though—he divided the page in two. Then he stopped."

"Like two parents," I say, and she looks at me, smiling. There is something in her eyes. Appreciation? Recognition? Patrick glances from me to her, and back again.

"Yes, like two parents," she says. "Or like two parts of the same parent—good and bad, or before and after." Teresa goes on to explain theorists who describe the way infants and young children can process things in two parts, and can push away from the bad parts because they can be too difficult. For them, the complexity of having good and bad in one person can be unbearable. And not just for them; she gives examples of the "only good" of the person we fall in love with, sometimes closely followed by the "only bad" of the other person in a breakup. She draws a link to the universality of games with good guys and bad guys and how easily a situation of conflict like separation or divorce can become that good guy/bad guy split. "The problem for the children we see," she explains, "is that neither parent is perfectly good or perfectly bad. When tensions rise, however, everyone wants the comfort of knowing who the really bad guy is so we have something to fight against. But what a tragedy when it's your own parent."

The supervision wraps up and we are all released out into the early dark of mid-October in Ireland. On the way to the bus stop, Patrick ditches me and jogs ahead a few paces to where Róisín is walking, bundled into a long, belted coat. I see her laugh and lean in a bit; perhaps his persistence is paying off. She turns to look at me and then says quite clearly to him in a voice I am meant to hear, "I don't think the ears are *that* bad, Patrick."

The bastard has sold me down the river. "Very funny!" I call out and their laughter washes back over me.

26

It turns out that once a term we have what is called "group support and process day" on the course, when they get an outside facilitator in to work with us on a number of things that are not very clear to me. This was explained to us last week, and they've asked us to wear comfortable clothes into college. My daily uniform of dark jeans, slim-fit button-down, and sweater aren't going to work, so I'm feeling a little like a drug dealer on my walk down to Trinity in the Adidas sportswear that Georgia had encouraged me to pack "just in case" I decided to exercise at some point in the year. When I get to class the chairs are stacked against the wall, and there are yoga mats and small round meditation cushions tumbled in the corners. As we come in, we are encouraged to grab a yoga mat and find a space to lay it out on the floor. Already, several of the women have begun doing yoga stretches and I take a space along the wall and sit up against it, trying to look around without looking like I am checking out all the positions they are moving in and out of. I end up closing my eyes because it is easier, and I can look like I'm meditating. Downward facing dog can present such a problem to the casual observer.

When class starts, I open my eyes and everyone is sitting on a mat, no asses in the air. The facilitator for the morning, a short woman in her forties named Diane, is a trained mindfulness teacher who plans to take us through a series of meditation practices. We begin with an exercise where all we do is pay attention to breathing in and out. I've done this before, with sports teams at home, and I'm expecting to relax. Sure enough, after a few inhales and exhales, my breath moves into an easy rhythm and my mind starts to wander. I remember doing this sitting on the bench in the dugout with the batting coach alternating between shouting at whoever was up and turning back to the rest of us with soothing, focused attention.

The exercise ends, and the mindfulness teacher takes comments from the class. I am surprised to learn how difficult it was for a number of my classmates. Skinny Nancy talks about how tight her chest was during the breathing, and how she found it hard to catch her breath. Rose says her leg fell asleep, but she doesn't sound distressed by it. Meredith starts talking about how her mind wandered to problems she is having at home and tears come to her eyes, making them shiny and bright. Meredith crying is nothing new to me, or any of us, but there is an intensity that is different, probably because we are all sitting on the floor like we're on a sleepover in a teen movie. Silence falls, and the mindfulness teacher gazes benevolently around at us and then goes into the next exercise, mindful walking.

The morning passes like this, moving from one exercise to the next, and I can see that several of my classmates are completely zoning out into relaxation while others are less so. At one point, Nancy makes eye contact with me and does an enormous eye roll, but I keep my expression carefully neutral because I am sitting directly across from Diane. Eventually, the exercises come to an end and there is a lot of sharing and then, finally, we are released for lunch.

Most of the class are heading off together and I'm on my way with them, when I check my phone and see a message from Sailí: *Meet for lunch?* Gratefully, I text back, *Hell, yes.*

We meet on Grafton Street and Sailí takes me to a café in the back of a church around the corner. I'd say we bring the average age of the clientele down by about thirty years, but the food smells great and there are plenty of tables. We order at the counter, and I pick up the tab, which turns out to be so low I'm a little embarrassed at offering, and we sit down. In the corner is a grand piano that is available for anyone to play, and as we've moved through the line, I've heard a hatchet job of Gershwin and a pretty good rendition of "Für Elise."

The piano falls silent and as we sit down, I gesture over to it and lift an eyebrow at Sailí. "Any requests?"

"Do you play?" she asks.

"Do you have a request?" I ask again.

"Not really," she responds, and doesn't sound amused.

"Well then, yes, I play beautifully." I grin at her and we sit, but the joke hasn't landed. To fill the space between us, I recount my morning of mindfulness and she tells me she is working in Temple Bar at a gallery and print workshop there. She shows me her hands, embedded with dark ink around the nails and fingertips. For some reason, this is a turn-on to me, and I am about to say something suggestive when she surprises me with a question.

"How's your girlfriend?" Sailí's head is cocked, and her eyes are wide. I can't tell exactly what she is feeling, but it isn't friendly.

There's a pause while I take this in. We are sitting across from one another, and she does not look away as I digest the question. I make an effort to maintain eye contact with her and think. Frustration rises in me and tension crawls across my shoulders—I haven't made any promises. What is she expecting? Rose must have passed on the information from the cheerleader conversation the other night in the pub. Why did I answer truthfully?

"Playing the field, I assume," I say, finally. Talk about an ambush.

Sailí leans back, takes out her phone, and starts tapping.

"Are you texting my answer to someone?" I'm a nanosecond from walking out. I like this girl but I'm not going to pretend that I've done something wrong here.

"No. I'm Googling what the exact definition of that is," she says.

I wait while she reads the answers, caught up in how strange this situation is. I've never had anyone Google something I've said in the middle of a conversation, or argument, or whatever this encounter is.

"I'm assuming you mean '*to become romantically involved with a number of people*' and not '*a television show about a woman's football team in Yorkshire*?'" The spark is back in her eye and the ice beneath my feet is not quite so thin. She is just trying to figure this out. She's not the first.

"Yes."

"Okay," she says. "That's good to know. I'd hate to misinterpret what is going on here. I'm assuming what we are doing is also playing the field, together?" I can see her dimples, now, but there are layers to the question.

"Well," I say, adopting a mock serious tone, "I don't mean to be pedantic about this, but two people don't really play the field together, if you know what I mean. Each person plays the field individually. Sometimes, people's fields intersect, I guess, and that is what is happening to us. We have intersecting fields. Or perhaps, to be more accurate, we visit each other's fields at times."

"Like a right-of-way?" she asks.

"Hang on," I Google right-of-way. After a bit of reading I respond, "No. Not like a right-of-way. More like a tourist, I'd say, or an invited guest. And I have to admit, I've really enjoyed my trips to your field. And your mountain range can't be beat."

Sailí puts down her phone. "Shocking!" she says, and I know I am back on solid ground. Jesus Christ. "The thing is," she continues, "sometimes people put walls around their fields. And sometimes they deny access altogether. I want to make sure I'm not visiting a field that somebody has already built a house on. I'm all for being a tourist, but I do *not* want to trespass."

This is a smart girl. "Okay," I say, looking at her. "Point taken."

She holds my gaze. "Okay." She smiles. Perhaps that ground isn't quite as solid as I thought.

After lunch, Sailí gives me a kiss I would describe as a clear invitation for another visit to her field, and I agree to swing by the studio after class. When I get into the seminar room, I'm a couple of minutes late and everyone is sitting on chairs in a circle. There is a small woman with thick glasses talking and she pauses when I take the last empty seat and silently watches as I put my bag behind my chair. When I stop moving, she begins talking again, and it becomes clear this is the "process group." We are encouraged to talk about anything that has come up for us so far on the course, in class, on placement, or in therapy. As if.

Eventually, she finishes her introduction and, in the silence, I reach back for my bag to take out a water bottle. She tracks the entire movement with her steady gaze and while this would normally make me a little self-conscious, something about the experience is starting to piss me off, so I take my time with it. I take a long drink of water, and then turn and slowly put the bottle back in my bag, closing it carefully. When I turn back, she continues to watch as I stretch out my legs and then crack my knuckles. By this time, I am aware everyone is watching me, but I continue moving as I reach forward and loosen the laces on the sports shoes I don't want to be wearing, first the right foot, then the left. When I raise my gaze again, she meets it and there is an interest in her eyes that is neither warm nor cold. I look back at her with what I hope is also a neutral expression and my body falls still, partly because I can't think of another movement that won't make it look like I am trying too hard to be disruptive. My frustration has also largely dissipated and become a very low hum of unease. When the facilitator finally looks away, I chance a quick glance around the room and catch an almost imperceptible wink coming from Rose who is sitting next to openly smiling Nancy.

No one speaks for a while and then Meredith says, "I feel like you are not really here yet, Jonah." I wasn't looking at her and when I do, I see her frustration. While I'm frozen in surprise, and wondering what to say next, Meredith continues, "I mean, here in the room with us. At all. That little routine you did is such a great microcosm. You have one foot out the door all the time." Silence falls and I just sit, trying to figure it out. I am tempted to stay quiet, but perhaps that would look like I'm taking it all too seriously?

Eventually, I speak. "I'm sorry I was late, and that I started messing around with my water and my shoes, if that bothered you." Probably I was being disrespectful, and I don't mind a quick apology if it'll get her off my back. I'm expecting Meredith to start crying, but she doesn't.

"I don't care about your water," she says, her eyes narrowing, and her frizzy dark hair framing her face like a nest, "but I *would* like to know who you are. I mean, behind the charming mystery man persona you bring in here when the rest of us are trying to be real."

I don't move a muscle, but suddenly I am made of stone. I have an urge to tell Meredith I would like to know *less* about who she is, about her history of childhood difficulty, about the conflict in her current relationship, about whatever today's crisis is, but I hold back. I don't need to engage with this. What do I want? More water from that faucet? A few beats pass. "Meredith," I say, "what if behind that persona, there's just more charm?" No one says a word. Meredith turns away from me with a look of disgust and I chance a glance at the facilitator, who is looking at me. Neutral, neutral. I have an impulse to stand up and walk out, but I refuse to rage quit and keep my seat. Nothing more is said in this interaction and the afternoon passes with other students' exploring one drama after another, and gently side-stepping anything to do with me or Meredith, who also remains surprisingly silent. I listen, sure, but I keep going back in my mind to Sailí's questioning, and the random hostility with Meredith, and part of me is braced for more. By four thirty I am exhausted and the process group comes to a close. We finish with a short mindfulness exercise and then I stretch, letting the tension release in my back and shoulders.

On my way down the hall, Rose sidles up next to me.

"Are you okay?" she asks, looking up at me.

"Of course I am," I say, holding her gaze.

"Of course you are," she says. "I can't believe I implied anything else." I laugh and look at her face, where there is openness and humor and maybe concern. It is clear to me that she is offering support, but also having a joke at my expense. I deserve it.

"Well," I say, "we mystery men don't like to let a lot of our deeper, more complex emotions too close to the surface. It interferes with the charm factor."

"It's good to have a clear policy on the issue," she says as we exit into the cold air.

"But seriously, thanks for asking." It occurs to me that maybe they all think I'm a shallow asshole. After all, she and Sailí have clearly been discussing me or I wouldn't have been blindsided with that girlfriend business. "I'm trying to be sincere here."

"It's really no big deal," she says, and now she is openly teasing me. "Stop being so emotional, Jonah. Pull yourself together."

I laugh and we part ways, and the irony is not lost on me that I am heading over to try to convince her daughter to share some very intimate moments with me in the extremely near future. At the thought of intimate moments with Sailí, the exhaustion disappears and is replaced with a sense of building energy as I stretch my legs in a fast walk across Front Square and out through the gates of the college.

27

I wake in Sailí's bed to the sound of the emergency ring on my phone. I have it on *do not disturb* at night, but Georgia and Dad can get through at any time, and the adrenaline that starts when I hear it is tempered by a tiny bit of relief that it is Dad and not Georgia calling, given my location.

"Hi, Dad," I say. "Everything okay?"

"Hi, Jonah," he says, and he has on his ultra-calm voice, which tells me there's a mom problem. "Your mother is here, and she is a little worried about you, so I thought it would be good if she could talk to you. We've been going over the memory board a bit but, well . . ."

"Is that him? Jonah, is that you?" My mom cuts in. Beside me, Sailí gets out of bed and heads for the bathroom. Dad hands over the phone.

"Hi, Mom?"

"Oh, thank God, Jonah. Are you okay? Where are you? Can you turn on the picture thing?" I switch to video call, and there she is, peering into the phone. I can see myself in the corner and I am not looking my best. I sit up a little and smooth down my hair.

"Hey Mom," I say. "I'm good. I'm in Ireland. I'm at a friend's house."

"You look tired," she says. I catch my dad's knowing look behind her, clearly guessing what I'm up to. Their faces pull at me a little. Seeing her always wakes up the guilt.

"I've just woken up, Mom, that's why I look tired. I'm in Dublin and it's the middle of the night here. Really, I'm fine. All good. Are you okay? You don't need to worry about me."

Tears spring to her eyes and I get a sense of what my dad has been working with tonight. "Oh, Jonah, I know I don't have to worry about you. I love you so much, I don't know what I'd do if anything happened to you. You are so important to me, Jonah." The tears are coursing down her cheeks now, and her breath is fast and shallow. "Poor Amy," she says, and cries harder. "Poor Amy."

Sailí comes back to the bed, but she is careful to stay out of the frame. My gut turns over, and my body heats up, sweat breaking out on my forehead. According to the accident report, Amy died instantly from the impact. My mom was alive, but trapped in the car until someone found her, and we assume she was unconscious, but we don't know. She may have been there, awake and trapped with her dead child. The car was totaled—every window broken and the whole passenger side crushed in the flip. They had to cut them out. No clear cause was found at the scene. No doubt it was gone by then.

"It's good to see your face, Mom." I try to pull her back, pull us both back. Dad has disappeared from the screen. "What did you have for dinner?"

"I couldn't eat, Jonah, I was so worried. Your father kept trying to get me to stop worrying about what could happen, but I needed to see you. I love you so much, Jonah. Where are you? I haven't seen you in so long. You look so tired."

Caught in a loop. I can tell her again or I can go for distraction.

"Hey, Mom, guess what happened to me today?"

"What happened, Jonah, what happened?"

"Well," I start, "I went to class, and we did this whole day on talking about our experiences on the course, really examining our feelings—it was so weird. Not what I'm used to from engineering!" My mother's face is riveted to the phone as I tell her about my day in minute-to-minute detail. I explain about the mindfulness, the lunch with Sailí, leaving out the awkward conversation but keeping in the piano, and then back to class for group.

I tell her all about my water bottle moves and knuckle cracking, and then tell her about Meredith being so upset about how shallow I am, and Mom interrupts:

"What a bitch!" Her fury is real but brief, and I downplay my own reaction and add in Meredith's backstory to temper the bite to the story. Then I tell her about meeting up with my good friend, Sailí, again, and my tour of the print studio, and our dinner. Luckily, before I can get to the going-home-together part, Mom loses interest.

"Okay, Jonah!" she says, midsentence. "Good to talk to you! Here's Dad." Suddenly she is gone, and he is there, center frame.

"What happened after dinner with Sailí?" he asks, with big, fake-innocent eyes.

"Very funny, Dad." It's good to see him relaxing. But even as he lets the tension go, I can see the fatigue settle in. He shouldn't have to do this on his own, without me. He shouldn't have to do this at all.

"Good night, son," he says.

"Good night, Dad." We hang up, the familiar sinking feeling settling somewhere below my diaphragm.

I lie back on the bed and Sailí leans into my shoulder. "Everything okay?"

"Sorry about the sleep disruption," I say. "I had to play it like that so she could calm down, but I probably should have gone into the other room. I didn't want to throw her by moving the phone around. She gets into these moods and the best thing is to keep it simple." There's a pause while I stare at the ceiling. The silence is hanging there. "Amy is my sister. She died when she was eleven, in a car accident with my mother. My mother had a brain injury." There are those words again. "That's why she's like that. Emotional, changeable, rude, forgets stuff."

Sailí takes a deep breath, and I expect her to ask a question. "Not a problem," she says, instead. "I liked hearing about your day. I mean, the director's cut version." There is warmth in her voice as she shifts in a little closer. "In fact, I'm proud to have been part of the production, in the role of *good friend*."

"I should have done a pan-around, that would have got them talking," I say, and she giggles.

I am so grateful to her for letting the whole thing go I could kiss her, so I do. It might be the middle of the night but we're young; we don't need that much sleep.

28

Only a couple of hours later, I am standing at Roberts' office door at seven fifty-nine, waiting for the magical buzzer ringing time, and resenting it. Obviously, I am embarrassed about Friday, about what I said and about vomiting on his doorstep. I stand there reviewing what happened, how close I came to talking about the accident. What would he do if I told him? Who would he tell? That first day he went over the rules about confidentiality, and I didn't give a shit, but he definitely spoke about having to report some things. But internationally?

Before I have a chance to ring the buzzer, the door clicks. He must have a camera out here. I don't make eye contact as I enter and take my position on the couch. I'm not inclined to talk, but after a few minutes of silence Roberts says, "It can be difficult to begin," and then I am just as annoyed about being silent. I mean, what do I care?

I start talking about the kids' group and how strange it was to be in that situation, and also how much I enjoyed their openness and humor. I describe the different characters and the drawings, and that leads me on to talking about Teresa. I'm surprised at how much I have to say about her, about how she was with the children, but also about how she talked to the team afterward about the meaning in the work. It is hard to mention her without referencing how beautiful she is, and before long I'm relating the talk we had over the photographs and it's like I know how ridiculous I sound but I'm still caught in the intimacy of the conversation.

"I really felt something pass between us, like a moment when I could have leaned in to her, if you know what I mean. That vibe of something being available—but it passed quickly." Roberts is silent, and I go on, "And then again when everyone else was in the room and we were talking about the group, I felt it again. Like, an intensity between us." I am warming to this subject and in my mind, I can imagine what that might have been like, if I had leaned in. If I had rested my hand on her shoulder, or her waist, or stepped closer. Jesus Christ, get some perspective. "I mean, I'm not going to come on to her or anything obvious like that." I'm saying this to convince myself I'm not some weird predator. I mean, what is wrong with me? "She must have men making a play for her all the time. I'm not going to be another dickhead pervert, but the thought of it is nice." Somehow this sounds even worse. Is it nice? Am I a dickhead pervert?

Still nothing from Roberts and I lie there, thinking about Teresa's finer points and how I shouldn't be thinking about them.

"Some things are nice to think about." Roberts says, with the emphasis on "some." Clearly, he is making the point that other things are not nice to think about. Fuck him.

"Yes, Doctor," I say, my tone thick with sarcasm, "fantasizing about seducing Teresa is nice. That's what I said. I am very happy to focus on that. I can picture putting my hand on her ass all day long." I know I sound like a prick, but I don't care. He wants me to talk about the accident. He can't leave it alone.

Roberts does not react. After a long pause, he says quietly, "Some things are unbearable."

"Nothing in my life is unbearable, Roberts," I say, and I sit up to look at him. Roberts looks calmly back at me. "I am fine." Even as I say it, I am aware that if I was fine, I wouldn't be this damned hostile—I wouldn't have to stress every syllable of *I am fine*. Fine people don't do that. Roberts is completely still, and I stay sitting up. "I am here because I have to be here for my course. I was really, really sick on Friday, so I left."

Roberts looks back at me and his eyes are unreadable. "If you want to, you can leave."

Jesus Christ. I sit there looking at him and then I turn and lie back down. I don't say anything for what feels like an eternity. Then I say, "Or I can just not say anything." And still pay the damned fee.

Roberts says, "That's our time, Jonah." I get up to leave,

resisting, as always, the urge to touch the fireplace, the cool marble. If it is marble. For some reason, it takes a lot longer to get to the door than it has before. When I walk out onto the street, I stand there, breathing in and out. After a few breaths, I am reminded of the mindfulness yesterday and then Meredith's complaint, and suddenly I'm laughing at the thought of how happy she would be that I hate therapy so much. I bet she loves it. All that talking to someone who *has* to listen.

The walk to college takes me past Christchurch Cathedral and down along Dame Street, passing tourists everywhere even at this early hour. On the way, I stop to pick up the best coffee I've had in Ireland at a tiny Italian coffee shop that is packed with people on their way to somewhere else. There's a tap on my shoulder and I look down into a face that is vaguely familiar.

"Jonah?" she says, and it takes me a second, so she follows up with, "It's Aoife, Margaret's daughter. Hello? Rotary family?" She's grinning and I remember her flirting style. Oh, yes.

"Aoife!" I say. "Can I buy you a coffee?" I should have recognized her by the short skirt alone.

"Oh, no," she says, "I'll get my own. How are you getting on in college?"

I buy her coffee, anyway, and fill her in on my progress thus far, being frank enough about my lack of enthusiasm for the course as we walk to the college. Aoife laughs out loud at my description of having to sit in a circle with a bunch of women and talk about my deep feelings and about how, it turns out, I'm surprisingly shallow. Her laugh is so warm and open, I do what I can to make it happen over and over, mimicking the drama that seems to unfold in every class. The constant tears. The attack on charm. We walk across Front Square together, and then have to part ways.

"We should meet up," Aoife says, holding my gaze as people pass by.

"We should," I agree, and she offers her number, which I promptly put in my phone. Nobody says a word about poor Ciarán. I text her right away, so she has my number, and I get back an instant thumbs-up emoji.

"See ya," she says, then turns her back to me and saunters away in a manner that suggests she knows I am watching her go.

I still have that vision in my mind as I cheerfully walk into class and a chill promptly descends. I can tell there is something going on—I'm not getting a lot of eye contact from anyone, and after we sit down Meredith gets up and walks out, purposefully. I send a look toward Rose and she smiles back at me, but something in her expression puts me on my guard. I am surprised that there is such an emotion hangover from yesterday's group, particularly since everything seemed finished before we left. Weird, but over.

Our lecture today is on psychoanalytic psychotherapy, and the woman describing it is a fellow American who reminds me of my high school English teacher—all business. She describes the "frame" of therapy: the consistency of the room, the time and length of the appointments, and how important that can be to help the person in therapy feel secure enough to "take risks." She also talks about the feelings the client has for the therapist, called "transference," and the feelings the therapist has for the client, "countertransference."

I'm thinking about Roberts and his office when the door opens, and Annemarie sticks her head in. "Jonah? Can I see you for a moment?"

In a split second I am back in elementary school and have that sudden, familiar foreboding of trouble. I get up and walk through the door and around the corner to Annemarie's office. When we go in, there is Meredith, crying. What the fuck else is new? Anger rises through my chest and tightens my shoulders. Annemarie has miraculously made space in her office for Meredith to sit on one of the chairs, and she quickly clears another chair for me, moving a pile of paper from its seat onto a different pile of paper on the floor. I fight an intense urge to walk the hell out, but I stay put, and sit down.

"Is everything okay?" I ask when the silence goes on forever.

Annemarie answers me, her face neutral. "Well, no, it's not, not really. I'm a little concerned about what Meredith has shared with me this morning, and I want to have a conversation with you about it. I don't really want Meredith to be a part of our conversation, but she has agreed to speak with you directly about her concerns now, if you are okay to listen? Then, you and I can talk about it." Do we really need such a clear road map for such a ridiculous situation?

"Sure," I say, "I mean, she spoke to me already in the process group, but if you want to say it again, Meredith, knock yourself out." I start the sentence nearly sincere, but by the end of it I know I sound flippant.

Meredith looks at me and says in a low, steady voice, "Jonah. This is not about what I said in group yesterday. This is about me hearing you this morning when I was walking into college go on and on with some friend of yours about how stupid our class is, and how much you hate it. I feel very undermined and invalidated by your behavior, and I think it was very disrespectful to all of us. How are we meant to share our experiences in such an unsafe space?" This takes me by surprise, all right. Aoife.

"Okay, Meredith," Annemarie says, calmly. "Jonah, are you okay to have a conversation with me about this or do you want Meredith to stay?"

I speak back in the same calm voice. "I'm good with just me and you talking." Quite possibly, Meredith is expecting me to be angry or worried about this, and I am not giving her that. In fact, I am forcing a completely calm expression, and looking forward to Meredith leaving the room. She is clearly the crazy person in this scenario. Why would I want to talk with her here? No wonder there was a chill in the air—who knows what Meredith told them. Rose, I think. I didn't mean Rose.

"Fine," says Meredith, and she leaves the room, still tearful. She closes the door carefully.

Annemarie turns to me and raises her eyebrows. I wait for her to speak. "Okay, Jonah. What's the story?"

"Listen, Annemarie," I say, leaning forward, "Meredith is completely right. I was bitching about the class with a friend I met on my way in this morning. I was most assuredly disrespectful about the people, and the course, and complained specifically about something Meredith said in the group. I'm really sorry." I was caught red-handed. Might as well take the honest road if it's the only road available.

"Did you mention anyone's name or describe them in any way? Did you say the word *Meredith*?"

I have to think about that for a minute. "No, I didn't," I say, and I'm pretty sure that's right. "I did mention *one lunatic* but I don't think anyone could narrow that down to Meredith." Annemarie looks at me and I realize humor is not my best option here.

I'm nervous. I crank up serious. "No. I didn't say anyone's name, and I'm sorry I was disrespectful but mostly I was just joking around with this girl I met once before, who I think might have been hitting on me. I'm sorry that that upset Meredith." Annemarie looks at me again with her steady green gaze and I repeat it in a more sincere-sounding voice. "I *am* sorry, even though I don't sound very sincere. This is an unusual situation for me. I'm caught off guard." Also, I think but don't say, Meredith was already pissed off with me and probably relished the thought of turning me in. It doesn't take a psychologist to figure that out, for Christ's sake. There's no way to say it without coming across as vindictive, so I keep my mouth shut. I know how to do that.

Annemarie leans back and looks at the ceiling. "I get that, Jonah, but it *is* important that people feel safe. It's okay to process what your experience is with your friends, or whoever, but you have to temper that with respect, or at the very least, discretion. People are trying very hard on this course to learn and grow. I'm sure you see how hard they are working."

"I do," I say, and I do. "I'm really sorry." Maybe I mean that one.

"The thing is, Jonah, these kinds of incidents are important to address in the wider class. You all will have another process group next month, and you might think about bringing in this incident, even if Meredith doesn't." Annemarie is speaking to me as if there is a chance in hell I will bring this up, or more ridiculously, that Meredith won't. I nod at her. "You might be surprised at how important a rupture like this is in the development of the group process." I nod again and sense the end of the meeting coming.

Annemarie looks at me and then stares out the window for a minute. Then she looks back. "Is there anything you want to discuss with me, Jonah?" Not the end of the meeting, clearly.

I think about her question. "Not really."

"Are things going okay for you? This is really a trial by fire for someone who isn't particularly driven in the field of psychology." She leaves a pause. Trial by fire? What happened to the stupid one hundred percent effort?

"I think it's going okay," I say, "I mean, apart from the past few minutes." She doesn't respond to this. "I don't particularly like going to therapy," I continue, "and I am different from the other people on the course, so yeah, I was complaining, for sure. But it's interesting and I'm okay; you don't need to worry about me."

"I'm not worried about you, Jonah." She looks out the window again. "People act out in different ways when they are under pressure, sure. I wonder about what you said, though. Are you so different from the other people on the course?"

I don't say anything because what I have to say seems so obvious. We sit there for a minute or so and then she takes a deep breath. "I think we might be done here?" she asks, and I agree with a nod. I leave her office and stand in the short hallway. Turn right and head back into class, or turn left and blow the whole thing off? The last thing I need is a room full of annoyed women watching my every move, but then, what the hell do I care? Instead of going straight in, I turn left and go down to the foyer to buy a nice Americano. Once it is in hand, I'm happy to walk back into class, the smell of hot, well-made coffee coming in with me as I sit down.

The lecturer smiles at me and says, "Welcome back," in a way that suggests she overheard some of the drama earlier and wants to put me at my ease.

"Thanks," I say, and smile back like I don't have a care in the world. The class continues for another few minutes, and then there's a short break called. Everyone files out until it's me, Rose, and the lecturer. Why would I go anywhere? I have my coffee.

Rose looks me in the eye. "Did you complain about me, too, to this leggy blonde?"

"Only about the boots," I say, and she laughs.

The lecturer laughs too. "Classic American mistake, assuming anonymity. You have to remember that this is a very small country—discretion is always the best policy. I'd say if you hooked up with the blonde, she'd have at least one or two cousins who are on the course here with you."

Rose looks at me knowingly, and I have to swallow. "That is a mistake that I keep making."

29

After a full day of awkward class experiences, I walk over to Temple Bar and ring the bell on the studio door. Sailí didn't respond to my text so I decide to turn up and see if I can buy her a drink along with the dozen or so I am planning to ingest. A guy with a beard answers, and tells me that Sailí has left for the day but might be down a few doors in the Elephant and the Castle with a friend. Sure enough, she is there in the window listening intently to another guy with a beard, who is gesturing wildly. I'm in an awkward decision-making moment where my options are to turn around or casually walk past, when she spots me and waves. I wave back and she gestures for me to come in and join them. I start shaking my head and walking backward and run directly into a street musician who is setting up his amplifier. Luckily, there is no damage done, but by the time I have righted myself and all his equipment, Sailí is by my side, dragging me into the restaurant to sit down with her and her friend. Aidan, she tells me, is also a printmaker and they share the studio space. He has a warm, open face and genuinely doesn't seem to mind me joining them, so I give in and order a drink.

"How was class?" Sailí asks.

"Not terrific," I say, "but better than therapy." There's a sentence I never expected to say.

"Poor Jonah, the reluctant psychologist." Sailí laughs. "I was just telling Aidan about that crazy group with your classmates you were describing yesterday."

Jesus Christ. A wave of panic rises in me and I put my head down on the table.

"What?" says Sailí.

"I literally spent the entire day with a group of women who are furious at me because one of them overheard me complaining about how nuts they are, and then that lit the fuse for the rest of them to be seriously pissed off. And now here you are, passing it on to some guy you work with in the middle of a restaurant!" Aidan chuckles so I know he isn't taking any offense. My voice is hushed and anxious.

"Let me guess," says Sailí, her voice as clear as a bell, "was it Meredith who started it?"

"Sailí, you are killing me." I look around at the other diners in our immediate vicinity and no one appears to be paying any attention to us. "I'm serious, they were ready to lynch me, and I even had to have a meeting with the course director about my indiscretion. Then the lecturer told me everyone in this tiny country is related to one another and your mother was sitting right there."

My drink arrives and I wait for the Guinness to settle. Sailí and Aidan have a good laugh at my well-earned paranoia but thankfully drop the subject and move on to talking about the artists and managers they work with, who sound as difficult as my classmates. As they talk and the alcohol works its magic, the tension leaves my body. I'm watching Sailí in profile as she animatedly describes some drama of the day to Aidan and thinking that she really is beautiful when she looks at me and pauses.

"Are you all right?" she asks.

"Perfect."

"That must be the fastest working pint in history," says Aidan.

Just then, my phone buzzes and when I look, it's Georgia.

Sailí says, "Go ahead and take it," and I know she knows who it is, probably by my expression. I don't take the call, but the vibe has changed. Whatever resolution I felt we had come to is a fantasy at best, and a coolness descends. I finish the drink, and excuse myself to walk home. Sailí doesn't object, staying with Aidan and offering me only a friendly wave as I leave the table. On the way back home, I call Georgia.

When she answers, I ask, "How are things in the Big Apple?"

"Good, good," she says, and describes what is happening on the course she is doing. They have a placement assignment on her course, as well, and Georgia has an internship with a woman who is meant to be extremely difficult, a dragon of the fashion marketing field. True to form, Georgia is having no problem at all with her. In fact, her boss has invited her out to Martha's Vineyard for a few days over Christmas, to work on a social media campaign. Typical Georgia—blossoming where others wilt. "I wanted to check with you what was happening for Christmas before I confirmed with Maggie," Georgia says, and there is a pause. I haven't thought about it.

"Aren't you going home for Christmas?" I ask. Her mom lives not far from my parents, with a boyfriend. I've lost track of where her father is living.

"I'm not sure what I'm doing," says Georgia, and I know I have missed a cue. Georgia is not a woman who would ask twice. She changes the subject. "Speaking of home, I got a call from your mom."

"You did?" This is unusual.

"Well, from both your parents," says Georgia. "She was upset about you and wanted to know if you were with me. Your dad told her where you were, but she wanted to check. You know." I did know.

"I hope she didn't say anything that upset you," I say. Strange that my dad didn't mention the call to Georgia. He usually gives me the heads up on that kind of thing. Maybe because I was in Sailí's place. He's a smart man.

"Frankly, I was glad she thought to ask me," says Georgia. "She talked about you for a long while. She told me about you as a baby, and then as a teenager. She bragged about how popular you were. How all the guys wanted to hang out with you. It was cute. "

I stop walking and lean up against the wall of a building, the red brick solid against my back. I close my eyes so I can concentrate on her voice. "That's so funny," I say. "You know how she is. I couldn't really have guys over. I remember one time I did she practically came on to one of them. He didn't know what the hell to do."

Georgia laughs and the deepness of her voice hits a nerve below my navel. "I bet he didn't. She's quite a hottie."

"Hey, that's my mother you're talking about," I say, but it is good to be having a little fun. "Do you want to come over here for Christmas?" I ask impulsively.

"I'm not begging, Jonah."

"I'm the one begging, Georgia." And I am. Something calm and uncomplicated. I do miss her. Her smell. The length of her body against me. Her blanket refusal to make any demands.

"I'll think about it," she says. We chat a bit longer, and she finishes up. Standing against the wall I think about the day, and I am exhausted. What I need now is some mindless time with straightforward people who expect nothing from me. Luckily, I am heading in the right direction. When I get to the apartment, I open the door and there are the twins, parallel on the couch, deep into some PlayStation game.

"Jonah!" they shout in unison, and I am so pleased to see them.

30

Thursday, and I'm back in the Castleknock kitchen happily inputting data from the questionnaires when Teresa comes in looking for me. This morning, she's in a figure-hugging black knit dress, gray tights, and knee-high boots, with her hair pinned up. The dress has some ruffles around the neckline that draw the attention to the V at the front. I work hard to keep my eye level above the neck.

"Do you have any time this afternoon?" she asks. "I need to have a meeting with one of the parents from the group, and I'd like you to be there if possible. It should be interesting, anyway."

"Teresa," I say, "my time is your time. Whenever suits you, I can be available. I'm doing this all day." I gesture at the stack of paper and the laptop.

"Okay," she says, and explains that Seán's mother, Tríona, has asked to meet with her before she can let him come back to the group next week. In her experience, this is not an unusual situation—parents can sometimes get cold feet about having the kid discuss the family in a public forum. "Or maybe something came up for Seán after the group that she is worried about, you never know. It's much better that she contacted us for a meeting, because she could have pulled him out of the group altogether." She pauses, considering. "Why don't you come up to my office at two, and we can go over the group for Monday. I'll see if she can come for two thirty or three o'clock."

"Sounds good," I say, probably keeping an unusual amount of eye contact.

Teresa walks out and a few minutes later Patrick comes in. "Hey," he says.

"Hey," I say. "I was just talking to Teresa." My face is as neutral as I can make it.

"Nice dress," he says, matching my expression. It's good to know you aren't the only one noticing.

Later in the day, I climb the stairs to Teresa's office. She had one client after another all morning and didn't come down for lunch. When I stick my head through the half-open door, she is opening a thermos, and before long the smell of good coffee fills the room. "Hi, Jonah," she says. "I hope you don't mind if I drink this while we talk. I'm not trying to be disrespectful—I need the caffeine." I think of my behavior with the Americano yesterday, and I'm glad I don't blush easily.

The focus for the group on Monday is "Marriage and Divorce." It turns out we follow the same structure as last Monday with the opening activity, and then working with the drawings to create some group discussion, with my specialty: snack. Obviously, Teresa points out, we need to be careful with the word "marriage"—it can be a bit tricky because many of the kids' parents aren't married, so we work with "getting together" and "breaking up" as well. The first sheet in the workbook for Monday is on "Getting Together for Life" and they can draw a picture or make a list of reasons why people get together.

"So, Jonah," says Teresa, "why do people get married?" There is a pause and I realize she is really asking me. It isn't a rhetorical question.

"Because they love each other?" As soon as I say it, I know I sound ten years old. The influence of all those Disney movies I watched with Amy, over and over again, because she loved them so much. Probably because we both loved them. I catch myself before the thoughts of her land properly. "Or because someone gets pregnant?"

Teresa is looking at me intently and I know she can see something happened. "Any other reasons? I'm not sure pregnancy is a motivator anymore."

"Because they think it means something—a commitment for life. Because they think it is important. Because they want other people to think it is important, to take the relationship seriously. Or political or economic reasons, I guess." What do I know about commitment? But then I think about my father. All those years by her side, adapting, caring for her. Protecting her from the world and its confusion. That's commitment. I've seen it in action.

"Okay," says Teresa, "and why do they break up?"

"Incompatibility? Money? Sex? Or it's too hard, too complicated. Or they are fighting all the time. Or they meet someone else, and they can't help themselves. Infidelity. Betrayal." This is a bit easier for me, surprise, surprise. Teresa is nodding, and a little shadow passes across her face. It's quick, but I see it.

"All of those reasons are likely to come up on Monday, Jonah. You might be surprised at how insightful the participants are about what is happening between their parents. People think that their children aren't paying attention, but they forget—parents are fascinating to their children—any change is noticed. Any tiny crack in the foundation is felt. Children hear more, see more, and think more than most of their parents give them credit for." As she is speaking her color is rising, and now there are high pink patches on both cheeks.

"Do you have kids?" I ask, and immediately regret the question.

"No," she says, and then again, "no." There is another pause and I don't make a joke. She looks at me and I can see the sadness in her face.

"Sorry for asking," I say.

"It's okay, Jonah," she says. "Just a little sore point. There's a lot going on. The baby thing is a project I'm working on."

I immediately get an image of her working on that project and once again am glad that I don't blush. Teresa laughs. "You look so much like a psychologist right now, Jonah. All intense listening while containing your reaction. You really are wasted on engineering."

Thank God she cannot read my mind.

The phone rings, and it is reception. Tríona and Seán are downstairs. Teresa is surprised that she has brought Seán, and suggests that I keep him down in reception and work on an activity, if Tríona agrees. She hands me a board game, and tells me to stay where we can be observed in reception. We go down together, and Seán looks up at us like we are executioners.

The waiting area is empty except for them, and they are taking up the least amount of space possible, huddled together on two small chairs. "Would it be okay with you, Tríona, if Jonah works on this game with Seán for a few minutes, while you and I talk? Then I can invite him in, in case there's anything he wants to say?" Tríona agrees and Teresa turns to Seán. "Is that okay with you, Seán?" Seán takes a long time to consider this, and then nods.

The two women head upstairs, and I try to look like this is a normal thing. "Okay, Seán," I say, "let's have a look at this." My enthusiasm sounds ridiculously hollow to me, like a frustrated camp counselor. I sit on the floor and open the box. Inside there are about four dozen metal rods of different shapes. There's a stand you put together, and the object of the game is to hang all the metal rods, one by one, on the stand. It's about balancing the weight so the whole thing doesn't fall over. I read out loud the "Getting Started" card and set up the stand.

I'm dividing up the metal rods when Seán speaks.

"Whatever she's saying is not true." I look at him and he does not look upset. His eyes are dry, and he is completely focused on this message. "My ma, up there. She is telling lies. She always tells lies."

Immediately, I am completely out of my depth. Like, in the middle of the ocean out of my depth. "Seán," I say, "I have no idea what is going on up there. I don't know what she is saying because I am here with you."

"But she is lying." His eyes begin to fill. "You have to tell Teresa. She's a liar. She's always trying to get me into trouble."

I look straight back at him. "Listen, Seán, I will tell Teresa what you have said here to me. Definitely. One hundred percent. Also, you can tell her when we go up there. I know she will listen to you because she listens to everyone."

He swallows, working hard to keep himself from crying. There is something about the effort he is making that makes my own throat tighten. I take a deep breath and then he breathes deeply, unconsciously following my lead.

Seán sits down and picks up one of the rods, hooking it onto the horizontal piece of the stand. The stand shifts dramatically against the vertical base but doesn't fall over. I hook one of my rods on the opposite side, and it stabilizes the structure. Seán looks at me and picks up another rod. Minutes pass, and piece by piece we construct a complex sculpture that sways but does not fall. One more rod from Seán, and the whole thing spins. We hold our breath until the spin stops and the balance persists. "That's so good," whispers Seán, and I am equally transfixed.

"Okay, Seán?" says Teresa, and we both look up. She is smiling but there is something else in her eyes. "Okay to come upstairs, now?" We stand and suddenly we're brothers being called in from outside for some bad news. Seán looks at me, and I start walking toward the stairs. He follows.

When I reach Teresa I ask, "Do you want me to come in?" Seán looks over like he didn't expect the possibility that I wouldn't be with them.

"Yes, I think so, Jonah," says Teresa, who has not missed a thing.

In the office is Tríona, her eyes and cheeks damp with tears. She glances at me when Teresa asks if it is okay for me to sit in, and nods. I am on high alert from what has happened downstairs, and there is something about her expression I don't like. But what? Seán sits next to his mother but does not respond to her outstretched hand. She lowers it.

"Okay," says Teresa, her voice steady and warm. "I really appreciate you both coming in. Seán, your mother was asking a bit about what we covered in the group together and I filled her in on the stuff the group talked about, in general, although I left out the bit about Jonah's ears." Seán smiles, visibly relaxing, and I grin back at him. "I hope that is okay." Seán nods. "Also," says Teresa, "your mother shared with me some of the worries that she has about how things are in your house, and she asked my advice on those things." At this, Seán stiffens. I see anger and fear pass across his face, and he glares at his mother before looking down at his lap. He crosses his arms and tucks his fingers in close to his body, his entire posture closing down. "Is there anything you want to say about anything?" Seán does not look up and remains totally silent. It's like someone has pressed "mute."

Tríona blows her nose on a rumpled tissue and takes another from the box in front of her. I feel a strange hostility toward her from what Seán said to me—like this is all for show. Tríona looks up and sees me staring, so I look away, focusing on Seán. Teresa lets a few moments pass before speaking again. "I know that you are in a tricky spot here, Seán, but I want to make sure you can tell me something if you need to." Again, Seán is silent. Tríona looks at him, but he does not look back.

"Sometimes it can be really hard to say something," says Teresa, and I hear an echo of Roberts. Jesus, I can't think about that here. Again, there is no response from Seán. "And this isn't your only chance. It might be that you need to think about things. In the meantime, I am going to talk to some people who might be able to help out with some of your mother's worries, because I think that is important." We can all see Seán begin to cry but he remains silent and nearly motionless. "Oh, Seán," says Teresa, "I'm so sorry that you are upset."

Moments pass with no one saying anything. I glance over and see that Tríona is now looking at me. She turns away when I hold her gaze. I keep running over in my head what Seán said downstairs but I'm not sure if I should say anything now about it. There is no indication from Seán—no eye contact, no sign that he wants me to speak. Finally, Teresa starts talking again. "Okay, well, today is Thursday and our next group is on Monday, so I'll see you there, Seán. Thank you, Tríona, for sharing your concerns with me. Let me do a bit of work now on my end, and I'll give you a call about our next meeting together. Anything else from anyone?" Teresa looks at the two of them but does not look directly at me. There is no way for me to signal to her unless I say something, and I don't. I picture that first meeting with Gary, the dad, and how fucked up that was. If I say something wrong now, I could make the situation so much worse. Teresa winds the meeting up and Seán and Tríona slowly walk downstairs. Teresa and I follow as far as the bottom of the staircase but then turn to head into the kitchen.

In the doorway, Teresa says to me under her breath, "Quick cup of tea and then back upstairs to debrief, yeah?" I nod and we walk into the melee of afternoon break with everyone looking for sugar and caffeine. I don't think about what Seán is walking into. I can't.

A few minutes later, we head back to the stairs, but before I get up a step the receptionist calls out, "Hey Jonah! What's the story with the waiting room?" Remembering the game, I head in to put it away and see that there are metal rods everywhere—across the floor, on the chairs, under the table.

"What happened?" I ask, and she shakes her head.

"That little Seán ran in on their way out. I thought he'd forgotten something until I saw this. He must have given them some kick."

Kindly, she helps me pick up all the pieces, and put them back in the box. Tension starts to curdle the tea I just finished as I carry the game upstairs.

I find Teresa looking dejectedly into her thermos, even though we just had a caffeine hit. "Wait a minute," she says, and rifles through her desk until she triumphantly pulls out a huge Dairy Milk Fruit and Nut bar. "A-ha!" Carefully she breaks the bar into several pieces and then opens it completely on her desk, motioning me to help myself. Teresa puts a piece in her mouth and closes her eyes with pleasure. Distracted for a moment by the scene, it is only the weight of the game in my hand that reminds me what I'm doing here, and I explain to her how I found it downstairs.

"Oh, poor Seán," she says, as I put it back on the shelf, and sit down next to her desk, my back against the wall. She takes another piece of chocolate and I studiously avoid watching her eat it. There is only so much I can take.

"There's more," I say, and explain the whole episode when Seán told me about his mother lying. I include everything I can remember in my description and attempt to relay the conversation verbatim. I try to get across the intensity of Seán's communication—even his attempts to control his emotions to get his point across clearly. Such a little guy, trying to hold himself together.

"Well," she says, leaning forward, "that is interesting, considering what happened in my meeting." Teresa then describes her time with Tríona, who talked about her fear of her husband and his angry outbursts. "She said that Gary quizzed Seán about the group, about what he might have said, and it frightened her—which is why she wanted to meet with us." Teresa leans back in her chair and stretches. "Tríona told me he has a history of abusive behavior, emotional and physical abuse against her, but she has never told anyone about it. Now she's worried about Seán. That puts us in an awkward position." She looks at her watch. "It's after four; I'd better make the call now. Can you please write down what you remember from your discussion with Seán?" Teresa hands me some lined paper and looks around. The only place in the room I could possibly work is at her desk or at one of the tiny tables. Reluctantly, she moves the chocolate.

"What call?" I ask. "Are you calling Gary?" I'm trying to figure out how that would help.

"No," she explains, "I'm calling Tusla, the government's child and family agency. I have to report any suspected abuse situations that involve children. I'm what they call *a mandated person*. Mandatory reporting requires me to make a report if I suspect a child could be at risk. If I think it is immediate risk, I can call first and do the online form or the paperwork later." This is ringing a bell. This is what I was trying to remember with Roberts.

"And do you think Seán is at immediate risk?" I ask. "What if Tríona is lying, like Seán said?" I think about Gary and Tríona. Gary is an asshole, no doubt. But Tríona seems off as well. That poor kid.

"What if Seán is lying to protect his father? I don't know what the truth is here, Jonah. How could I? Something is happening in the family, that's for sure, and I had a woman in here reporting that her husband, who she says has a history of verbally and physically abusive behavior, is frightening her and their son. The parents are splitting up, so there is heightened tension in the house, and now everyone is possibly feeling exposed because of poor Seán coming to our group and talking about it. Not that he is, really. He hasn't had a chance."

"But we barely know them, Teresa!" There is a note of panic in my voice but I don't understand it. "I mean, can't we wait and see how it goes, or at least let Seán talk to you one-on-one?" I wish that kid hadn't trusted me. I wish he had spoken up with Teresa in the room. "You didn't see his face, Teresa. I'm telling you that kid was certain his mother was lying to you about something."

Teresa looks at me, concern in her eyes. I don't know if it is for Seán or for me. "Anyway, what can Tusla do about it?" I ask. I keep digging in.

"They can drop in to the house to do an assessment. They can refer the family to a support worker, who can help them manage conflict better as a couple, or refer them for parenting classes. They can get *An Garda Síochána*, the Irish police force, involved if they have to. They can take Seán and his mother to a safe location. They can separate Seán from his parents if it is in his best interest. Or, you know, they can make a note of it and add him to some list. Whatever happens next, I don't have a choice about this. It's the law." She has on her calm voice.

"The police? Seriously? Or foster care? But what if she is lying? It's one conversation. One conversation with a woman whose own kid doesn't believe her." I am trying to put the brakes on, slow down the process. This official report seems totally out of proportion after a few tears and a fifteen-minute meeting. I think about Seán's resignation in the room. How was he supposed to object, with his mother right there?

Teresa puts her hand on the phone and looks me in the eye. "Would you lie to protect your mother or father, if one of them turned against the other?" I have an immediate memory of my father's arms, bruised from having to hold my mother during one of her tantrums in the early days. Or the scratches on his face. Or my own bruises, when I was home alone with her. I would, and did, say anything to cover up what was going on. Lie? I've spent my whole life lying. Teresa sees the answer in my face and picks up the phone, her notes open in front of her.

"Wait, wait," I say, and she puts the phone down. But I have nothing to say. What the fuck am I doing in the middle of this? I know what it is like for a family to explode.

Teresa looks at me gently. "Jonah," she says, "this is the hard part of the job. Not knowing what is going on and having to decide one way or the other. I don't know what the reality is in that house. I don't know what might happen because I am making this call. But I have to do it, and then I have to manage the consequences as best I can." She lifts the handset again.

All told, it takes about a half hour of conversation. There is a lot of discussion of "risk factors" and "consent." Clearly, Tríona knows Teresa is reaching out to the agency, but no one has told Gary, as far as we know. Teresa describes our contact with Gary, and summarizes my interaction with him, repeatedly stressing my lack of experience. She also describes him physically, and looks up to confirm with me her estimates of his height and weight. I am more and more uncomfortable about Seán at home in this mess. I keep thinking about how quickly he moved from kidding around to total withdrawal, and then back again to playful. The social worker asks Teresa to put me on the phone, and I describe my conversation with Seán. I'm conscious of Teresa in the room with me, and I don't want to openly contradict her, but it doesn't seem right. I'm like a teenager reluctantly calling a parent from the school office.

The social worker sounds exhausted but professional. She asks me to repeat what Seán said and how he said it. I do my best to be clear, and hand the phone back to Teresa. When we are finished with the call, Teresa leans back in her chair and stretches, accentuating the narrowness of her waist under the tight dress, among other things.

"I know it's difficult, Jonah. I really thought this group would be a straightforward experience for you, and instead we are knee-deep in a very distressed family. Even for an experienced clinician, a case like this can make you feel helpless and overwhelmed." She prints off the forms we need to fill out and leaves them in a stack on her desk. "Let's do these in the morning along with the online forms." She pauses. "Oh, wait, you aren't here tomorrow. Friday already."

"I can come in, no problem. I have therapy at eight, but I can be in here by nine thirty or ten. Or I can cancel therapy and meet you here early if you want. I hate it, anyway. I'd happily pay the guy to leave me alone."

Teresa laughs, and it cuts the tension. "What's wrong with him?" she asks, and then immediately puts her hand up. "Don't tell me, don't tell me. There is nothing worse than talking about your therapist. Therapy is hard enough without someone else's perspective. If you can, come in for ten. We'll do it then. Thanks."

We straighten up the office and walk down together. She runs back upstairs for a minute while I take our cups into the kitchen and take a few long, deep breaths, trying to shake off the tension. When she comes down it is impossible to miss the fact she has brushed her hair out—it now falls in soft waves past her shoulders. She's done something with her makeup, too, and she looks fresh and awake, even after a long and difficult day.

There isn't a sound from any of the other offices, and although it is only just after five the parking lot is near dark. I walk her out to her X5, the last car in the lot. In the light breeze, I get the slight smell of her perfume, familiar and comforting. Leaving the building behind us, I'm reminded of how she has a whole other life, away from this place and her work. She's wearing a light jacket over the knit dress and as we stop by the car I wonder if she is cold. "Are you okay?" I ask her. I'm suddenly aware this whole drama could be upsetting for her, too, including all my whining and emotion. It's hard for me to read her expression in the low light but maybe she is feeling helpless and overwhelmed, like she said.

"I'm fine, Jonah," she says, putting her hand on my arm and looking into my face, her eyes clear and beautiful. The warmth and weight of her hand through the sleeve of my shirt surprises me, and it triggers a deeper heat reaction of its own. "This is my bread and butter. But it is kind of you to ask. Take care of yourself tonight—make sure you have a big steak and a good sleep." Something in her voice pulls at me. Affection? A deepening? I take a half step toward her, holding eye contact so she has to tilt her face up a little, and my hand reaches the arch of her back. There is a short pause when my palm is on fire against her and then Teresa takes a step back, dropping her hand and her eyes.

"See you tomorrow," she says lightly, and quickly hops into the driver's seat. I stand there in the growing dark as she pulls down the driveway and, with a little beep, turns left. Did I just do that? What the fuck is wrong with me?

31

Friday morning, I wake with a sense of dread, a dry mouth, and a headache. It takes me a minute to find my bearings and I do a little inventory in my head. Home. College. Therapy. Georgia. Sailí. The clinic. Basically, it is all fucked up. Teresa. I think about that moment in the parking lot in vivid detail and a wave of humiliation washes over me. What was my plan, there? A dark parking lot? My supervisor? I force the thought away.

Last night I came back to the apartment via the corner grocery store and bought a steak, as ordered. I also bought some beer. The twins were out, and I sat and watched bad television, ate steak, and drank until an early bedtime. I shower and shave, and head out to see Roberts.

On the couch the only thing I can think about is that moment with Teresa. I don't have the stamina to sit there in silence looking at the fire, so I tell Roberts the story of how the day went with planning for the group and then all the drama with Seán and his family. When I am describing constructing the game with Seán, tension builds in my throat and chest, but I keep moving forward with the story and it passes. Roberts starts to say something, but I cut him off.

"Wait, wait," I say, and keep talking. The accusation, the discussion with Teresa about the mandatory report, the social worker and her tired, robotic voice. Finally, I get to the moment in the parking lot. I describe the lead up, the walk to the car. The darkness. I tell him about asking her how she was, and how she responded, putting her hand on my arm, looking into my eyes as she spoke. I describe how attracted to her I was in that split second, how every inch of my skin was alert to her, and how I stepped in toward her. That moment when her face tilted up, and the length of her neck. Even how good she smelled. And then I stop talking. My heart pounds and I am covered in sweat. I can't say it. Her little step back. Her swift movement into the car. The friendly tap on the horn as she left the parking lot. All perfectly the right thing to do. The right thing to do when a confused kid you are supervising makes a clumsy and weird play for you in a dark parking lot after a shitty day at work.

I am still not talking, and Roberts doesn't say a thing. I lie there, breathing and sweating. Teresa is a pro at this. She knew what she was doing, the gentle redirect, the kind and subtle brush off—how many times has she had to do it? Even the little beep on the horn to tell me everything was okay. Knowing I have to go back in there today makes me physically sick. No way am I describing all that to this asshole. Let him think it all worked out; let him think we went at it right there up against her SUV. Let him think what he wants.

Roberts is there, waiting, and I let him wait. Finally, I say, "I don't know what I'm doing here." He says nothing. A familiar anger rises up in me along with the urge to walk out, but what would that help? I am exhausted and a tight sensation behind my eyes tells me I am close to tears. The thought of crying on this fucking couch with Roberts silently staring at me in his stupid shoes snaps me out of the exhaustion and I take a deep breath. I can wait him out. Minutes pass. Then I ask my question.

"What about this mandatory reporting business, anyway?" I sit up on the couch, and I look at him directly. Gray pants, gray shirt. "What if somebody did something wrong, but it was an accident? Like, if someone left a candle lit and a house burned down. Would you have to report that? If they told you they had done it? If people died? A child?"

Roberts looks back at me. "Is that your question, Jonah?" We both know this isn't about a candle. I breathe in the burning woodsmoke, and start to unravel.

"Yes, that's my question. Please answer it. Don't repeat something I've said." I am ready to launch across the room at him. His body looks completely relaxed, and I am a coiled spring.

"No, I wouldn't have to report it. Not unless they meant to burn down the house and kill the child, and were planning to light more candles in more houses with children in them. Not if they had just made a mistake." His voice is low and smooth.

My heart starts pounding, and the smoke is all around me. "What if it wasn't a candle, Roberts? What if it was the scariest fucking spider you've ever seen?" Suddenly I'm there. Ten years ago, at a camp I didn't even want to go to. I was so *over* Boy Scouts with their stupid oaths, and their community service, and their obedience. I had a mother who wanted to get rid of me for a week of peace—that's the only reason I was there, and everyone knew it. And then a few days in, a miracle. I spotted some fine gauze under a dry log and there it was, a wolf spider. Nearly impossible to find or capture because of its dark brown body and speed, but I found one and caught it. Not only that, a large female, nearly three inches across, with about a hundred baby spiders clinging to her back, hatched but not yet ready to live on their own. The only spider that carries its young. In the net, we turned a flashlight on her, and she lit up like a disco ball, a million little eyes glowing back at us. Easily the most impressive creature ever captured, at any camp. I remember my scout leader's praise. And his heavy hand on my shoulder, squeezing.

We took her to the specimen room to watch her and the spiderlings in the terrarium, and dropped a couple grasshoppers in. The best hunter in the forest, she advanced quickly, and just as she approached, I heard my name called. I looked up, and there was the regional director, holding a pack of cigarettes we all knew were found in my bunk. Everyone cleared out for the explosion. Everyone but me.

I am close to throwing up again in Roberts' office. "What if that asshole kid stole the spider and all her fucking babies from the specimen room at camp while he was waiting to get kicked out?" I'm angry now, and shouting. "And what if he left it in the car with his mom and his little sister? A *hunting* spider, a *wandering* spider. In the car? A spider that was ready to explode into a hundred little spiders?"

Roberts does not move a muscle. I am so weak. I couldn't stand now if my life depended on it, and my arms weigh more than I can lift. When my eyes close, I can see myself scoop her into the only container I could find—disposable coffee cup with a plastic snap-on lid—and stash it in the side pocket of my backpack, so she could breathe. The mesh pocket held the cup part firmly but didn't reach as high as the top. I didn't think that mattered. I thought I'd be there, with the backpack. I thought I'd be able to keep an eye on it. Notice if the top came off. But I wasn't. I was home, safe, and they headed out.

It's played out a thousand times in my nightmares. The spider in the car, and one of them sees it. Amy. Mom. A scream, a jerk, somebody swats at it, and then spiders, spiders everywhere.

I put my head down and slowly my breathing returns to normal. Minutes pass in silence. Why is this session a hundred hours long?

"That's our time, Jonah," he says, and I walk out without looking at him.

32

Forty minutes later, I am buzzed through the security door of the Castleknock center at nine thirty, feeling like the day should already be over. Despite my shower earlier, I am clammy and uncomfortable in my clothes, like I've been wearing them for days, and I am walking like a zombie. Luckily, Patrick was on the same bus and distracted me by describing the headway he is making with Róisín, who is not as uptight as I had predicted, particularly when there are a few drinks on board, or so Patrick claims. I listen to him and do not think about Roberts, and what he might be thinking, or Teresa, and what she might be thinking, or anything besides Patrick and Róisín and the minutiae of their budding relationship.

"Are you all right?" Patrick's question catches me by surprise. I thought I was paying attention.

"Me?" I raise my eyebrows in a pantomime of nonchalance and Patrick narrows his eyes.

"Seriously, are you all right? You don't look great." He has paused his narrative and is observing me closely.

"I'm fine. I'm fine," I claim. Passing the waiting room, I catch a glimpse of Gary, Seán's dad, sitting on a chair and staring at the ceiling, his arms crossed. The size of his torso makes the chair look like one of the little ones up in Teresa's office. I keep walking, but instead of heading to the kitchen with Patrick, I go straight up the stairs to Teresa's office. I am so surprised to see Gary, I forget about being embarrassed until the moment I push her door open. She's there, sitting at the desk with a file open, looking fantastic in an all-white outfit, and glances up when she hears the door opening.

"Jonah!" she says, warmth and pleasure in her voice.

I step into the room and close the door behind me. "Do you know Gary is downstairs?" I ask in a hushed voice, as if he has followed me up. My unease is like a cloud around me, hard to see through.

"Yes," she says, "I do know that. Would you be okay joining us? He turned up here, absolutely furious, about fifteen minutes ago, and I asked him to wait downstairs. He wants to talk to us about yesterday's meeting. I'm thinking this is going to be unpleasant." She smiles to let me know she is aware of the understatement. Fitted white cashmere sweater, white pants, white leather ankle boots that give her a good four inches.

I have an impulse to apologize for last night, but the timing isn't great, and I'm not sure what to say. I get a flash of what happened in Roberts' office and have a sudden desire to tell her about it, like a dam has burst inside me. What would she think? I stand there, paralyzed for a moment, and then realize she is waiting for an answer. "Okay, no problem," I say, and I'm sure my voice has given me away. That she will ask me what's wrong. That I'll be able to tell her, and she'll say it is going to be okay. That I'm not a bad person.

"The thing is, Jonah, this is an excellent opportunity for you to watch your own internal reactions, right? All that stuff from the last encounter with Gary, all the male hierarchy, the body language, all of that, your job is to pay attention to it. If I make any suggestions for you to leave the room, for whatever reason, you leave immediately, okay? This is going to be a tricky enough encounter without me having to worry about you, but I think it could be good learning. In summary, as you Americans would say, please keep your shit together."

"That, I can do," I say with confidence, despite the fact that I've already lost my shit today and am unmoored and disconnected from everything around me. What is Roberts thinking? What is he doing? But I don't want to think about that. Not right now. Not if I don't have to.

Teresa grabs the extra chair from the assistant psychologist's desk in the hallway for the meeting, and walks down to collect Gary, who comes into the room behind her, having no doubt observed her walk up the stairs. His body is stiff with anger and he sits down heavily, leaning forward, the thick muscles at his neck tense, straining against the fabric of his shirt. Teresa sits in her desk chair, swiveled around to face him, and I sit in the chair next to her desk. Nobody shakes anyone's hands, and I might as well be invisible.

"Thanks for coming in, Gary. I know this is a difficult situation and I'm glad to be speaking to you." Teresa is in management mode, but she sounds sincere. "You said you wanted to talk about something?"

Gary looks directly at Teresa, and says in a low, measured voice, "I am going to ask you the same question I asked you fifteen minutes ago when I walked in here, and you made me wait downstairs with your little power play. Did you contact anyone and report me as a problem in the house, a risk or a danger, after a conversation you had with Seán's mother yesterday?"

"Yes, I did contact Tusla, the child and family agency," Teresa says, "but I wouldn't call it *reporting you*. I contacted them to discuss my concerns about your family, and to make sure everyone was safe and getting the support they need. Because of my position here at the clinic, I am mandated, by law, to contact them if I have any concerns about a child that could be at risk. This means you, as a family, have access to additional supports, Gary."

"Do you have any children?" Gary asks Teresa. Second time she has been asked in the past two days.

"No, I don't," says Teresa, looking Gary directly in the eye.

"I'm not even going to ask the boy wonder here," says Gary, nodding in my general direction. He could say anything to me right now. I'm nearly entirely focused on his body language. On his tense arms and shoulders, and his restless, huge hands.

"Please don't be disrespectful," says Teresa. "What are you trying to say?"

"What I am trying to say is that you have made a difficult situation a million times worse. By making that report, you have potentially distanced me from my son, and I am the only stable thing that child has in his life. If you had children, you would get what that means a hell of a lot better than you do. Seán's mother is not well. She hasn't been well for quite some time, maybe forever. You'd know this, if you had bothered to contact our general practitioner, or me, or the school, or anybody but her. One thing that she does is lie—she'll lie to anyone, about anything. But especially about Seán. It's like a perverse game to her. How much chaos can she create? How many appointments? How many professionals? The more problems she says he has, the more attention she gets. Ask any doctor in the children's hospital—he's been assessed in every clinic. I'm sure her name is on a watch list in there. And now this Tusla business is feeding into it. Any community social worker is going to go with the mother's story, at least at first—the statistics are with that scenario, and who is going to believe a small child trying to defend his father? Seán's the victim and she'll get the attention. Perfect. Here we are, in the middle of a legal separation and now there is an abuse question mark hanging over my head. Don't give me some line about doing me a favor, madam. You took a short cut, and you know it." Gary leans back in his chair but does not break eye contact with Teresa.

Teresa is looking back at him and hasn't moved. "I'm glad there are other services involved, Gary," she says. "I'm glad you aren't alone. I'm happy to talk to your GP or the school, or even community mental health, if you'd like, but I'd need Tríona's consent if it is about her."

"Consent?" Gary leans back in. "Now? Good luck with that. I want you to know that I am going to do everything I can to fight this. I will not let that woman, or the naïve professionals who listen to her, come between me and my son. I will use this little stunt to finally pry her sick fingers off my son for good. I just hope to hell he is okay until that happens. My solicitor will contact you on Monday. You think you are protected by all this?" He waves his hand, gesturing around the office. "Think again. Every bureaucracy turns on the individual, eventually. You might want to be ready." Gary stands up. There is a short pause and then Teresa stands up, so I do too. I notice a little satisfaction in being taller than Gary, but I keep my posture loose and casual, the opposite of how I am feeling.

"That's fine, Gary," says Teresa, "and I'm sure that between us all, we can figure out what is best for Seán. Support for the family is a good idea wherever it comes from. I appreciate that we see different angles on this thing at the moment, but clearly everyone has his best interests in mind. Is there anything else that you want to ask me?" Somehow, Teresa still sounds like she is in charge of the meeting.

"No." Gary turns and walks out of the room. Teresa follows him and I hear first his, and then her footsteps on the stairs. I go to the hallway so I won't miss anything that's said, but nothing is, and Gary simply walks out of the center, the security door banging behind him.

Teresa does a swift U-turn and comes back up to where I am standing at the banister.

"Whew!" she says. "That was intense." Her color is high but she doesn't look upset. If anything, she looks invigorated.

"Tea?" I ask.

"You are becoming Irish so quickly, Jonah." She smiles. "Tea? Really?"

"I thought it might be too early for chocolate."

"No such thing," says Teresa, "but we can start with tea." We join the tail end of the breakfast rush in the kitchen and then head up to her office to complete the paperwork, which is surprisingly brief. Teresa compiles a short report on our contact with the family, what was said to her by both parents, how Seán behaved in the group, and what he said to me in the waiting room. She also suggests contact with the GP, and adult mental health services.

When it is all written out in black and white, the report is so straightforward, but when I think about what Seán is going through, I am overwhelmed by sadness. I remember to retrieve the questionnaire with the purple ink, and sure enough, it is Tríona's original information about Seán. Teresa thanks me and adds a paragraph to her report, stressing that it is Tríona's opinion, not independently observed information. She returns it to me, for the data.

By noon we are finished with the online form, and Teresa signs a hard copy of the full report and has reception scan and send the material over to the social worker in Tusla by email, before she puts it on her desk to send in the regular mail, later.

"Well," she says, "that is a piece of work done. Or several pieces of work, really. What do you think, Jonah?"

I wait a moment while I think, and I'm a little cautious about expressing an opinion.

"I guess the more people keeping an eye on that family the better. I thought you were amazing in the meeting. It could have been so much worse." There was something else too. I believed

Gary. I agreed with him, but I'm not saying that here. I'm in deep enough water.

"I'm glad that he came in," says Teresa, "and he isn't my first angry parent, or my first threat of lawyers. When you go, I'm going to send the online form and call Tusla again, updating them on this morning's meeting in case it increases the risk. Then they'll have the online copy and our report, soft and hard copy. To be sure to be sure, as my mother would say. The fact that Gary is talking legal action is good, in a way, because he has a pathway set out to channel all that anger and get his voice heard. I'd rather have him plotting revenge against me than blaming Tríona completely. Or Seán."

"That makes sense," I say, but I noticed the *when you go* part of the sentence. "I guess I'll head off now, and let you get started."

"Okay, grand," says Teresa. "Unless there is anything else you need to discuss." Her expression is open, and I have no clue what she is expecting.

"Is there something else *you* want to discuss?" I say, after a short pause.

Teresa smiles and turns back to her desk, already preoccupied with her next task. "No, Jonah. I'm good. Thanks for coming in today. See you Monday."

I smile back but she doesn't see it. On the way down the stairs, I have a fleeting image of Roberts this morning and I'm hit with a wave of exhaustion. Was that today? It's almost hard to remember. His office, the couch. I concentrate and pull my thoughts into the here and now, walking into the weak autumn sunlight, heading into my Friday.

33

On the bus I text the twins but get no response. Either they are in class, in bed, or sucked into some PlayStation reality. Considering their night out, bed is the likeliest option. Being on my own is not an option. Every time my mind starts to wander, it heads for a cliff edge. I text Sailí, offering to take her to lunch, and get a swift reply. She is teaching a day-long seminar at the Trinity Arts Workshop on printmaking and only four people have turned up. I am welcome to come along, and start late. An art class? Anything is better than what's happening in my head. It's a short walk from the bus stop to the studio, and for a three euro membership fee, I am ushered into her classroom, where Sailí and four women over sixty are wearing aprons and standing around long tables.

"Hi Jonah!" says Sailí, with her professional voice on. "Glad you came along. We are working here on screen printing. I was just saying that it is the only form of printmaking that pushes the ink through a fine mesh directly onto the print surface." The women with her look at me with frank curiosity and respond to my greeting with friendliness. In front of Sailí is a stretched mesh canvas with a stencil under it of what looks like buildings. The tables around the room support other rectangular screens, stencils, and tons of plastic bottles of ink in different colors. "We have time now, before lunch, for a quick demonstration on working with color so you can be thinking about what you want to do when we come back," says Sailí. She takes a very dark blue ink and squirts some on the edge of the frame, and then, using a flat and flexible blade, works the color over the surface of the mesh screen. Her movements are strong and confident, and it is difficult for me to keep my attention on the artwork. Sailí has her hair piled up high on top of her head in a twist, held in place with chopsticks. Stretching out across the canvas accentuates the curve of her neck and jaw, and there is something compelling about the quality of her concentration. I look around and two of the women are watching me watching Sailí, rather than her demonstration. That leaves two people paying attention to the instructions. I grin at my observers and we all look back down at Sailí's strong hands and arms, working the ink. She gently raises the screen to reveal the dark blue image of a building off-center, with less detailed blocks to the left, on stark white paper, perfect. A small round of applause follows and Sailí takes a bow. When I look at the detail of the buildings there is something familiar, but I can't quite place it.

"Okay," says Sailí. "I'm going to leave this to dry on the rack with the fan next to it, so I can show you a second layer after lunch. The work on the stencils this morning was painstaking, but you can see how it pays off, here, because of the detail. Where the stencil is, the ink doesn't get through. When we come back from lunch, we'll do your first layer and then, if we have time, we can do another layer in a different color. Is that okay?" The women nod and head off to lunch in a pack, taking their bags and coats. On their way out the door one of them looks back and gives me a thumbs up. I'm not sure what to do with that.

Sailí gently releases the paper from the steadying hold of the clamp and places it carefully on one of the drying racks that line three of the walls.

"That's really cool," I say, "and it looks familiar. Where is it?"

"It's the Stag's Head," she says, "remember?" Sailí has moved over to the sink to wash her hands and I step up behind her. She leans back and I can feel the warmth of her body through her jeans and sweater. I wrap my arms around her. Something to hold on to.

"Oh, yes," I say. "I remember. That place where all the local women troll for innocent tourists."

Sailí swivels in my arms so we are face to face, and rises up to kiss me.

When I get a moment for a breath, I say, "You might be the first woman in an apron I have ever thought about undressing." She laughs and steps back.

"Not a chance, cowboy, I'm at work." Sailí takes off her apron by herself and suggests we get some food. She is teaching for the rest of the afternoon and needs some energy. We head out of the back of Trinity and end up in a little Italian café. The coffee is so good it rivals the other little Italian café I frequent.

"How is your work going?" I ask, and she laughs.

"Better than yours, if I remember right," she says. "It's good, but stressful at the moment. I'm behind on that office commission, and I seriously don't have time for this class today, but I had already agreed to it, so I'm stuck. I like working with students, and the Trinity Arts Workshop is worth supporting, but teaching isn't my passion. I'm too impatient. Especially when I'm under pressure with actual, paying customers."

We finish our sandwiches and head back to the studio. Sailí shows me what the other women worked on in the morning—the stencils they want to use for their prints. There are simple outlines, one that looks like a chicken, and something more complicated that might be two people in silhouette. She puts me in an apron and sets me up with heavy card, pencils, and an extremely sharp knife. "Go ahead," she says, "do some art."

The last time I did anything remotely linked to art was a required class in high school where I spent most of the time arguing with the teacher about the extreme importance of white space, thus limiting what I had to do. He used to wear his button-down shirts with one too many buttons undone, and possibly had glitter in his chest hair. The guy nearly cost me my grade point average.

"Seriously?" I ask Sailí.

"Get to work, Jonah," she says, and walks away. Before long, I am drawing random lines on the page, top to bottom. Not straight, but close. The first one I draw reminds me of Seán's picture—the two halves of his parents—but I shake it off and add more. While I'm working, the women come back in and begin the process of clamping and taping their stencils to the screens. There is much hilarity in the back-to-front mistakes and the difficulty in spreading the ink evenly. Sailí made it look much easier than it is.

I go to work with the knife and begin to cut away some of the paper. There is something satisfying about the pressure of the knife and the smooth parting of the fibers. When I'm finished, I look at what's left and there is grass, rising from a solid base to gentle, tapering, and uneven points. Sailí takes the stencil and places it on another clean page, instructing me to trace it, and then cut again so that I have a stencil of the part I have cut off. The two should fit together like puzzle pieces.

"Couldn't I have done that in the first place?" I ask, as if I am suddenly an expert at this. She pats me on the back and walks away again, not even honoring my petulance with a comment.

The other students have their first colors done and have racked them to dry next to the fans. Sailí takes back her place at the screens and demonstrates the use of a second stencil, adding a strong yellowy orange to the windows on her buildings. The detail of the stencil is not lost on us, compared to our amateur attempts, and a clock face has emerged from the blue.

34

I wake in Sailí's place and lie there, orienting myself. No sign of Sailí, so I stare at the ceiling. Suddenly, I am homesick. I check my phone and there are several missed calls from Patrick, no doubt wanting to discuss his short girlfriend. It's very early morning at home on a Saturday. I can't call. I picture my parents asleep in their big bed, the framed photos of me and Amy on the wall. Me, getting older, graduating from high school, graduating from college. Her, forever eleven. The first thing they see in the morning.

The muscles in my shoulders constrict and I think of Roberts, sitting there yesterday, listening to me confess. Taking notes? Coming up with theories? All the times I didn't say anything to my dad, to anyone, and now I'm talking to this stranger. What am I supposed to do on Wednesday, when I go back? I know he won't bring it up, but he also won't let it go. Panic rises, and with it pressure behind my eyes. God, I hate him. The first shudder catches me by surprise, and soon I am wracked with sobs.

When I wake again the light is much brighter, and Sailí is sitting on the bed, fully dressed. "Well, hello, Sleeping Beauty," she says, handing me a hot cup of coffee.

"And here I thought I was Prince Charming," I say, and sit up. It's not like me to sleep in like this. I'm worried Sailí can tell I've been crying, and set down the cup to give my face a vigorous rub.

"Ha! That'll be the day," she says, "you've been sleeping like a log while I've been working my tail off in the studio. I brought in some food, in case you are hungry, but I'm off again—I need to keep my shoulder to the wheel at the studio for the rest of the day. That workshop yesterday cost me so much time. Stay as long as you like, and help yourself to whatever. The door will lock itself after you." She kisses me on the cheek and retreats before I can reach for her. "Thanks for last night," she says, with a parody of a lascivious wink.

"My pleasure," I say, and wink back.

When she is gone, I have another look at my phone and it is nearly eleven. Patrick has called again and texted *Call me right away.* Jesus Christ.

I text back: *Everything okay?* Less than fifteen seconds later, my phone lights up; Patrick is calling.

"Hey Patrick," I say, "I'm sorry I didn't get back to you sooner. I think I was a bit all over the place after all the difficulty with that family." Sure, that was it.

"What are you talking about?" asks Patrick. "Where are you? The twins said they haven't seen you since the day before yesterday."

"The twins?" I'm confused. "Were you talking to the twins? What the hell?"

"Jonah, something's happened at Castleknock. I've been trying to get in touch with you. Can you meet me?"

I catch the tone in his voice. Something serious. "I can meet. What happened? Are you okay?" An image of Gary flashes in my mind.

"I'm fine," he says. "Let's talk when we meet. I'm on Wicklow Street. Can you come here? We can get coffee."

"Don't be a drama queen," I say. "I'll come in but tell me now, what happened?"

"It's Teresa," he says. "She's dead."

35

When I meet Patrick at Butler's Chocolate Café, the place is crowded, and we sit side by side at a long counter looking out at the street. He has an extra coffee beside him, and there is a small dark chocolate to go with it. Something about the scene looks absurd. This is not a place for bad news.

"Is this for me?" I sit down next to him. Did he buy me a piece of chocolate?

"Yeah," he says. "They come with the coffee, here." I thank him and look around. Sure enough, everyone has a chocolate with their drinks. Why am I so distracted?

"I got a text from Vera this morning. Teresa had an accident in the center," he says. He looks terrible, with dark circles under his eyes. His naturally unruly hair is matted down in places and when he drops his head into his hands, I can see exactly how it happened.

"Who is Vera?" I ask. "What accident?" It's like he is wrong, that somehow there's been a misunderstanding, and Teresa is fine.

"Vera, the caretaker. You know her. She's a keyholder, and she went to the clinic early this morning and let Teresa's husband in when he came looking for her. She hadn't come home last night, and he was trying to find her at the clinic this morning, but he couldn't get an answer at the door. You know—Vera, she's there in the mornings, cleaning."

An image of the small woman I terrified on my first day springs to mind. "Why does Vera have your number?" I ask, but immediately see that is not the point of the story. "Never mind."

"She was there when Teresa's husband went in; Vera had to let him in with her key because it was locked. You know the way it locks automatically, the security door. She said they found her at the bottom of the stairs. Teresa was working late, and they were there together until about five thirty but then Vera left. Her husband came looking for her this morning and eventually called Vera when he couldn't get in. Her car was still there, see, but no answer at the door. And when they finally went in together Teresa was dead at the bottom of the stairs." He is speaking to me like I am having trouble understanding even very simple sentences. He isn't wrong.

I want to ask how the husband had Vera's number, but I don't. I am focusing on the wrong things, trying to find a hole in the story that will make it untrue. "Jesus Christ." I can't think of anything else to say.

"I know, I know. Vera said the husband tried to pick her up, but he couldn't because . . . " He stops, mercifully. "Vera was crying her eyes out when she told me. Can you imagine? The trauma."

"Jesus Christ," I say again, and I can imagine it, like I am right there watching him, like every crime drama I've ever seen when a body is discovered, stiffened. "I can't believe it."

"They had to call the *Gardaí* as well, the police, and they came and examined the place for hours. Vera thinks they're treating the death as 'not suspicious.' Apparently, it was clearly an accident. She had even lost one of her shoes."

"Stop. Stop," I say, and he does. I know those shoes. They were white leather, and high. I can picture them so clearly in my mind. If Patrick says another word, I'll lose it. He waits. My chest is tight. For some inexplicable reason I feel like punching him in the face. I take a deep breath.

"Are you okay?" he asks. "I can't believe it, either." He looks at me carefully. "You look pale, Jonah. I think you should eat the chocolate."

"I can't believe it," I say again, but I do believe it. Terrible things happen. I know that. Patrick keeps talking, going over what he knows and saying the same things in different ways. He has been in touch with his course director, with the assistant Róisín, with Vera, and with the social worker on the team. He has talked about it with his friends, and even mentions something his mother said about it on the phone. For Patrick, this is well-covered ground. It's no wonder he looks like shit, he's been talking nonstop for hours. I am caught by the thought of her, broken at the bottom of the stairs. The shoe. He says something about a funeral, and I ask him to repeat it.

"Today is Saturday," he says. "I wonder will the funeral be on Tuesday or Wednesday? I think she lives down on the south side of the city. We will have to check RIP.ie for the details." Patrick shows me on his phone how to navigate the website that hosts service information for bereaved families and friends. Nothing yet. The chocolate is like ash in my mouth. I wish I hadn't eaten it. I was just with her. An image of the parking lot flashes in my mind, and I push it away.

"I'm not going to the funeral, for Christ's sake," I say, and it sounds harsher than I mean. "Anyway, I have class on Tuesday and Wednesday."

Patrick looks shocked. "Oh, you are going to the funeral all right," he says. "This is Ireland. Everyone goes to either the removal or the funeral, and you are going, because you are going with me. You can't not go. Trust me on this."

"What the hell is a removal?" I'm not sure I want to know.

"It's when they bring the body from wherever it is to the church, usually the night before the funeral. You have to go to one or the other. Or they might have hours in the funeral home, that's possible too."

When Patrick says the word "body," it sits like lead in my stomach. Teresa.

I suddenly remember about Monday. "What about the separated parents group on Monday?" I ask Patrick. "All those kids are going to be turning up." It's weird to be even thinking about it at the moment, but with Teresa gone, who's in charge?

"I was talking to Anna," Patrick says, and I hold back from asking who Anna is. "She is devastated. She is going to go in tomorrow to do all the cancellations for the week for Teresa, including the group." I remember, now, that Anna is the other psychologist working there. The one from the photo with Teresa. "I gave her your number, I hope you don't mind, in case she has any questions about who to call. I offered to go in with her, but she said no. I think the receptionist is going in to help with the calls. I haven't talked to her, yet." So, there is one person he hasn't spoken with. He looks at me for a minute. "Anna is the other psychologist. I'm not sure if you've met her, she's been on personal leave."

"Patrick," I say, "I know it's early, but can we get a drink?"

He looks at me. "Like I said, this is Ireland." We stand up and walk across the street, and into the International Bar.

Two hours later, and the assistant psychologist, Róisín, has turned up, tearful and jumpy. She sits in next to Patrick and he puts his arm on the bench behind her. The twins arrive and Patrick goes through all the details again, periodically pausing to send or receive update texts from various sources, or do a run to the bar. There are exclamations of disbelief every few minutes and even the twins are respectful, asking me how I'm doing. "I'm fine," I say, staring into the glasses in front of me. Sailí texts during a break and I text back where I am and why. Before long she arrives, and the twins make space next to me for her to squeeze in.

"Are you okay?" she leans in and asks me. The space in the booth is tight and I can feel the heat of her body up against mine. It makes me want to pull her closer, to put my face against the soft skin of her neck. "My mother is worried about you."

"I'm fine," I say, like a mantra. "It's just weird. It's not like I know her, really. I mean, not for long, anyway. It is so strange that I was there with her yesterday and now she's dead." Sailí takes my hand and holds it in both of hers. I have a quick flashback to those hands last night and a heat rises through me. Then I think of Teresa at the bottom of those beautiful stairs and my gut lurches. Jesus Christ.

"I'm not feeling great," I say to Sailí, and in no time she and the twins are shuffling me out of the pub. It isn't until I stand up that I realize how unsteady I am and I'm grateful that she flags down a taxi because I'm not sure my legs will carry me. There is some discussion on the sidewalk between them about where I'm going and eventually Peter gets in the taxi with me and we head up to the apartment in Christchurch. I make it in the door and collapse on the couch. Peter offers to make toast and I decline but he makes it anyway and we eat it, along with cups of strong tea. We are both largely silent and he switches on the television to watch soccer. Before long I am asleep.

When I wake, I am still on the couch, but lying down. Peter is on the PlayStation in the chair next to me, whispering commands into his headset. Total carnage on the screen and I lie there thinking about Teresa. I get up to get a glass of water and a wave of nausea crashes over me. Peter grabs my elbow and propels me into the bathroom in time. When I come out, he is back on the PlayStation. "Are you okay?" he asks while landing a helicopter on a city rooftop.

"I'm fine," I say, yet again. "You were pretty fast, there. Thanks."

"I have a lot of experience with daytime drunkenness," he says. "It's a special skill I'm working on."

"I think there's a future in it for you," I say, but neither of us can work up a laugh.

"My mother is on her way here, so you know," says Peter. "Brace yourself." He explains that Moira rang to check on the laundry situation and when he told her about Teresa she went into maternal hyperdrive. Surprise, surprise, she was aware I am living here full time and is coming with food and suffocating affection. "I'd hate to be the driver in front of her on the motorway," says Peter. "We should get her one of those flashing lights for the top of the car. And a siren."

As if the joke summoned her, there is a quick knock on the door, and she comes straight in. The buzzer on the gate was obviously no match for her today. "Peter! Jonah!" The timing is so perfect we break into laughter and she immediately looks annoyed. "What is wrong with you boys? Peter, help your father unload the car. Jonah, into the shower. You should see the state of you." The transformation from affection to frustration is so quick I'm caught by surprise and head straight for the shower, as instructed. In the mirror I see what she saw and I'm grateful to step under the hot water.

When I come out of the bathroom, Dave is on the couch and Moira is packing the kitchen cupboards with food. The sheer volume of material she is able to put away seems impossible. "Jonah," she says, "get your laundry ready to go in some of these bags." I start to politely decline and the look in her eye hardens, so I grab a bag and move into the bedroom I'm using. Dave greets me with a nod from the couch.

"How are you, Jonah?" he says. "I won't get up in case I bash your head in, again." The size of the man makes the room a lot smaller.

While I'm in the bedroom picking up clothes and feeling embarrassed about handing over my dirty laundry, Moira comes in and shuts the door behind her. Before I can say anything, she has her arms around me in a tight hug. “Oh, Jonah. I’m so sorry this has happened. You must be in shock.” The strength of her arms is reassuring, comforting even though I didn’t think I needed that. Emotion rises in my throat as she releases me and steps back. I surprise myself by wanting to talk.

“I don’t even know her, really. I can’t believe it. I was just there, yesterday, talking to her. I walked down those stairs.” I pause. “She was so nice to me.” I still feel drunk and there is a chance I could cry.

Moira sits down on the end of the bed, which thankfully is made. I didn’t sleep in it last night.

“I know, I’m so sorry,” she says. “The twins said she was very nice too. What a tragedy for her family. Her poor husband. Did she have children?” I shake my head. Hearing that the twins described her as “nice” to their mother and knowing that is actually “hot” in their minds has pulled me back from the brink and I am okay again. “Do you know when the funeral is?” she asks.

Before I can answer, there is a quiet knock on the door and Dave comes in.

“Are you going to let the fellow out again, Moira?” he says, and she walks past him into the living room, clearly annoyed at the interruption and not responding to his question. “Are you all right, Jonah?” he asks, and I tell him that I’m fine. His face gets serious. “Jonah. I rang a cousin of mine, who’s in the *Gardaí,* the police here in Ireland, and he says they’re most likely ruling it an accident, so . . . Such a tragedy.” I agree with him that it’s a tragedy, but he isn’t done saying what he wants to say. “All the same, Jonah, and I’m sorry to be saying this now, but you need to contact your Rotary host family to let them know what happened. After all, they’re responsible for you over here, right? I mean, they’re the ones to help you out if something happens, right?”

“I guess so,” I say. “I mean, nothing happened to me, Dave.” I’m confused by what he is saying. I don’t remember talking to him about my host family, but maybe he discussed it with the twins.

“Well, yes,” says Dave. “You are right there, Jonah. All the same, it’s a good idea to keep them in the loop, wouldn’t you say? I mean, just in case.”

There is a commotion in the living room, and we head back in.

Michael and Sailí have arrived and are trying to look sober in front of Moira. It is possible that Sailí is pretty sober, but Michael is not. "This," says Michael, with a grand wave of his arm, "is the lovely Sailí." He waves the other arm and bows. "These are my beloved parents."

"Well," Moira says, standing with her hands on her hips. She is facing the other way so I can't see her expression, but going by Sailí's face, it is unlikely to be friendly and welcoming. Dave moves forward quickly and shakes Sailí's hand, then deftly puts an arm around his son, which might be seen as a gesture of affection but is actually providing him with essential support. They start moving toward the couch.

"It's lovely to meet you," says Sailí. "I wanted to check on Jonah, and Michael kindly brought me up. I hope I'm not interrupting anything. Jonah has told me a lot about you."

Moira looks from Sailí to me and her gaze softens a little. "You're not interrupting!" she says. "We are doing the same thing. That and collecting laundry." She rolls her eyes and Sailí gives a wry look back, so they are instantly united in their acknowledgement of the ridiculousness of men, and we can all relax.

It turns out that Dave and Moira were going to take us out for dinner, but Michael is in no condition for that, so they leave us with pizza money and head home with our laundry. Peter and I help carry down the bags, and Dave reminds me to call my host family. Moira asks me to fill her in if anything else happens and gives me another hug before getting into the car. I am beginning to feel like the third twin.

I head back upstairs with Peter and hear Michael laughing before we even open the door to the apartment. "Did you see her face?" says Michael when we walk in. "I thought she was going to turn Sailí to stone, right then and there."

"Thank God you mentioned Jonah," Peter says with a laugh, "or we'd all be dead in the crossfire."

Sailí nods. "She isn't my first Irish mammy. I know that look."

"Is it any wonder we're single?" says Peter. "With that hellcat waiting to pounce on any woman who might chance her luck with one of us?"

Sailí and I exchange a look. "Really guys?" I say. "You're blaming your mother?"

While the others are organizing the pizza, I scroll through my phone and find Margaret, my Rotary host's number. I step into the bedroom again and call. When she answers it sounds like she is caught in a sandstorm. I try to explain to her what happened but I'm not sure what is getting through when the phone goes dead. About thirty seconds later, the phone rings and her name comes up on the screen. I answer and this time it sounds like she is in a bathroom.

"Hi, Jonah. I'm in the changing room at the club. You caught me standing at the side of a pitch, and I couldn't hear a word you said. These blasted floodlights mean the matches never end."

I apologize for disturbing her, and fill her in on what has happened even though it is overkill. Margaret repeats back to me what I've said to her as if she has been taking notes and tells me she is going to have Mick call me back. I tell her there is no need for him to call back and she asks me to keep my phone handy. The conversation leaves me with a sense of foreboding, rather than relief. I'm not sure what the point of that was.

About an hour later, the phone rings with a number I don't recognize, and I step back into the bedroom, away from the suspense movie we are all watching. All of us besides Michael, who is passed out in the chair, asleep. It turns out one slice of pizza was the final ingredient.

"Hello, is that Jonah?" he responds to my greeting. "This is Mick. How are things?" We pass some small talk and it turns out the kid won the match, so there are celebrations underway at their place.

"I hope I'm not inconveniencing you," I say. "I didn't plan to call you at all about this, but my friend's father said I should, because you are my host family. I'm not really sure why."

"No, no, I'm glad you called. Now, tell me what happened."

I go through what I know, which is very little. I mention Dave's conversation with his cousin and explain that it was Dave who told me to reach out.

"Very sensible," says Mick. He says a few things about how tragic it is, and asks me how well I knew Teresa. I explain the placement and how it fits in with the course. I'm surprised at how brief my time in the clinic has been; so much has happened.

"What time did you leave there, yesterday?" asks Mick. "What did you do after?"

I tell him I left around noon and start describing the art class with Sailí when I realize what is going on.

"Are you asking me for an alibi?" I say. "Do you think I need one?" Wait a minute. Is this what they are thinking about? Patrick had asked me where I was too.

"Not at all," says Mick. "I'm just trying to get the lay of the land, so to speak. Sometimes things are more complicated than they look at first glance, that's all. I work in the area, so I tend to overthink these things." His tone is light, and he explains that he works in the Director of Public Prosecutions's office and has a lot of contact with the courts and police procedure. "Have you had any contact with the *Gardaí* on this, Jonah?" I don't say anything because I am trying to figure out why he is asking. I feel like there is sand under my feet and I'm slipping.

"Jonah?"

"No." I manage that word. "Sailí, my friend, was with me from about twelve thirty."

"Till when?"

"All night."

"Grand," says Mick. "Were you out together? Sorry to be asking. Is she a good friend, would you say?"

"We were out," I say, feeling like I am in a movie. "We had dinner, and a drink. I was exhausted so we went back to her place early, around eight, I think. We are seeing each other, I guess. Dating." It feels like an awkward time to define my relationship with Sailí.

"Grand," says Mick, again. "That's good. I don't think you should be surprised if the *Gardaí* contact you, Jonah. They'll probably talk to everyone from the clinic. Do me a favor and give me a ring when that happens, yeah? Save this number now; it's my personal mobile and I'll answer it."

"Okay, yeah," I say casually, but there is an alarm signal racing up my spine.

"Tomorrow's Sunday," he says, sounding cheerful. "Do you want to come out to us for some grub? We should have had you out by now, anyway. We're neglecting our Rotary duties."

"No, no," I say without thinking. "I'm going to Tipperary with my friends tomorrow." This is a complete fabrication. The only thing going to Tipperary is my dirty underwear. "But thanks, anyway."

"Okay, well, another time." He's relieved, I think, and then casually asks me for the address where I am living. I give it to him and then he asks for next of kin details—who he should call if there were an emergency. He says he has it in the Rotary stuff, but telling him now saves him having to sort through the paperwork. At this point I am on autopilot as I rattle off my father's details. Finally, he wraps up the call. "I'm glad you called to let us know, Jonah. I'm sorry this is happening; I'm sorry for your supervisor."

We hang up and I am left wondering about what he has said. Questioning by the police? In case of emergency?

I have a text from Patrick: *Tuesday at eleven. Church of the Assumption in Dalkey. Removal Monday night. Both or just funeral?*

I text back, *Funeral.*

36

On Sunday morning, I walk Sailí down to the studio. Waking up with her in the twins' place was strange, and luckily, we didn't cross paths with them before we left. I cast an eye over the pizza boxes and empty bottles but decided to leave it all where it was in case cleaning it up might wake them. Sailí must have been thinking the same thing, because she showered and dressed without a word, and it is only when we hit the fresh air that we start talking. I can't face another conversation about Teresa, so I ask her about her project when we are buying coffee, and she describes the work all the way down Dame Street.

"I'm sorry about yesterday," I say. "I know you're behind with the commission and you had to quit early for me. That must have cost you some time."

"Honestly, Jonah, don't be silly. Besides, I got a load done the night before, so I'm mostly back on schedule." I'm distracted by how pretty she looks in the morning air, so I almost miss what she has said.

"The night before? But I was with you the night before."

Sailí cups my cheek in her hand. "Don't you remember, Sleeping Beauty? I had to wake you up at eleven with your breakfast. You passed out so early I went back into the studio. I basically worked all night, although I'm pretty sure I dozed on the couch in there for a couple of hours because I ended up a little groggy and disoriented."

She sees my expression change. "What? What did I say?"

So, I wasn't with Sailí. I wish I hadn't said it to Mick. "Nothing," I say, and try to relax my expression. "Everything's fine." I don't need an alibi.

We part ways and she heads into Temple Bar. When I am at the gates of Trinity College, my phone rings with an unknown number. It is Anna, from the Castleknock clinic, with a low, hoarse voice that I have to concentrate to make out. I pass through the arched entrance and swing away from the tourists to try and catch what she is saying, ducking into a wide doorway in the corner of Front Square. We pass a few words about Teresa and how amazing she was. Looking out at the students and visitors milling around, dutifully staying off the short grass, I feel like I am on a different planet.

Anna lets me know that she has contacted everyone from the group to cancel for Monday and tells me not to worry about them. The whole building is closed for the next few days, on orders from the *Gardaí*. I imagine them in there, looking around. The crime shows flash through my consciousness again—detectives searching for evidence. But it wasn't a crime, was it?

"How are you doing about all this, Jonah?" Anna asks, and I can picture her clearly now in the photo with Teresa. Looking so happy.

"I'm okay, Anna," I say. "How are you? I'm so sorry this has happened."

"Thanks, Jonah," she says. "I'm a mess, to be honest. I mean, I can do the whole professional thing on the phone with the clients, but inside I am completely torn up. I can't believe she is gone. It is such a fucking waste." The emotion in her voice brings a knot to my own throat. There is silence on the line from her end, and I am conscious of the sound of students coming down the stairs behind me.

"I'm so sorry," I repeat myself. There is nothing else I can say, really. I have to move to let them through the doorway.

"She liked you, Jonah," says Anna. "You made her laugh." Heat rises up my neck as I wonder what else she might have said to Anna. Clearly, they've been in touch.

"I liked her too." I try to keep my voice neutral.

"Everyone did," says Anna, and we sign off. I wanted to ask her about the funeral or the police, but I couldn't break in. Her grief seems so potent it would have felt callous.

I'm off the phone for about a nanosecond and it rings again, another unknown number. I haven't even stepped out of the doorway.

"Hi Jonah. It's Annemarie." From the course. She's calling to check on me and to tell me not to go into work tomorrow.

"Are you planning to go to the funeral on Tuesday?" she asks.

"Yeah," I say. "I'm going with Patrick, the clinical trainee. I wasn't going to go, but he says everyone here goes to funerals." It's out before I catch it. The cultural tourist.

"That's true," she says. "We are all going from the course, so your classes are cancelled. It's a mark of respect, and a lot of us knew her." I can hear the depth of her answer and I feel like a jerk. "We'll have to meet, you and I." She sighs. "We'll have to figure out the placement, but I'm not there, yet." I hadn't even thought of it. I wonder if all the other students have met with Annemarie as often as I have.

The rest of the day passes in a blur. I spend some time in the library with my phone turned off but end up staring at the walls. When I come out, there are so many update texts from Patrick, I ignore them completely. Sailí wants to meet up after work, the twins invite me to join them with their friends, but I simply don't have the energy to talk about Teresa to one more person. Climbing back into bed, I'm worried I'll lie awake, but I don't. Not for five minutes, even.

37

Monday early I wake up knowing that I dreamed about the accident—the bedsheet twisted around me. I think of Teresa immediately, my chest tightens, but I'm okay, I tell myself, I can breathe, I can move forward, I know this experience. There is an insistent beeping coming from the twins' room—some futile alarm system—but no movement. I've showered, made coffee, and eaten cereal when I hear the familiar buzz of the front gate. By the time I get to the release button, there is already movement in the hall, and a series of bangs on the door signals the arrival of Moira.

"You're up!" she says, standing at the door with two massive bags of neatly folded laundry.

"It's early. What time did you leave the house? Or have you been secretly outside all night? You really take this mothering thing very seriously." I help her lift the bags in.

"Oh, Jonah, you poor thing." She skates right over my attempt at humor. "I couldn't stop thinking about you. Dave made me wait until this morning to drop back the laundry, but I wish you boys had come home with us on Saturday. Are you okay?" She has put on the kettle and is checking the already overstuffed cupboards for any potential needs we might have. She's warming up for a big conversation, and there is no way I'm doing that. The phone buzzes in my hand at the same time Moira hears the beeping coming from the twins' room. She's distracted and I check the message:

Annemarie here. The Gardaí *phoned for your contact details. Call me.*

I hit the call back button immediately, but it goes straight to voicemail, so I leave a message. The pressure in my chest has spread to the rest of my body and I have a bizarre thought about that woman skinny Nancy saw in the clinic. Am I going to start throwing up all the time? Or sweating? Or shaking? What is happening to me? Moira is harassing the twins in the room next door, and I am staring at my phone wondering what to do when it rings.

38

"Is that Jonah Smith?" The *Garda* has a friendly, upbeat voice, like she is calling with good news.

"Yes," I say. "It's me." Guilt grips me and it is so familiar. Those memories run deep. Like bad news at school. Like talking to the police after the accident. I haven't thought about it in years, but suddenly I remember the broad shoulders and sad eyes of the uniformed officer on our front porch at home. Waiting for us when we drove home from Denny's.

The *Garda* explains that they are making a few enquiries about the timing of things on Friday in the clinic. She says she understands I was in there early in the day, and can they please talk to me? Could I come into the station? She makes it sound like an appointment to get my teeth cleaned.

"Of course, Officer," I hear myself say. "No problem." I make an appointment for lunch time and hang up.

"What the fuck was that?" I look up and Michael stares at me with incredulity. He is looking at me like I'm the idiot, while he stands wearing boxer shorts with a cup in his hand, pillow creases tracked across his face. "Did you just make an appointment to go into the *Garda* station? Don't you fucking watch television?" His hair is plastered to one side of his head and sticking out on the other side. It is hard to respond to his question without openly ridiculing him.

"I did," I say, and I suddenly want to sit down.

Immediately, Moira and Peter are in the mix and everyone is talking. It becomes obvious they've covered this ground between them before, and they know that Dave talked to me about it. I remember Mick gave me his number and I call it.

Within two hours, a flurry of activity has resulted in conversations between me and Mick, Mick and Rotary International, Rotary International and the US Embassy, and Mick and some solicitor linked to Rotary for just this purpose: students abroad in need of legal advice. I wonder how busy the solicitor is, especially since she agrees to meet with me immediately. Moira is refusing to leave the apartment and there is a lot of tea made. Everyone agrees I should keep my appointment with the *Gardaí*, but I shouldn't go alone. Moira insists I call my dad, even though it is very early morning his time. I call and he answers. He is never off duty.

"Are you okay?" he asks, when I have filled him in. His tone is even and measured—he is a guy who keeps his reactions under control. Like I used to be.

"I'm good," I say. "There is a surprising number of people involved at this end. A real machine." I'm sure he can hear my confusion.

"Listen to them," he says, "follow their advice." He takes their numbers. Mick, the solicitor, the embassy contact, Dave and Moira. I feel the international parent network tighten around me, and it makes me feel worse—like I am actually in trouble. He offers extra money, to call our family lawyer, to call Georgia, to talk later. He does not offer to come over. He won't leave Mom. He never would.

I insist on walking down to Pearse Street *Garda* Station on my own. Moira would be a liability at this point, and anyway she is deeply ensconced in the apartment kitchen, sleeves rolled up, and spray bleach slowly poisoning the air. The twins stay with her, and I arrange to meet the solicitor, Ciara, on my way down Westmoreland Street at the Italian coffee shop.

I wasn't thinking about what she might look like, so it is a nice bonus that she turns out to be an attractive blonde. "Are you Ciara?" I say to the only woman wearing a suit in the café, and she responds with a quick nod before launching into a monologue that takes my breath away as we collect our coffees and step back into the fresh air. Ciara covers the nature of meetings with the *Gardaí*, the systems they use to record interviews, the common pitfalls, and the importance of being honest if you choose to say anything, at a speed that would make a game show contestant proud. The entire time she is talking, her long, straight ponytail is swinging along with her nodding head. Her eye contact is so intense, I'm a little afraid to look away to glance at the pavement in front of us. I'm not sure how she is managing to walk.

Despite looking like a high school cheerleader, Ciara projects considerable legal confidence and information, and by the time we are walking up to Pearse Street Station I am feeling prepared.

"It's grand," she says, "totally grand, a good thing to do it right away. I know these lads and we are in good hands. Grand, grand." Any happier and she'd be skipping.

39

The most remarkable thing about Pearse Street *Garda* Station is the parking. There are about fifty cars parked at improbable angles directly outside the door. It seems like the least likely place to park illegally, so I have to assume they are police vehicles, but I honestly don't know how they get anything done that requires driving, it is so chaotic.

Within minutes of our arrival, we are ushered past the front desk. We meet with *Garda* Mairéad, a small woman with dark hair wearing a snug, blue suit. She reacts with surprise that Ciara is with me, but rolls with it. Ciara explains the US Embassy has been in touch, and Mairéad shrugs in a very convincing "whatever" way as she types something on her phone. We begin by talking through my movements throughout the day on Friday. We are sitting on chairs in a corner room that must have seen a lot of human misery. I go through my schedule on Friday and Mairéad writes it all down, carefully.

"So, you were with Sailí the whole time? From twelve thirty in the afternoon on, is that right?" Her pencil poised above the page.

I pause, and both Mairéad and Ciara focus on me. I can nearly feel it like a spotlight, hot.

"I was at Sailí's place, yes. But she went out. She went to her studio to work—I'm not sure what time she left." Ciara is too professional to react, but I'm afraid to look in her direction. I forgot to mention this on our walk, and I think Mick probably told her different.

Mairéad doesn't react, either. Nice and friendly. "Was there anyone else there when she left? Were you on your own? Did you go out, see anyone else?"

"I was alone, asleep the whole time. I fell asleep before she left. You can ask her." I feel like I'm lying, even though it's the truth. Maybe being in a police station does that to you.

Mairéad asks for Sailí's phone number and address, and the names of the restaurant and pub we went to. Each is carefully recorded in her tiny, even script. I am reminded of Dr. Roberts, and my gut twists at the thought of him. Jesus, that was Friday too. As she is writing, I wonder what he might have in his notes about me. And what he might do with them.

Eventually, Mairéad sits back in her chair and I take a breath. Ciara is studying me, a steady look on her face.

"What was she like? Teresa," *Garda* Mairéad asks.

"She was great," I say, and it's good to say it. Back on solid ground. "She was nice and funny and smart."

"And fit?"

"What?" I'm confused. "Like, athletic?"

Garda Mairéad looks at me like I'm an idiot. "Sexy?"

"Oh, yes, yes, sexy." I suddenly sound like a pervert. I'm paying attention again—this ground isn't so solid. Ciara's focus sharpens on Mairéad.

"Was she happy?" Mairéad asks.

"Happy?" I say it before I think. Was she? I think about the blushing, the frustration. The discomfort about the baby project.

Before I can answer, Ciara breaks in and starts asking about what is happening in the investigation—why are they questioning people, and why is the funeral Wednesday if there are so many unanswered questions? The sheer volume of her talk is a weapon. Sentence after sentence flows out until she finally stops at: "Should you be releasing the body if you are still questioning people?"

Mairéad squints. There is a long silence. Then, "Who says we are releasing the body?"

I freeze. What the fuck is going on, here? Is this actually an investigation?

"Jonah." Mairéad is suddenly made of steel. "Who is Gary?"

I inhale sharply, and Ciara is off again and this time she doesn't stop until a short, bald guy opens the door to come into the room and exclaims, "Hey, Ciara! How's things?"

Ciara jumps up and hugs him. "Hey, Tommy!" What follows is a surreal catch-up chat between fast-talking Tommy and much-talking Ciara while Mairéad and I sit and watch. I learn a lot about Tommy's golf game and Ciara's challenges with getting a membership at his club before eventually Tommy casually asks her if she'd mind looking over some testimony he has from another case she might be able to help him with.

Without missing a beat, Ciara gets serious. "If you think I'm leaving this room, you are one sad bastard, Tommy."

"I told them it wouldn't work." Tommy shrugs at Mairéad and walks out, giving Ciara a quick peck on the cheek. Mairéad's face tightens.

Ciara smiles, showing her teeth. "Okay, so, what's next?" she asks, but *Garda* Mairéad is done with us. For now.

On the sidewalk, surrounded by haphazardly-parked cars, we debrief and I imagine all the lawyers and all the criminals who have stood right where we are, doing exactly what we are doing. Except I'm not a criminal. When we've gone over what was said, Ciara looks at me with concern. "Jonah," she says, "what was going on in there? Were you nervous?"

I do a quick review in my mind. "Of course I was nervous, Ciara—I was being questioned by the police. Why?"

"There was something going on in there. I don't know what, but there were a couple of moments there that I thought to myself, *This guy looks like he is hiding something.* And if I was thinking it, you can be sure Mairéad was thinking it. Is there anything you need to tell me? I mean, apart from having no alibi, which it would have been good to know before we met with them. Anything else? Any more fun surprises?" Her tone is light and she is smiling, but she is not happy.

The only thing I can remember is thinking about Roberts and his written notes. What I said to him before all of this happened, about me and Teresa. About me and the accident. "No, Ciara. There's nothing. I was just nervous."

Ciara nods and calls Mick. It all sounds very positive and when she gets off the phone, she gives me her business card and tells me to call her if I have any more contact with the *Gardaí*.

"What is going on with Teresa's body?" It's like I am betraying her for even asking.

"Jonah, I have no idea," says Ciara. "I don't know what is happening. Sometimes it can be slow with an accident, or it could be that they are investigating her death as suspicious even though nobody is saying it. I can't imagine the coroner is releasing the body for the funeral tomorrow if it is still under investigation, but sure nobody is clear on that, so who can know? Maybe the funeral will be a memorial service or something, without her body? I don't know. I heard Mairéad asking you about a Gary person and I need to remind you, as well, that in case that might be a patient or client or whatever from the clinic, and don't tell me anything about it please, but in case it is someone from the clinic I want to remind you that the Health Service Executive is involved here, as well, and they have systems in place around patient confidentiality and all that, and you'd want to mind your manners around all that because there are plenty of solicitors on that end, as well, and patients can have their own solicitors as well so in case that is a patient, I want you to keep your mouth firmly shut when you are on your own, meaning without me, do you get it?" She takes a breath and I nod. There is enough speaking happening already.

"If they, the *Gardaí*, call you or turn up somewhere you are, and if they start asking questions, you mention the embassy right away, do you understand that? Mick is linked in there already, and they'll be careful if you say right up front that you want them to contact the embassy. And you call me right away, yeah? Right away. Literally, turn your back on them and call me, right there. Don't you get all nice and helpful because there is something going on here, now, that we don't know what it is, so you keep your mouth shut except to say you want them to contact the embassy and then you call me. Right?" Another nod from me.

"Any questions?" Ciara asks.

I shake my head and she laughs, her ponytail bouncing. "It'll be grand," she says, back to cheerleader.

40

With Ciara gone, I sit at a table in the corner of a Starbucks and call my dad, filling him in on the meeting and Ciara's thoughts. He reports he was talking to the embassy, and they are well aware of my situation and happy to step in if there is a need. They knew Mick and Ciara's names when he called, so he has no doubt they are staying informed. He has clearly been playing backup.

"It's a mess, Jonah," he says, his voice low and sad, "but it's not your mess. That poor woman." As soon as he says it, my chest tightens, my heart pounds, and my throat constricts—I can't catch my breath. I push back my chair and lean forward, trying to take slow, deep breaths, my elbows against the table and my head down. The phone is still at my ear, and I can hear my dad talking. "It's okay, it's okay, son." His voice and the wave of fear hook into familiar pain and suddenly I'm trying to not think about Amy and my mom and poor Teresa. I want to say it to him, but I can't. I never could.

It passes eventually and I sit up again. The woman at the table next to me is studiously looking at her phone, but there is a glass of water in front of me that wasn't there before. I take a sip and let out a deep breath before reassuring my dad I'm okay. More soothing talk from him and we finish the call with me saying I'll keep him updated. I set the phone down on the table and notice the dampness of my shirt and the palms of my hands. Jesus.

I pick up the phone to leave and there is the voicemail symbol in the top corner. I dial and Georgia's voice asks me to call her, tells me she loves me, lets me know that my dad has told her the news about Teresa. I call back and she answers, pure compassion in my ear, giggling when I describe the farce of Ciara and the *Gardaí*.

"Should I throw the towel in over here and come to Dublin?" she asks. "I can be there to bail you out of lock up, or whatever they call it over there. I've always wanted to date an outlaw. Get some motorcycles. I could rock that."

"How reassuring." The thought of her next to me here in this foreign city is so pleasant and comforting I nearly say yes. But not quite; she deserves her opportunity too. "Come for Christmas," I say. "Please. This will all be behind me, and we can spend some time in a castle with other American tourists drinking Guinness and eating Irish stew. It'll be great."

"Eating and drinking?" she asks. "Is that all you can think of to do? I must be losing my touch."

"Don't make me say it in this café," I say. "There are children present." A small smile appears on my eavesdropper's face. "I'll talk to you later." We hang up and the woman beside me gets up to leave. I thank her for the water, and she shrugs, her hand giving me a quick pat on the shoulder. No problem. The kindness of strangers.

Glancing at my watch, I realize that this time last week we were in the separated parents group, me and Teresa and all those little kids. I remember the photos of her, and how she spoke about her father with such openness. This brings me to thoughts of Seán, and then Gary. Why was *Garda* Mairéad asking about Gary? He was so pissed off in that meeting on Friday—somebody must have put that together with her death. When I talked to Mairéad about my timeline, I mentioned a meeting with a parent but I didn't say anything else about it. "Gary" she got from somewhere else. But who? It was just me and Teresa in there. The receptionist? Or the social worker from Tusla? Could Gary have come back to the center and pushed her down the stairs? I think of the way he threatened legal action and his angry, intense language. I think of Abel and the one hundred percent asshole debate. Gary might be a dick, but that doesn't make him a killer. Poor Seán. He must have gotten one of the cancellation calls from Anna. As if that kid needs more tragedy.

I stand up and the stickiness of my sweat-soaked cloths tells me it is time for a shower, and for that I'll have to brave Moira and the now excessively clean bathroom at the twins' place. Turning to leave, I think of the photos again. Where are my photos? Did I stick them back in that box, mixed in with Teresa's? The chill sets in.

41

I have a number of missed calls from Patrick early Tuesday morning, but I ignore them because I really don't want company on the way to the funeral. It's weird enough as it is, going at all. He texts me: *Are you going? You had better go*. I've declined the company of Sailí, both twins, and Moira, who have all offered to come along, and I'm dressed and out early, to avoid any complications. I decide to walk down to the city center before taking the train out to Dalkey. The day is cool and clear, and would be perfect if it weren't for the obvious. An email from the course last night confirmed the cancellation of our classes today, and repeated the details for the funeral. Teresa is described as "a great supporter of the program" and I think of our first conversation, and her delight that I wasn't interested in learning psychology. Those students must have been a pain in her ass.

Another text from Patrick. I respond: *I'm going. See you there*. The phone immediately rings and I answer it. Turns out he is in the city center already, so I agree to meet him. He has Róisín the assistant psychologist in tow, and I imagine he may have used recent events to grease the wheels there, so to speak. We meet at Brewbakers for coffee and when I sit down, I'm actually glad for the company after all. Róisín looks like she is going to cry at any second and Patrick looks exhausted. Seeing their faces, I know I'm not the only person all over the place.

True to form, Patrick has talked to everyone, and he fills me in on how people are doing. He tells me that the *Gardaí* have been out again to the clinic and have been checking the daily timelines of everyone there, although they haven't spoken to him or Róisín. I don't share my meeting, for some reason I can't quite put my finger on. Ciara, probably. I'm surprised they haven't been contacted. What does that mean? Why did they want to talk to me? Gary, maybe.

"Do you know why they are asking? I thought it was a clear accident." I try to keep my voice neutral. Patrick is no idiot.

"No, I don't," he says, looking at me. "Do you?"

Before I can answer, Róisín cuts in. "I remember when a psychologist was knifed a few years ago by some client—but I think that happened in the clinic in front of everyone. She was fine in the end, but it was a real shocker. The *Gardaí* talked to everybody."

"What?" I ask, and it is the right move. Róisín goes into a long story about the event, and then starts quoting research about violence between therapists and their clients. She mentions some Irish research on psychologists being stalked by patients. It's obvious she has done some recent reading, so they must be talking about this idea a lot. By the time she has finished her macabre thesis, it's time to go and we head off. Patrick doesn't circle back to his question. Yet.

The train down to Dalkey takes us past some stunning scenery and to stay off the topic I ask them a few questions about castles in Ireland—where I could take someone.

"Sailí?" asks Patrick with a sly smile.

Luckily, Róisín breaks in again, and lists off a few possibilities of places she or her parents have stayed in. The know-it-all nature of this assistant psychologist is extremely helpful to me on a number of levels this morning.

When we get to the church, we are still about a half hour early. Despite that, it is completely packed. The area by the front door is so crowded I feel like I am being rude as I walk through, but when I get inside it is less than half full. Patrick picks up on my confusion and explains people are outside to meet the coffin as it comes in. What he had thought was a removal ceremony last night was open hours at the house for family and close friends. Anna had been there and filled him in later. She said it was terrible and beautiful at the same time.

We sit for a few minutes, while Patrick and Róisín spot various psychologists in the congregation who they know or who they've heard about. I'm thinking about the coffin arriving. Has Teresa's body been released? Is the investigation over? The pews are filling up despite what Patrick said. The receptionist from Castleknock is with Vera, the caretaker, and a red-headed woman who must be Anna, although it is hard to recognize her from the smiling photograph in Teresa's office. She looks drawn and pale, and even from where I'm sitting, it's obvious she isn't steady on her feet. The receptionist puts an arm around her, and they sit down heavily, close to the front of the church. Anna looks like someone who hasn't slept in days.

Suddenly, there is a swell of people coming in, everyone stands, and the main doors part. The pallbearers come in slowly, carrying a long coffin-shaped basket, the top covered in flowers. The basket is white, the flowers are white, and there is a cascade of blossoms flowing down the back of the coffin like a veil. It is as if the whole thing has grown out of the earth in some magical forest. Terrible and beautiful. The pallbearers have their arms stretched out beneath the basket to rest on the shoulders of the men on the other side, the dark suits in dramatic contrast to the white burden they carry. I think of her all in white on Friday, and the white boots. My heart is breaking at the waste of it, and my eyes fill. I try to remind myself that I barely knew her, but death is death, and it's all mixed up with Amy in my head.

The whole effect, white on white, is breathtaking, and a hush falls on the crowd. Róisín starts to cry next to me, and she isn't the only one. More and more mourners come in, following the procession until the church is completely full—every seat, every space against the wall, and a few lines of people deep at the back, standing room. More come into our pew, and we are packed tight enough I am uncomfortably close to Róisín, and Patrick's hand, attached to the boyfriend arm around Róisín, rests behind me as we sit down. I'm getting ready to shoot him a look when my attention is caught by a chain of children and teenagers walking up the aisle, each gently placing something on a low table in front of the altar. Everyone is straining to see, so I have to look around a few heads to take in the table of offerings—a paper flower, a drawing, books, painted stones, a cross, a stuffed bear. I don't recognize any of the kids, but my mind goes immediately to the clinic—are these former patients? Or extended family? It is impossible to know.

The children melt back into the crowd and the priest stands to begin the service, taking his place at the lectern. It is a little hard to hear his opening words and someone must signal him about it, so he adjusts the microphone and there is the usual screech and static as he tries to get it right. Rage sweeps over me. This overwhelming tragedy—all these people gathered for the senseless end of this woman's life—and nobody checked the sound equipment? As the flush of blood courses through me, I close my eyes, trying to slow down my reaction. I hear the priest get the sound under control and welcome up William, Teresa's devoted husband, for the eulogy.

I take a breath and open my eyes. There, gliding to the microphone, is Dr. Roberts. I am so shocked I nearly stand up. Roberts? As I watch, he buttons his suit jacket and tugs down his cuffs. Effortlessly, he adjusts the angle of the microphone.

Róisín reaches out and pats me on the leg. She must have felt me freeze. I don't look at her. I am focusing on breathing in and out, slowly. How is this possible?

Composed as ever, Roberts could easily be greeting us and gesturing toward a therapy couch behind him. A second wave of fury hits me as he begins to speak, his voice strong and steady.

"He's a doctor," whispers Róisín.

"And a psychoanalyst," says Patrick, who has noticed Róisín's hand on my leg. "Anna was telling me about him—one of only a few fully trained psychoanalysts in Ireland. He trained at the Tivoli, in London, she said." The woman sitting in front of me does a half-turn and they fall silent. Róisín removes her hand and Patrick reaches for the other one.

Roberts goes on. His speech is perfect. A balance of emotion and intellect. Poetry, memories, and loss. Perfectly delivered. Róisín's tears turn to sobs. Other people are crying, but I am made of ice. Stone cold. I glance around and see Anna, whose face in profile is also frozen, her eyes dry. She glances back and we make eye contact, something passing between us, and then we both look back at Roberts, who comes to the end of his speech with a word of gratitude to all who loved Teresa, and all who made her feel loved. Even through my fog of confusion and numbness, the power of that hits me as he moves from the alter, unbuttons his jacket, and sits. Right front pew at the far left. He crosses his legs. So familiar.

The service continues and I go through the motions, robotic, same as everyone, standing up, sitting down, responses to the prayers filling my ears. The entire time, I am watching Roberts, trying to figure it out. Her husband, the bigwig doctor. Jesus Christ. I start thinking more about therapy. My confession about the accident, but also Teresa. What did I say, exactly? What did I imply? That session Friday morning, describing Thursday evening in the parking lot. What did I say?

My heart beats faster and I try to lengthen my breath, but it is not working. I flash to the panic attacks in his office, in the coffee shop. It can't happen here. My palms are damp, and moisture beads on my forehead. "Are you okay?" I have to look at Róisín now, and she is all concern—her tearful eyes trained on mine. Her hand rests on my leg again, and the warmth and weight of it is a distraction. I remember talking about Teresa so much, so explicitly. Her husband, forced to sit there, listening. And feeling, what? Disgust? Jealousy? Rage?

"I'm okay, Róisín. Thanks," I whisper, but I am not okay. Gray is gathering at the sides of my vision, and I am lightheaded.

"You're grand, Jonah," she says, "you're grand. It's nearly over." I look at her kind face and it pulls me back. What must she be thinking?

Eventually, the service ends and the pallbearers reverently walk the coffin back down the aisle, mourners closely following. I can't see Roberts as he moves past on the other side of the coffin, and then everyone starts lining up in the aisle. I look to Róisín for instruction and she whispers, "To shake hands with the family." The perfect cultural guide. Where would I be without this girl today?

At first, I want to turn away, but then I get into the slow-moving line behind Róisín and Patrick. We shuffle forward bit by bit, and they have hushed conversations with people we meet on the way. Low music plays in the background. My eyes seek out Anna, but I can't find her. I do spot the big-haired speech and language manager from the clinic with streaks of makeup beneath her streaming eyes, next to Vera, also crying. We keep moving forward, and eventually I see Roberts standing in the doorway of the church, shaking hands, moving his head close to hear what people are saying. Down the line past him, there are people who might be relatives. A woman who must be Teresa's mother, long-limbed and graceful like her daughter, and some others with a passing resemblance. I could look at them all day, trying to see her again.

Eventually, we approach him. Róisín is first, her small hand extended "So sorry for your loss. We are students from the clinic—she was so good to us." Even to him, she is offering gentle guidance.

Roberts shakes her hand. "So good of you to come." He turns to Patrick and then to me, registering absolutely nothing on his face.

"I'm so sorry for your loss," I say, expecting to get some reaction with my voice. The voice that must be familiar to him. Roberts shakes my hand.

"Thank you," he says, holding my gaze in the most perfunctory way possible—I am just another person at the funeral. Nothing suggests he knows me from anywhere else.

I keep moving forward, and only then think I could have referenced our appointment tomorrow, but I missed my chance. Maybe he didn't recognize me. The thought crosses my mind, but it is ridiculous. If nothing else, I can be sure that last appointment was memorable.

Before I tune back in all the way, I am shaken back to Earth by the slender hand in mine and the soft voice. "Good of you to come." I look into Teresa's eyes in her mother's face.

"Hello," I say. "I'm at the clinic with Teresa. What a beautiful ceremony. I am so sorry she is gone."

We both pause at the mixed-up present tense. "Oh, yes," she says, "the good-looking American. She mentioned you." She is smiling without really smiling. What did Teresa say about me? "Thank you for coming."

I move on, carrying the weight of her acknowledgement. I can't be sure what she meant, but I am still trying.

When I step into the sunlight, there are two people it takes me a minute to recognize: *Garda* Mairéad and her fast-talking colleague, *Garda* Tommy. Both of them are in dark, formal clothing like every other mourner, and both of them are looking right at me. I give them a little nod, and they ignore it. Then I realize they are looking past me, and I turn to see Roberts staring back. He looks directly at me and then past me, at them. No reaction on his face; the same as when he shook my hand.

42

I can't stand the thought of more of this, so I decide not to follow on to the hotel after the funeral. According to the all-knowing Róisín, there is a reception in Tinakilly House to celebrate Teresa's life. It's not clear if there is a cremation, or an interment, or perhaps no body yet. I decline the offer of a ride to the reception by someone Patrick knows, and head for the train station on my own. Passing through the tiny, peaked building, I spot Annemarie and Abel chatting on the platform and can't face the thought of a long trip back, making conversation, so I make a quick U-turn. I pass through the station gate again, and end up at the side of the road, just in time to meet a *Garda* car, slowly coming to a stop in front of me.

I'm frozen in place as Mairéad's window drops.

"How are you, Jonah!" she says, with what could easily be mistaken for a friendly tone. "Heading back to Dublin?"

"Hi, *Garda* Mairéad," I say, sounding about ten years old. "Yes, I am."

"Not going on to the reception?" calls Tommy from the driver's side. "I bet it'll be a swanky do—plenty of grub, anyway. I thought you students were always looking for free food."

"No, I've got to get back," I say, but I can't think of a reason why. It's like my brain is trapped in fog. There is no good way through this moment.

"Do you want a lift back to Dublin, Jonah?" Mairéad is smiling at me and I can't tell if it is friendly or carnivorous. "Only, you appear to be going the wrong way through the train station, if you know what I mean." Is she really offering me a ride in the back of their police car?

"Are you all right, Jonah?" Tommy is leaning down, nearly into Mairéad's lap, so he can look at my face. "A bit upset, maybe? I know you and Teresa were close, yeah?"

"Very close, we hear," says Mairéad, and I'm sure now that the smile isn't friendly.

"No thanks, *Garda* Mairéad," I say, ignoring her insinuation entirely. "I like the train, and it's a beautiful day. I'm just heading over to get some cash from the ATM." I gesture inanely down the road toward some stores. There is no way I am getting in that car.

"Suit yourself, Jonah," says Mairéad.

"See you soon, lad," Tommy calls out. "Mind yourself!" The window goes up and they are both grinning now as they pull away. That must have been fun for them. Behind me, a train pulls up and I wait for it to pull out before heading back into the station, exhausted.

On the next train, I try to work it out. What were Mairéad and Tommy doing at the funeral? They must be investigating it as a murder. Murder. It's the first time I've entertained the word. And it sounds like they think I was involved with Teresa. Which I would have been, if I'd had a choice. How would anybody know that? Roberts? Presumably they've spoken to him—he's the husband—but would he tell them about me? Would he have to, because she died and maybe I had a motive? A spurned lover? But he doesn't even know she turned me down. Maybe he told them we were having an affair. Surely that would implicate him, though. But how else would they know?

I text Sailí and there is no reply. Luckily, when I get back to the apartment the twins are there and besides a cursory comment or two about the service, we drift on the level of PlayStation companionship and a well-stocked kitchen which, for some reason, I am now allowed to access. Turns out there is at least one benefit to a traumatic couple of days.

By late evening I remember to check my phone, which has been on silent since the church service. There are several messages from Sailí and a missed call from Patrick. I text Sailí back and she invites me over, but I am too tired to move so we decide to meet for lunch tomorrow. Wednesday. Am I meant to go for therapy? I can't imagine yes, but I haven't heard anything from Roberts directly. And if he turns up and I don't, what does that look like?

Guilt? I think about calling Patrick for advice, but I don't really want to get into it with him. The problem with Patrick is that he pays attention to everything. There's a reason why he made it to clinical training—he's observant and analytical. Do I really want him in my business? Anyway, he doesn't know enough about it to give me good advice. And I'm not going to tell him any more than I have to.

Is there any point in asking the twins?

"Hey, guys?" They don't look over from the game, but there are a couple of grunts. Peter goes so far as to move one of the sides of his headphones off his ear.

"Turns out my therapist is the husband of Teresa who died." As soon as I say the word "therapist," I know I am not doing the right thing here, but no one has reacted so far. "I'm supposed to go to therapy in the morning, but he hasn't cancelled. Should I turn up and see what happens? If I don't turn up, and he does, I still have to pay."

No response. There is someone being hacked to death by an axe on the screen, so I assume that is taking their attention.

"Also," I go on. In for a dime, in for a dollar, as my old coach would say. "I talked a bit about her in therapy. I didn't know they were married. I think I may have even talked about a little coming-on-to-her move I made."

"What the fuck?" Peter completely removes his headphones and turns to me. "Did you just say that your *'therapist'* is Teresa's husband? The funeral from today? And that you tried it on with her? And that you told her husband, the *'therapist,'* you tried it on? What the fuck? Did you hear that, Michael?"

"I'm with you," Michael says, still staring at the screen. I think Peter may have been the person hacked to death. I wasn't banking on his full attention.

"Dude," I say, and decide to go for a distraction technique. "I really don't think you should be doing air quotes and a baby voice when you say the word *'therapist.'* It's disrespectful all round."

Michael lets out a guffaw, and Peter goes ballistic.

"Oh, yeah, the baby voice is the real problem. Not the fact that you were riding your supervisor and telling her husband about it and now she's dead. It's the baby voice. Oh—and the air quotes. That's the fucking problem here. *'Dude.'*" He does his air quotes.

There's a pause.

"I say go to therapy," says Michael. "What's the worst that could happen?" He's found a cache of weapons and I'm guessing that's why he sounds so cheerful about it. "How far did you get with her? Oh, shite."

We all watch as Michael navigates a tricky encounter on screen. He makes it.

"Nowhere. Total brush off. I don't even know what got into me. It was a dick move." I'm glad to have said it out loud. It seems a little more normal, even if it isn't.

"Literally," says Peter, and gets up for a beer. He brings me back one and sits down again.

"You do realize this gives the husband a motive, if he thinks she was cheating on him with you. Did you tell him about the brush off?" Michael says this in his happy voice, making good progress on the screen.

"He watches a lot of *Murder, She Wrote,*" says Peter, gesturing at his brother. "It gives him big ideas."

"I also watch *Making a Murderer,* you fucker. You'd better watch your step, Jonah. Hence my advice about getting the solicitor in early."

Peter laughs. "Did you say *hence*? Shut the fuck up."

"You shut the fuck up."

"Guys." I've heard how this goes about a thousand times. Not helpful. "What about tomorrow? Do I go? Do I text him?" I pause. "I didn't tell him about the brush off, I think." I know I didn't. "I left it open, like maybe something happened."

"Oh, man. No texting. Nothing in writing," says Michael.

"Jesus Christ. Text him about your '*therapy*' appointment the night of his wife's funeral? Now that is a dick move." Peter does the therapy air quotes to annoy me, but I don't bite. There was no baby voice, so we are moving in the right direction.

"You could go in tomorrow and tell him about the brush off," says Michael.

"After he's killed her? What the fuck? What would Jessica Fletcher say to that, moron?" Peter is clearly warming to the *Murder, She Wrote* theme.

"You guys are really helpful." I'm done. "Thanks so much for your carefully considered opinions. You've given me a lot to think about. I'm so glad I brought it up. I'm surprised more people don't come to you with their problems." Peter nods and drinks more beer, but he is looking at me.

"Oh, man," says Michael, and we all tune back into the game. "That was a close one."

43

I'm up and ready for therapy in the morning, all the same. I can go and see if he's there. It took me a long time to fall asleep last night, despite a crushing fatigue. I started thinking about Roberts and Teresa. What if he did think something happened? I can picture her in her wedding dress, from the photo, and it is hard to imagine Roberts in the same ceremony. Late to it, I remember her saying. What if he is there today? What will I say to him? What if Tommy and Mairéad are there? I push the thought out of my head. Now I'm getting paranoid.

To my surprise, when I come out of the bathroom, Peter is on the couch, fully dressed. I'm not sure I've ever seen a twin up this early, unless it is from the night before.

"What's the story?" he says to me. "Are you going?"

"Yep."

"Sure, I'll walk down with you."

I don't want that. "I'm fine, Peter. He won't be there. And even if he is, I'm fine."

"Is that right?" says Peter, putting on his jacket.

"Yeah, seriously. I'm fine. I'm going to walk down, and if he's there I'll cancel any further sessions. I don't want to hang out with the guy anymore—I can't deal with the Teresa thing. I just want to see if he's there." As if that's what we are doing, hanging out. As if I didn't vomit on his doorstep or confess my worst moment in the middle of a panic attack. I don't want to think about that now, so I don't.

"Perfect. Sounds good." Peter is standing by the door.

He is missing the pertinent information. "Peter," I say, slowly and clearly, "I don't want you to come. I'm fine on my own." I don't know how to be more direct on this point.

"Have it your own way," he says, and takes out his phone.

"What are you doing?"

"Calling Ma."

"Why the fuck are you calling your mother?" It is too early for this.

"Listen, you bollocks." Peter stands up and takes a couple of steps toward me. I haven't seen him like this before, and I can recognize his father in him. "If you think I want to be your fucking therapy babysitter you are a complete nutter. But if you think I'm going to let you go into the lion's den on your own when I know, for a fact, I am going to have to fucking hear about it for the rest of my fucking life from my mother, you are even worse than I thought. I am sick to death of minding Michael all the time, and now she is lecturing me about you." He takes a breath and seems to force himself to be calm. "Either I go with you now, or I call her and the siren goes back up on her fucking Range Rover. You decide."

We stand there in silence while I'm trying to control my temper and decide my next move.

"And," says Peter, "you may have noticed: no air quotes, and no baby voice. That is my little gift to you this fine morning."

Jesus Christ. We leave together.

44

We get to Roberts' door at seven fifty-three. Because I'm annoyed, we walked fast and now I have seven minutes to kill. Peter wants to knock on the door, and I have to explain the system to him. He stares at me and says nothing. I am so used to it by now, I want to defend Roberts. At eight exactly I ring the bell and we hear the door release. I can't believe it now that it's happened. How can he be here? I push the door open, and Peter pushes from behind me so we both end up going in. I was hoping to force him to wait outside and now I am completely off balance. Roberts is standing in his usual position by the fire, next to the couch. I hear Peter close the door behind us.

"Jonah," says Roberts, "and a friend?" Peter is looking around and I don't introduce him.

"Dr. Roberts," I say, "I'm so sorry about Teresa. I'm so sorry."

"Thank you, Jonah. It was kind of you to come to the ceremony." I'm relieved he acknowledged I was there, even though I shouldn't care. Now that I'm here I'm all over the place—my legs are weak and I am shaking. Like I've done something really wrong. Again.

"Dr. Roberts, I'm so sorry, I feel like . . ." Before I can finish the sentence, Peter has grabbed my arm in a vise grip.

I pull my arm back and throw him a look. His face tells me he is not going to leave it alone.

"Jonah," Roberts says. "Are you staying?"

I'm afraid if I say anything ambivalent, Peter will break his silence, and I do not want anyone to hear from him right now. I certainly don't want a Peter/Roberts mashup.

"No," I say to Roberts. "I think I need to finish therapy here. I mean, I think I need to change to someone else. I'm sorry."

Nothing changes in Roberts' face. "Sometimes, when finishing work together, it can be good to have a final session to end. You and I have had a very powerful conversation in the last week. Would you be interested in staying to complete our work properly?" He is looking at me intensely, and I want to stay. I really do. I want to talk about Teresa. And the accident. And my mom. He's the only person who knows.

I hesitate, and Peter inhales sharply. Before he can say anything, I cut back in. "No, thank you, Doctor. Sorry for being so abrupt. Can I ask, what happens to your notes? I mean, if I start with someone else, do you send those on?" As soon as I've said it, I think about my mother, and then Teresa. What is my problem? It's like I've stepped into quicksand. What could be in his notes? My God.

Roberts opens his hands. "What notes?" he says. "I have a record of dates and the number of sessions you attended I can forward the college, but I have no notes, bar your next of kin, and you saw me write that down. Whatever was said in here is just between me and you. No one else." The breath leaves my body before I realize I was holding it.

There is a pause. "Okay, so," says Peter. "Lovely to meet you." He is attempting to open the door we came in, and there is a farcical moment where I'm trying to point him in the right direction and he is confused and then we make it to the exit door, and I press the button. The door clicks unlocked and I immediately think of Starbucks.

As we leave, I turn to say goodbye to Roberts and he looks back at me through the closing door, his expression perfectly composed, as always.

45

"Jesus, fuck," says Peter, "what the fuck was that?" We are sitting with two flat whites and banana bread. "You were fucking useless with Count Dracula in there. Are you alright?"

There is real concern in his tone despite the frustration. "I'm fine, it's weird. The whole thing is so crazy."

"Crazy is right," says Peter. We sit in silence for a minute. "I mean, sorry about this, but I had my phone on record the whole time. You know, just in case. But now I want to delete it because you were such a fried bastard. I mean, why were you apologizing, for Christ's sake? You sounded like you killed his wife." He stops himself there and looks at me, waiting for a response. I have taken a look around the café, to see if anyone I know is there. I may be slow, but I learn.

"I don't know," I say in a low voice, and I really don't. The whole thing was so disorienting. I could have stayed there in the clinic with Teresa on Friday, and maybe she wouldn't have died.

"And all that business about the notes? I didn't know what was going on there." Peter's eyes are narrowed. "I mean, whenever anyone says *just between me and you* that's not a good thing, you know? I'm sorry, but basically, he can say anything he wants about anything you said and he's the doctor, right? You're some fucked-up student. That is some creepy shite, that is. Right?"

"That's very reassuring," I say, getting pissed off again. I don't think that is what Roberts meant, but now I am starting to wonder. Maybe Peter is right? Was he threatening me? I try to review the conversation in my head, but it is all mixed up. I should listen to the recording.

"Look, I'm sorry," says Peter. "No wait, that's fucked up. I'm *not* sorry and you shouldn't be sorry, either. What the hell? You have *nothing to do with this*. Even if he thought you were riding his wife it's not okay to kill her over it, right? I mean, seriously. Did you tell him you were with her?"

"No, no I didn't. I described a moment that could have led to something, but it didn't. But I didn't clarify that it didn't lead to something. I just left it hanging. I ended up talking about something else." How did I get into this? How did I tell Roberts about the accident?

"Well, then." Peter is on a roll. "First of all, that is seriously fucked up, but you didn't know it was his wife. Secondly, even if you freaking *left it hanging* it's no reason for a flipping death sentence on the woman. Thirdly, we don't even know for sure she didn't fall down the stairs."

I am strangely comforted when he says this. "Speaking of fucked up, what are you going to do with the recording?"

"I'm going to put it on repeat in the apartment so we can laugh our asses off at you, what do you think I'm going to do? Michael is going to love it. Now, can I please go back to bed, or do I need to supervise another meeting between you and your '*therapist*'?" The air quotes are back.

46

Annemarie catches me in the hallway before class, her expression impossible to read. "Jonah," she says, "just the man I'm looking for. Can you come in my office for a moment?" I walk in and immediately remember that scene with Meredith. What a joy that was.

We sit down in the same spaces and look at each other. "How are you doing? I am so sorry about poor Teresa." We chat a bit about the funeral and how beautiful it was. She comments on the tenderness of the husband's eulogy, and I nod in agreement. "Speaking of Dr. Roberts," she says, "I didn't understand you were attending his rooms until I received an email from him a few minutes ago. I can't believe he was in work this morning."

There's a shift in my gut. "Yeah," I say, totally neutral. The guy works fast.

"Yes," she says, and looks like she is thinking, or choosing her words carefully. "I think it is wise of you to change therapists at this point. The work is hard enough without the added complication of an overlapping relationship. And a bereavement."

Or murder. "I'm glad you agree with the decision." I'm thinking about what else may have been in that email.

"In fact, you might want to take a break from therapy for a while. If you aren't continuing with psychology in the long term, and given what you've been through, I think we could suspend the requirement for therapy or even for the work placement, and still allow you to complete the year." She is looking at me carefully.

"What?" I am completely taken aback. "No placement? No therapy? Is that what you are saying?" A couple of weeks ago, I would have been only too delighted with this option but now I'm wondering. "Did Roberts say something about me in his email?"

"I'm suggesting you might want to ease up on things. This has been a difficult time. Obviously, you've lost your supervisor. Now you've lost your therapist. We are happy to keep you on the course, if that's what you want, but you don't have to push yourself at the moment. That's all I'm saying." Annemarie sounds so sensible, but she didn't answer my question. I think about it for a second. If I agree in this moment, then everything pretty much goes back to normal—back to engineering, back to what I know. Just keep skating on the surface. There is something appealing about that. But. What has Roberts said about me?

"Annemarie, did Dr. Roberts write something in his email that has made you rethink my position on this course?" I'm wondering about my mother and Amy. Who knows how he could spin that. Or the mess with Teresa. Did he say something about that to Annemarie?

"Jonah." She looks right back at me. "I really didn't think you would feel so strongly about this. I thought my suggestion to take it easy would come as a relief. I am very happy to follow your lead on this. If you want a new placement, fine. If you want to source a new therapist, grand. I will support you either way."

"You still didn't answer my question." I'm leaning forward and she leans in toward me.

"No, I didn't." There's a pause, but not because she's intimidated. "Now, tell me what you want."

I sit back and think. Fuck Roberts. I suppose from Annemarie's perspective I'm trouble at this point—everyone on the course pissed off at me, confused, inexperienced, supervisor dead. It's no wonder she wants to be done with it. Plus whatever Roberts said. But I'm not here to make things easy for Annemarie, and I am not going to let Roberts spin this so I look like a problem. "I want to continue with the course, and I want to continue with the placement. I like it there. It's a nightmare what happened to Teresa, but I don't want to leave." I'm saying this mostly because I'm pissed off at Roberts and Annemarie but now that I'm saying it, it's true. "What about Anna? Could she supervise me? Could I stay in Castleknock?"

Annemarie sits back and looks at the ceiling. "Well," she says. "That's grand, Jonah. It is a surprise to me that this is what you want, but I'll try to make it work. I'll talk to Anna when she is back at work." She looks at me again and something has shifted.

"Are you going to tell me what Roberts wrote about me?" I am seriously pushing now, but it's worth it to me.

"Jonah." Annemarie sighs, and leans back. "You are very welcome to submit a Freedom of Information request if that information is a priority to you. I will not stand in your way, and I'll even give you the form. You have to submit it through the Graduate Studies office. Is it that important to you?"

It feels important, but is it? What would it change? Anyway, do I really want to draw more attention to whatever it is? "Forget about it," I say, and stand up. "Thanks, Annemarie."

"Time for class, Jonah. And try not to annoy anyone today, okay? Unless it is completely necessary for your growth."

47

Turns out Annemarie didn't need to worry. Having a supervisor die apparently gives you special status on a psychology course and everyone treats me as if I was made of very thin, very precious glass. Even Meredith is solicitous, so by the time the morning is over we are chatting away as if she had never called me out as shallow and I had never bitched about her to Aoife.

Sailí is waiting for me at the weird old person café with the piano, and I am so glad to see her. She refuses to talk about her work until I have filled her in on the funeral and what has happened since, so I tell her about the Roberts connection but not my part in it, obviously. Even without that she is freaked out.

"Jesus, Jonah. Talk about a small world. I wonder did they talk about you?"

"I know," I say. "I keep having to learn that lesson—how small this country is. She must have been talking about me because her mother knew about me. But I don't know about him. He doesn't seem like the type that would talk about his patients." Obviously, I hope this is true. Teresa didn't know who my therapist was, because she had asked, if only briefly. That sounded sincere, but who knows? Maybe Roberts discussed me at home. Did Teresa go into detail? Did she mention that clumsy move? Did he ask her about it? Did they argue? I try to imagine being in Roberts' position. Me, on that stupid couch, talking about her, implying that something happened, and then he goes home to her. How could he have ignored that?

While we eat our ridiculously underpriced meal, Sailí talks about the commission and how hard it is to produce what they want and still be an independent artist. Even though I'm interested, it is hard to stay focused; my mind wanders back to Teresa and Roberts, then Roberts and Annemarie, then Gary and Teresa. What the hell happened? I snap back into the conversation when Sailí starts discussing scheduling her work over the next couple of months and I can feel it coming. Christmas.

"So, what is the story with Christmas for you? Are you staying in Dublin? Shall I tell my mother to set another place at the table?" she says, and although her tone is light, she is watching my reaction.

"Last I heard, Georgia is coming over." There is no point in not saying it. Now or later, it's coming out. "They're all a bit worried about me, over there, and I think she is coming as the point person."

"Right," says Sailí, "that could be awkward with the three of us in the field." She laughs but it's not joyful.

"I could work with that." The space between us is widening.

"Right. No doubt." Sailí puts down her fork.

Lunch is clearly over, and she gives me a light kiss on the cheek in the doorway. We walk into the fresh air together and I have my arm around her, but she's not really there.

"See you later." A little wave and she walks up Grafton Street toward Stephen's Green, looking confident, beautiful, and already remote. It isn't the way back to her studio, but it is the opposite direction of where she knows I'm headed, so that could be the point. I want to call out to her, but what would I say? I think of all the people who have stood in this exact spot and watched someone walk away.

48

What starts to bother me as I sit in class is the fact that the *Gardaí* don't know about me and Roberts. Unless he's told them, they don't know that we have a connection, so if they are treating what happened to her as a murder, then it's an important piece missing from their investigation. Mairéad and Tommy were at the funeral, watching Roberts. I mean, what if he did kill her? What if he killed her because he thought I was screwing her? I try to think back to what exactly I said in that last session, but it is all mixed up in my head, with Amy, with my mother, with the scout pack. Could the *Gardaí* be looking at those notes? Even if it is just the list of dates for our appointments—would it look like I'm hiding something? Or maybe they came to the funeral to watch *me*.

"Jonah?" I look up and Rose is looking at me. "Are you okay?" I look around the room and they are all looking at me. I wonder did I say something? Did someone ask me a question? I have no idea.

"I'm fine, thanks." I sit up straighter in my chair and notice the slick damp of my palms. I reach for my water bottle and they get the message. Move on.

What I really want to do is call *Garda* Mairéad and explain the whole thing to her. She and Tommy have some idea about me and Teresa. But if I do that, I have to admit to her that I did come on to Teresa, but she blew me off, and how I told Roberts enough to possibly make him think something happened between us but not enough to explain that nothing did. It isn't a great position.

Also, if I tell Mairéad what happened, it could end up looking like I was in love with Teresa and when she blew me off, I killed her. Except I have an alibi. Or do I? Sailí can only vouch for me from twelve thirty to what, nine? Eight thirty? Then it occurs to me that my alibi just walked the wrong way up Grafton Street to get away from me.

There is the option of simply not saying another word. The familiar option. How could I be in this position, again? What the fuck is wrong with me? When I come out of class it is coming up to five o'clock and Annemarie is waiting at her office door.

"Jonah? Can you come in here, please?" I should be used to this by now, but I still get the jolt of fear. I tell myself that she must have heard from Anna, so I am completely unprepared when she closes the door and hands me the *Herald* newspaper. On the front page is Teresa's smiling face. Next to it, Gary scowling. The headline: "Man Questioned in Death of Psychologist." I sit down and read the entire article, which essentially reports that Gary is a suspect ("helping the police with their enquiries") in what is presumed to be Teresa's suspicious death. The article quotes "a source close to the story" as saying that Gary was the subject of a mandatory reporting incident in relation to his wife and son. Then another few paragraphs on what mandatory reporting is. The implication is that Gary is both an abuser and a killer. I'm not a fan of the guy, but this is rough. Unless he *is* the killer.

"Do you know anything about this, Jonah?" Annemarie asks, and she is not happy.

"Yes," I say, "I know a lot about it. I was with her when we met with this guy. I was with her when she made the report." I think about the confidentiality thing and I'm a little surprised she's asking me about it. "Am I supposed to be talking about this?"

"No, no, no. That's not what I meant," says Annemarie. "Do you know anything about the article?"

"What?" I am truly perplexed but then it hits me: she thinks I am the source. "No! Hell, no. I don't know anything about this article." Her shoulders relax and the storm clouds leave her expression. "You would not believe how crazy this day has been. You think I'd make it worse? No way. I have trouble talking to myself about this, much less anyone else."

"Grand." Her calm expression is back. "I believe you. Please don't talk to anybody about this. I'm sure the HSE is going to be all over our cases. Lovely. In the meantime, Anna has confirmed she would be delighted to supervise the rest of your placement. I'm not sure if she is going in to the clinic yet, but she said you could give her a call." Annemarie gives me her number and when I put it in my phone, I have missed calls and text messages from pretty much everyone I know. Except Sailí.

49

Five minutes later, I am sitting in a café across from the college. I simply can't face returning all these calls. And say what? More bullshit? More lies or half-truths?

Finally, I call Ciara, the lawyer.

"Where are you?" she says when I ask to meet with her, and I tell her. "Come to my office, will you?" I follow her directions across the Liffey and into an anonymous block of offices on Ormond Quay. She's wearing a T-shirt with Led Zeppelin on it, and dirty-looking jeans. "Sorry," she says, "I'm in the middle of moving premises." We sit on two nondescript chairs with an empty table between us. My phone starts vibrating again and I switch it off; a few minutes of peace.

"Now," she says, "what is going on?" There's a smear of dust on her forehead and so much has happened in the past few days I don't know where to start. I think about Amy and my mom, and Teresa and Roberts, and Sailí and poor little Seán, and nearly getting kicked off the course and I shut down completely. I close my eyes, and it is all I can do to sit there in silence. Ciara puts up with it for a minute or so and then says, "What is going on?" again, but this time, a bit softer.

My eyes well up and my breath shortens. "All right, all right," she says, and goes into a different room, leaving me on my own. By the time she is back with two cups of tea, brushed hair, and a clean face, I'm settled. The seams have come back together.

"Ciara, I want to talk to the *Gardaí* again." My voice is strong:

"Not a fucking hope," she says, and then launches into all the reasons why it isn't a good idea no matter what I did and on and on, until I cut in.

"No, wait," I say, and she pauses. "I didn't do anything. You are trying to shut me up because you think I did something. I didn't do anything criminal or even nearly criminal. I'm an asshole—that's it. I did an asshole thing that's embarrassing and wrong, but I think it might be important, it might mean something about what happened to Teresa. I swear, I didn't do anything *criminally* wrong." Even to my own ears, I sound guilty of something.

"Tell me," she says, and leans back in her chair. I have her complete focus and I use it, my mouth dry and a slight pounding in my head. For someone who talks a mile a minute, she can listen well. I start at the beginning with Teresa's connection to Roberts, and what I said, and what I didn't say. I include all the stuff with Gary and his family, the funeral, and this morning in Roberts' office, and finally the conversation with Annemarie about the newspaper. I put the whole thing out there, dumb move in the parking lot and all—telling Roberts half the story, and even Anna's look at me across all those mourners, like she knew something. All of it, except what I told Roberts about the accident. If he is going to use that against me, so be it. If what he said about his complete lack of notes is true, it's his word against mine. If not, well, I don't want to think about that. After a pause, I remember that Sailí is annoyed, and I throw that in for good measure. Also, why she is annoyed. And then the little chat with Mairéad and Tommy in Dalkey. At that, a little smile crosses her face.

Ciara listens and then sits, thinking, her lips a tight line. Eventually, she speaks. "What time is it?"

I'm surprised but not unprepared. I look at my watch. "Six thirty."

"Okay," she says, and takes out her phone. "Do you think you can tell that story without getting upset? Like, no tears?" I nod and she scrolls through her contacts. The little smile on her face is back when Tommy answers.

In Ciara's world, people are immediately available. Tommy agrees to meet us in the Chancery Inn on the corner to have an "informal" conversation. We head down and order drinks that I pay for. I turn the phone on and I have several more missed calls from the twins but I don't want to tell them what I'm doing in case

I get more crime television based legal advice. Or they will turn up for drinks. I turn it off again. Silent isn't enough—I need to be able to think clearly.

The Chancery Inn is another pub that somehow avoids looking like a tourist venue despite its location in the center of the city. In fact, if it weren't directly on the river surrounded by commerce, government buildings, and the courts, I'd think it must be about to close down due to lack of business. Clearly whoever owns it has decided that "seedy" is a good niche market in a city of "olde-worlde" themed venues.

Tommy strolls in and there is another surprisingly long and warm greeting between him and Ciara that includes not only golf but also past and future holidays. I'm beginning to think that maybe something is brewing here that has nothing to do with me—it's hard not to notice the complete lack of *Garda* Mairéad in the mix.

Finally, Tommy gets a drink, scoots in next to Ciara, and turns to me. "What's the story, Jonah? What's the big confession?"

"Did you say *confession*?" says Ciara.

"I'm messing," Tommy laughs. "What have you got for me, Jonah?"

I say it all again and it is much easier the second time. In this version, I give the bare bones of what happened between me and Roberts. When I mention Gary, Ciara shakes her head, so I leave that bit out too. Tommy sits, drinking his pint. When I finish, his face is expressionless. There's a pause.

"So?" he says.

"That's it," I say. "I think he might have killed her because he thought I was having an affair with her. Or something happened, anyway. I thought it might be important. I mean, it was the same day, Tommy."

Tommy looks at Ciara and then back to me. "It's a good thing the Guinness is good in here, because that is a load of bollocks."

"Oh, Tommy," says Ciara, but she's smiling.

"Are you serious?" Tommy says. "What am I supposed to do with that? Thank you, good citizen, for your information, but it is of fuck-all use to me, to be honest. Of all people, if that fella wasn't used to people trying it on with his wife, I don't know who would be. I'd say you weren't the only stallion pawing at her stable door, for Christ's sake." He turns to Ciara. "Did you get a look at her, Ciara? Did you see her photo in the paper?"

Ciara gives him a look and turns to me. "Do you feel better having said it, Jonah?"

I am surprised at his reaction; surprised and annoyed. "Whatever. You guys are questioning that other guy and I've offered you another take on it. I get that I'm not the police and you all have your expertise, but Roberts is a complete dick and I have spent some time with him, which you have not. I guess I didn't get that this was a make-Jonah-feel-better meeting. I thought I was helping." I sound like a petulant child at this point. Luckily, I am not tearful. And it is out now. I've told him. Whatever happens next is up to him.

"Oh, dear," says Tommy. "Have I offended you?" He looks from me to Ciara, and then back again. "How about this theory, boy genius? This fine lady is living her life, doing her thing, and then a sick bastard starts working with her, a guy with a few fantasies, a guy who can't stop talking about her, who can't keep his hands to himself. Maybe this guy pushes himself on her in a parking lot. She says no, and he won't take no for an answer. Who knows what happens between them? The next morning, he turns up at work on his day off to talk with her. And then she ends up dead. And his only alibi is patchy, at best, and provided by some other woman he's riding. Or this theory: maybe this guy *is* having a consensual affair with his boss, goes back to meet her at the office, and something goes wrong, there's an accident—she falls and ends up dead, and now he's got to figure out a cover story, blame the husband, whatever. And here we are. There you go, Sherlock, at least two more theories for you to mull over as you try to *help*."

"Oh, for Christ's sake, Tommy!" Ciara playfully swats his chest and leans over to squeeze my frozen arm. I must look as shocked as I am. "Don't worry, Jonah. This is classic Tommy." She turns back to him. "We are here as a courtesy, Tommy, you could be civil and not scare the boy to death."

"Fair enough," says Tommy, "but I can't do a thing with this horseshite, so I'm glad for the pint all the same. If you wanted to have a chat about that Gary fella, that could be helpful, but I think this lovely solicitor is going to stop you from doing that, so really, it's no use to me." He pauses and looks thoughtful, leaning back into the booth. "I nearly didn't have a drink in case I had to arrest you."

"God, that was a close one," says Ciara, smiling. Frustrated, I get up to leave, and Ciara walks out with me. She leaves her coat behind, though, so I know she is going back to Tommy. We get to the door.

"Okay, Jonah?" she says.

"What the hell?" I say to Ciara now that I am finally able to speak. "That guy is an asshole. I'm trying to help, here."

Ciara looks at me straight, and although she is petite, I have the sense that we are eye to eye, and it occurs to me that I didn't see her drink the Guiness I bought her. "I get that you were trying to help, Jonah, and so am I," she says. "What we know, now, that we didn't know before this little meeting, is that Tommy and Mairéad have a few lines of enquiry. You've got your conscience clear about the connection with Dr. Roberts, and we haven't told them anything about you they didn't already know. You're welcome."

"Thank you," I say, trying to read her body language. Annoyed? "I mean it. Thanks. But he doesn't have to be a dick."

"Sounds like there are plenty of dicks around," says Ciara, "and one dead woman." Shame rises through my torso and onto my face. She's right. I wonder what she really thinks of me.

"Call me if you need me," she says, "again," and turns into the bar, heading back to Tommy. I honestly don't know who is playing who at this point, so I leave them to it.

50

Stepping out onto the quays, I turn the phone on again and there is another flood of missed calls, including my dad, and about fifty text messages. Jesus Christ, what's next? I hit the number to call him back but before it dials, the phone starts ringing and Peter's name is flashing.

"What?" I say, still on edge from the meeting with Tommy and my thoughts already on home.

"Your father is here." Just as he says it, I look up and there he is. Standing on the sidewalk, leaning up against the granite stone wall that borders the River Liffey, the familiar shape sparking a warmth in my chest. "I think he . . ."

"I see him," I say, and hang up while Peter is still talking. As I walk toward him, he is absorbed in his phone, the light reflecting on his face. Before I get too close, he glances up.

"Hey. Fancy meeting you here," I say. He reaches out, and pulls me into a hug. I am released quickly but he holds onto my shoulders and looks at my face.

"Okay?" His concern is obvious. He lets go, but looks me up and down carefully, like he is checking for physical wounds.

"Dad, what are you doing here? Where's Mom?"

"I've got it covered," he says, but he doesn't look comfortable. He looks exhausted. "Where have you been? I had to track your phone's location because you wouldn't pick up. You turned it off."

It figures. "I was with the police," I say, and his face hardens. "And the lawyer, in that pub," I add quickly, gesturing at the Chancery Inn. My brain is trying to catch up with the fact that he is here, in Dublin, standing in front of me in his Dockers and

L.L. Bean. He must have gone to the apartment first. No wonder the twins were panicking. I imagine them answering the door and trying to put it all together. My dad is a big guy, tall like me, but broader across the chest. Maybe not quite as huge as their dad, but he's intense.

"What the hell is going on, Jonah?" He's got his old voice on, his officer's voice. "Let's get you home. I packed what I could find." He hits a button connected to his key, and a car lights up next to us. "We have to be at Shannon Airport in four hours."

"What?" The whole thing is completely surreal. I'm several steps behind him, as usual. The alcohol doesn't help.

"Get in, we can talk on the way." He starts to circle to the driver's seat. "We are booked onto a hop and I don't want to cut it too close." He must have called in a favor on one of the military flights through Shannon.

"What are you talking about?" There is a whining tone creeping into my voice and I clear my throat. "Dad, I'm not going home." I haven't moved my feet at all. It's like if I lose contact with the sidewalk for even a second, I might as well be boarding the plane.

He fluidly turns and comes back up on the curb. "Jonah," he says, his voice low and steady, easy to hear even though we are surrounded by pedestrians and traffic. "I don't understand what is going on here. There is a woman dead, tragically, and you seem to be talking to the police every time you turn around. You don't need to be here, helping out, taking responsibility, whatever it is you think you are doing. None of this has anything to do with you—your life is somewhere else, doing something else. Not this. A year out, fine. A break from the insanity at home, that's what I wanted for you. This nonsense, no thanks. Let's go home. Everything will go back to normal." Normal? Does he think that is what that was?

"But, Dad." I start to speak and then stop. Why is he here? Why does he think I need to be rescued? My brain is finally catching up. He thinks I'm involved. The realization is like a sharp pain, and I gasp. He knows. He knows what I did back then, and he thinks I've done it again. Fucked up, and somebody dies. A wave of nausea hits me, but I keep it together. Breathing. I'm suddenly outside my own body, imagining what we look like to the people passing by. Just a guy standing on the sidewalk with his dad, disagreeing about something.

"Jonah." We are face to face and his looks older than it used to. I wonder how he is really coping at home. "Get in the goddamn car." His words are hard but he is looking at me with concern. His one surviving child. What happens next? Am I supposed to say something? Something about Mom, or Amy? Some tearful discussion? My law-and-order Dad, trying to get me out of the country before this blows up. Protecting me, like he always has.

"Dad," I say, my voice steadier than I expect. "I can't. I'm sorry." It's there, between us. I can't walk away, pretending I had nothing to do with this. Not again. I know what that's like.

"Jesus Christ." He takes a step back from me and leans his forearms against the cold stone, looking out over the dark river. The streetlights catch only his profile and I can't see his expression clearly. I take a chance and move my feet, shifting up next to him. "Did I ever tell you, Jonah," he starts and then stops. I can hear his breathing, but he doesn't look at me, just at the water. A little silver glints in the stubble on his jawline when he speaks. "Did I ever tell you that the car, your mother's car, needed repair?"

"No," I answer, but it is out of habit, because the question is rhetorical. Obviously, he never told me, we never discussed anything to do with the accident. I couldn't. I spent all my life avoiding that conversation.

But he isn't finished. "There was something going on with the brakes. She had complained about it, asked me to take it in. Fixing the car was on my list, and I hadn't gotten to it. Too much else got in the way. Can you believe that?" My mouth is bone dry and I look over at him, but I can't really see him. Maybe because of the dark, or maybe because the world is spinning. "Would you please just get in the damn car." He finally looks in my direction again and it hits me. He doesn't think I'm responsible. He thinks *he's* responsible. That he let us all down, and he has spent the last ten years trying to make up for it. It starts to make sense. Not duty. Not devotion. Guilt. I know what that's like.

"Dad," I say, "wait." It takes me a few moments to pull it together, and then suddenly I'm terrified he thinks I'm judging him. That I'm here, silently accepting his confession, and the dam breaks. "It wasn't you. It wasn't the car." It's like I'm twelve again, my voice is somebody else's and it all comes tumbling out. "I had a spider in the car from camp, I took it, I took it when she came to get me, and it must have gotten out of the bag. A huge wolf spider, Dad. The biggest anyone had seen. And it was carrying its babies." I pause, gulping air. "Mom had the bag in the car with Amy. In the back seat. She dropped me off and I didn't grab it in time. It was me, Dad, it was me."

"What?" He has let go of the wall and is now at his full height and I stand up too. I am not sure I can say it again. And I'm not sure he wants to hear it. He looks me in the eye, and then looks away, turning it over, taking it in. It's like I can see the scene playing differently in his head. I can't believe I've finally said it to him. And I can't believe what he said. Faulty brakes? The movie reel in my head is going to have to add that. The spider, the scream, and now the brakes that don't work. Is there any end to the horror of what they experienced? Any end that doesn't involve a dead girl and a brain damaged woman?

After a few moments of silence, of staring out at the dark water, he turns to me. It's hard to see his expression. "I've really got to get going. I'm not sure how long that woman can last with your mother." His tone is unreadable, and I am searching for what emotions could be riding beneath. Anger? Fear? Is he really not going to say anything else?

"Do you want a ride to the apartment?" I suddenly realize that he is really going, and leaving me behind. That he is not going to comment on what I have said. I have an urge to change my mind about staying, go home, beg him for forgiveness. I want him to tell me it's okay. That it doesn't matter. That it was a long time ago. But he isn't saying any of that.

"And force you to meet the twins again? I don't think so." I try to connect with him on any level, even our default wry humor, but it is not working. He pops the trunk and lifts out my bag, which looks even bigger than when Margaret picked me up at the airport.

"Good luck, son." He is all business, now. "Be careful." I understand. I get it. There was a moment, and now it's gone. Why would we talk about this now, when we never have?

"Thanks, Dad." I am glad that it is dark so he can't see me clearly, either. "Give Mom a hug for me." He embraces me quickly and is in the car faster than I expect. Swiftly pulling into traffic, decisive as always. And then he is gone, and I'm alone. With a bag I can barely lift, again. On top of the bag is a long white envelope, which I open. Cash.

51

One of the thousand or so texts that I'd missed was Anna, to let me know that the clinic was closed but she and some of the other staff would be going in on Thursday if I wanted to turn up. *No pressure,* she added. *It's up to you.*

I'm not particularly looking forward to going in, but I also don't want to stay away. Sitting on my bed, punch-drunk from the day I've had, I text back: *I'll be there.*

The night passes quickly. I don't talk much to the twins, and although they probably have a thousand questions about what's going on, they leave me alone. In my bedroom I scroll through newspaper stories about Teresa, photo after photo, and whatever information journalists could find about Gary. According to them, he's a successful businessman with a string of upmarket service stations developed along the Irish motorway system. There are photos of him cutting ribbons, shaking hands, and even celebrating a lottery win by a customer at one of the outlets. With a smile on his face, he comes across as warm and friendly, although one "unnamed source" says he has a terrible temper. It's quoted in every story.

When I arrive at the clinic in the morning, it is early enough that reception isn't open and Vera has to buzz me in. I ignore the kitchen and quietly move up the steps, studiously avoiding looking for signs of Teresa's fall. At her office, I only hesitate a moment before opening the door.

The office looks like someone, probably the police, have looked through everything, and the effect is a sense of messiness or disorder without disarray—everything slightly out of place. The workbooks are stacked on one of the little tables, ready for last Monday's group. A quick vision of bouncing curls comes to me, but I shake it off and move quickly toward the bookshelf to take down the box of photos, bracing myself for the images of Teresa, healthy and alive. I have a clear memory of her reaching up to get them and I am looking toward the top shelves when I'm startled by a voice. "They aren't there."

I turn around and there is Anna, who clearly should not be at work. Her face is even more drawn than at the funeral, and she doesn't look like she has showered in days. "The photos are gone," she says. "The bastard took them." Anna stands there and it is like she is completely open, completely defenseless. I can look through her eyes directly at her heart, and it is broken into a thousand pieces. She sits down on one of the tiny chairs and starts to cry like someone who is resigned to crying—no artifice, no shame.

"We nearly made it," she says. "We nearly made the break." I have no idea what she is talking about—I can only wait. Patrick sticks his head in the door, raises his eyebrows, nods at me, and goes back out, closing the door. Anna looks up and sees my bewilderment. She takes a deep breath. "The last two weeks I have been moving into an apartment down the road, here, on the edge of the Phoenix Park. Teresa was meant to join me at the end of the month. We couldn't wait to be together, for real. We wanted to start a family." Slowly, the pieces come together in my head. Teresa and Anna. Teresa's baby project. Jesus Christ.

"Anna, I am so, so sorry." I reach over and put my hand on her back, patting awkwardly, and letting the information sink in. Teresa was leaving Roberts. Did he know? I picture him giving the eulogy. Was he thinking of me in that parking lot with Teresa? Was he thinking of Anna and Teresa? I wonder how a guy like that would cope with humiliation. If she didn't come home on time Friday, could he have thought she was with Anna? But then, why did he come to the clinic looking for her? Anna shudders under my hand and it brings me back. I suddenly think of the twins and how much they are going to love this new twist, and I have to push that thought down on top of everything else. My brain is in overdrive trying to figure everything out and I'm losing all perspective.

"I'm sorry, Jonah. I shouldn't be like this. I shouldn't be telling you all this, either." She is sitting up, now, and breathing better.

"I don't know why, but somehow you know her husband is a real bastard. Was a real bastard. You know what I mean." The tenses are all mixed up, but I do know what she means. "I saw the way you looked at him at the funeral, and I knew it."

"I do hate that guy," I say, "you're right there. I was trying to convince the *Gardaí* yesterday that he had something to do with her death, but they think I'm crazy." Saying it out loud makes me sound ridiculous, and I remember Ciara's flash of anger last night. Do I hate Roberts? I'm not so sure. I know I'm afraid of him.

"He killed her," says Anna. Because she is so certain, and yet she looks so unhinged, with her matted hair and her streaked make-up, the foundation of my own belief shakes a little. On the other hand, this is a much better motive than the little pass I made. "And he must have taken that box of photos on the night she died. On the night he killed her," Anna continues, "because there wasn't any other time. The clinic only reopened today. She loved that photo of her and her dad. He won't even let me have that one little piece of her. God, he put her through hell. So cold. She said he never really loved her."

Late to the wedding. Maybe there was more to that story. It is hard to imagine Roberts late for anything.

I think of the photo of Anna and Teresa in there too. And the photos of me that I must have tidied into the same pile. Did it look to Roberts like she was holding onto them?

Anna stands up and brushes down her clothes with her hands, trying to take on the semblance of sanity. "I was so glad to get a call from Annemarie yesterday, Jonah. I'm delighted to be your supervisor and I am so relieved that you are staying with us here in Castleknock." She starts to straighten up the small tables and chairs, all business. I am so focused on helping her, I nearly don't catch her next sentence: "I'm going to need your help in proving that he killed her."

52

It's a good thing Anna has moved back into Anna-at-work mode because I have nothing to say to this. I push the little chairs in under the tables and Anna excuses herself, saying something about the bathroom.

"All okay?" Patrick is back, half in and half out of the door. I look over and whatever is on my face makes him come fully in and close the door behind him. "What happened? What's going on?" His voice is low, his expression open, and right then I have an urge to tell him the whole story. Maybe he could help me. He *is* a smart guy. But what can I say about me and Teresa and Roberts that isn't stupid? Does he even know about Anna and Teresa?

"It's so crazy," I say, and that is true. So true. This, but not just this. Everything. My thoughts swing to last night with my dad, but I push them away. I'm not thinking about that here.

"I know," he says, "even being in this room." We look around at the office. Whose office? Suddenly it occurs to me that Anna could come back and think we are having a big discussion in here with the door closed, about her.

"Toast?" I say, and he laughs.

"If all else fails, feed the beast. Emotional eating—the last resort of the sad psychologist."

"Not quite the last resort," I say, "there's drinking."

"Even at nine in the morning, that sounds good to me," says Patrick, and we head down to the kitchen. The door to the bathroom is closed and I hope Anna is in there, brushing her hair.

Breakfast is a much quieter affair than usual, and Patrick moves into position next to Róisín at the toaster. Several of the other clinicians, including the speech and language manager, ask me how I'm doing. These people have known her for years, and they are worried about me. There's a little debrief about the funeral and a quick segue into the newspaper article.

"Can you believe it?" says the receptionist. "That's the father who nearly flattened Jonah. I had to ring up for poor Teresa to come down."

I'm a little annoyed at this characterization of the meeting, although in all reality that is exactly what would have happened if there had been a physical altercation. I'd like to think I would hold my own, but Gary is huge. Annemarie and Ciara have made me completely paranoid about the HSE, so I don't say a word to change the narrative.

"The idea that he came back here, poor Teresa, it's so terrible." She lets out a little shivery breath. "I mean, if it was after hours, how did he get in past the security door?"

Anna comes in, and everyone quiets down even more. I don't know if it is because they worked so closely together, or because everyone knows they were a couple. I keep my game face on. Patrick glances around the room.

"Okay, everyone," Anna says, and I'm relieved that she looks okay. There is some puffiness around her eyes, but she has fixed her hair and makeup, and is in control of herself. "Here is what is happening in psychology. All appointments have been cancelled for today and Friday, same as everyone. We are back in business from Monday. I'm going to pick up the group with Jonah, because the kids know him, and I don't want to let it go. Even if we don't get through the material, we have to follow up. I'll call the parents tomorrow and make the offer."

This surprises me, but I keep my eyes fixed on Anna. I sense there's more.

"Also," she continues, "Risk and Legal from the HSE are dropping in to talk to us about the press, and to make sure the cases Teresa was working on can be made available to the *Gardaí* if necessary." We all know this is about Gary. "As far as I know, no one is obliged to come along, but I wanted everyone to know what is happening."

Anna turns to the coffee maker, and there is an attempt to have a normal conversation at the table, but it's impossible. Breakfast breaks up quickly, and it's me, Anna, and Patrick left.

"Do you need some help with the group?" Patrick asks Anna. "I can do it, if it's easier."

Anna shakes her head. "No thanks, Patrick. I think we'd better have an experienced clinician in there. I need Jonah because he's the constant from week one. I can't bear the thought of leaving it, Teresa's last group, even though it's tricky."

"Anna," he says, "I am experienced—remember, I'm finished with my training in a couple of months. It'll be fine, and it will free you up. Let me help." Patrick glances over at me, and then back to Anna. "Jonah can fill me in on what I need to know about the children."

Anna pauses, then shakes her head. "It's the optics, Patrick. I need the parents to know someone fully qualified is at the helm. The children could be very confused or upset with what has gone on, and the parents will be nervous."

"What will we tell the kids?" I think of all the potential questions, especially from that little girl. How did she die? Where did she die? What was she wearing? I don't think I can take it.

"The truth," says Anna. "Teresa can't do the group because she died, so we are doing it instead."

"But what about all the questions? You would not believe how many questions they asked about her wedding photo."

As soon as it is out, I think of the arrow I just shot at Anna. She doesn't react. She doesn't even look like she is holding back a reaction. "Jonah," she says, "I do have some experience with children." Patrick laughs and my panic eases. "I'll tell them that I can't answer their questions about Teresa, because I don't know, or because it is her private business. Don't worry, it'll be okay."

"Oh, right." Another full breath in.

"Or maybe you could mention Jonah's ears," says Patrick. "They love that subject."

53

Risk and Legal convene the meeting and they look exactly like Risk and Legal should look. Suits, briefcases, and a stenographer to take minutes. Luckily, it isn't a meeting so much as a briefing, so I can just listen. Despite Anna's casual comments, the entire building turns up to hear what they have to say.

PowerPoint slides flash up as they cover confidentiality and its limits, documentation, common mistakes with the press, liability, and procedures. By the time the slides are over, everyone is too exhausted or too frightened for questions. That, or nobody wants their questions recorded. The HSE team wrap up the group meeting and head up to Teresa's office with Anna to review the case materials. As soon as they are out of sight, Patrick and Róisín leave early, and most of the clinicians follow. I'm not sure if I can go, or if Anna wants to talk about the group on Monday. We haven't touched base since breakfast. I'm about to go back to my data in the kitchen when Anna calls my name.

"Jonah? Can you please join us?" She is at the top of the stairs and as I round the corner to go up, there is a moment, a pause. These fucking stairs. I bolt up and Anna takes me back into Teresa's office, where the Risk and Legal suits have set up at Teresa's desk.

Anna takes a seat on one of the little chairs. "We can't find the file on Seán and his family, Jonah." I think she is expecting me to sit down next to her but I'm not going to. I'm not sitting on the baby chairs. If I've learned anything from my father, it's never to volunteer for the one-down position. My father.

"Hang on a sec." I retrieve the desk chair from Róisín's space in the hallway. "Here, Anna, have a grown-up chair." She shifts seats while I dart next door and grab another chair from Anna's office. Now I'm ready. "The file isn't there?"

"No." Risk and Legal number one answers for her, possibly not happy with my little chair protest. "It's not. And it isn't in the filing cabinet either. Or the desk drawers."

"It wouldn't be in the drawers or on the desk." I'm pretty confident; I've seen Teresa with paperwork. "She filed everything away in the cabinet. I think it was locked when she wasn't in the room."

"Where did she put the key?"

Anna answers, "Under the flowerpot," gesturing to the orchid on the shelf. I never saw that. Maybe she did it at the end of the day. Maybe I missed it. I was with her late on that one evening, the Thursday. We were in the office together and she cleaned up. I can't picture where she put the key.

Risk and Legal are watching me. "Is that right?" Number one asks.

"I have no idea." It's the truth, but I also realize they are trying to find out if I knew where she kept it. "Do you have the key, now?"

"It was in the cabinet lock," Anna answers for them, looking at me. "She wasn't finished with her work." Poor Teresa. There is a moment when I think Anna might tip over into grief again, but she doesn't. Anna is all business. "I have no idea where the file is." She says this directly to Risk and Legal.

We all look at each other. Risk and Legal ask me to talk through all the contact with Seán's family, and I do. I think about Annemarie and the course, and the embassy, and Ciara the solicitor, and I go ahead anyway. At least they've sent the stenographer home.

We go through the whole thing a few times from different angles, and I'm like a child again, despite my adult-sized chair. My story is full of pauses and confusion, and I can't remember or don't know the name of the social worker, so I reduce her to "the lady on the phone." Eventually we finish, and Anna suggests I come back in the morning to organize the group, and help her with the calls. She's forgotten that I don't work here on Fridays, but I don't have the heart to remind her. I am reluctant to leave her alone with Risk and Legal one and two, so I head down to the kitchen to wait for them to go.

While I'm there, I remember Seán's mother's questionnaire

and quietly dart back up the stairs to dig it out of the stack I've stashed in Patrick's office, easy to spot with the purple ink. As I remember, everything is highly endorsed—the behavior and emotional problems listed are marked at the extreme ends: always or never. There isn't anything about family relationships or marital stuff on the form, but I wonder if it could be relevant. I wait until the two suits leave, and I head back in to Anna, the questionnaire in my hand.

I find her in Teresa's office, staring at the shelves again. Clearing my throat first so I don't startle her, I wait until she turns to face me, despair showing again on her face.

"I had this in the data," I say, and hand it over. Anna reads the name at the top and then flicks through the pages. "Teresa used it for her report to Tusla too."

"The poor child, he's a disaster. Jesus. Twenty-seven Park Manor. Pretty posh address. We don't see Park Manor kids here very often—not that they're not screwed up the same as the rest of us, but they generally go private." Money. That fits with what I read about Gary last night, but I don't want to mention my personal research. It occurs to me that is now in my search history. Perfect.

"How was he in the group?" I was expecting this to be about Teresa, but Anna is suddenly completely focused on Seán.

"He was fine. Completely fine. A little shy when he was expected to share, but he was good."

"Did he get on with the other kids?" She pulls out Teresa's chair and sits down again. It's strange to see her in that space. I sit down in the chair next to the desk. I have a picture in my head of Seán laughing with that other little guy at the table.

"He made a friend, I think. They were playing with a toy and they laughed about spaghetti turning into poo."

"Right, session one—change." Anna is thinking. "Sounds pretty normal, not like the child described in this questionnaire." She sighs. "I'm a bit reluctant to call the family tomorrow because of the dad thing in the paper, but I'd hate to exclude Seán. I mean, it's not his fault things are screwed up."

This takes me completely by surprise. Anna is going to call the house of the guy currently being questioned for Teresa's death? That can't be right. I mean, she is hardly a disinterested party.

"Are you sure that's wise?" I try to keep my expression neutral.

She is the supervisor here. "I mean, isn't it a conflict of interest or something?"

Anna looks me in the eye. "I don't have a conflict of interest, here, Jonah. I'm interested in helping this little boy whose parents are separating." There is a definite edge to her voice, a challenge. She waits for my response, but she hasn't really asked me a question. I look back at her in silence and it occurs to me that this is the second time I've questioned her judgement today.

Eventually she breaks eye contact and stands up, stretching. "Okay, Jonah. I'll see you in the morning." No way am I going to challenge her on the Friday thing. I offer to wait with her until she is ready to go, and she shakes her head at me. "I can take care of myself, thanks." I get the message.

54

The one time I am dying to talk to the twins, they aren't available. The apartment is empty. I send a text and hear back that they have cleared out for a long weekend that involves parents, grandparents, and a lot of ancillary family. Michael says his mother is eager to have me come down and join them, but he strongly advises against it. He says he can't be responsible for protecting me from the bowsie cousins, whatever that means. I take his advice. It has been quite some time since I have been alone, and I am exhausted.

On the counter is a note from Moira, telling me to phone her if I want to come down, that she would be delighted to come and get me. Also, she encourages me to eat everything that's in the apartment as she'll be bringing "a load of shopping" when she drives the twins back on Sunday night. I open the fridge and it looks full. Luckily, there's craft beer, so I can be of some immediate help in making room.

I crack a beer and start thinking. I've been going about this all wrong, bouncing from one drama to another, trying to extricate myself from being involved. But I am involved, and despite what I'm feeling, and how I'm being treated by everyone, I am not helpless. I can think this through. And maybe I can help Anna.

Why the hell would the photos go missing? Did Roberts take them? And why would he take the file? It makes no sense. I picture his office, or "rooms" as Annemarie called it, and there isn't even a desk for a file to be on. There must be a back room where he puts the extra chair, right? Maybe that's where the paperwork is. I think about the dimensions of the inside room, and of the outside of the building, framed perfectly by the Starbucks window. There must be another room. And I've seen an alley, with a high metal gate, from the intersecting street down the back of the building, so there must be another door. What do I do, break in? Tomorrow is Friday, therapy day. He'll be there. And very unlikely to leave that chair between the hour and fifty minutes past.

But it doesn't explain the file. Why would Roberts want that? Gary? But why would Gary take the photos? And then another question occurs to me, one I'd missed because of the wave of shame I'd felt in the pub. How does Tommy know I had a moment with Teresa in the parking lot? Did she tell someone? Roberts? Her mother? The shame is back, and I push the thought away.

I open the fridge again for another beer, and at the sight of all the food, I am suddenly starving. I take out salmon cutlets, salad, and a package of coleslaw of the type I've only ever seen in Ireland. As I'm shoveling everything onto a plate, I doubt very much that the twins would eat any of this. Ham, cheese, bread, and butter. Moira would have a very short grocery list if she were a realist.

Sitting on the couch after eating, I pick up the remote but then notice a brown paper package with my name on it leaning up against the wall near the door. I'd missed it on my way in. With more effort than it should take, I get back up and cross over. My name, no address. When I open it, it takes a second before I understand. It's a framed canvas, with layers of strong colors. Rising up from a solid base are long strands of grass, tapering off at the top. The way the shapes are repeated in different tones gives it depth and the slightly frayed edges of some of the lines suggests movement. Mostly, it is shades of blue, but there is red and a strong orange in it as well. In the bottom right corner is my own name, in unfamiliar handwriting. The print I worked on in Sailí's workshop. From the day Teresa died. I put it up, leaning on the mantle, and go to bed. I don't have the energy to think about any of this.

All day, I've had to work so hard to not think about my father. As soon as I lie down, it all comes flooding back.

55

Friday morning, I'm tired and groggy when I wake. I'd resisted texting Sailí last night, but I'm even lonelier now in the fresh daylight so I send a thank you message and suggest meeting up later for dinner or drinks. You never know.

Now, decision time. Do I head down to Roberts' office? Not for my appointment—I think we are clear on that after Wednesday's fiasco—but maybe he has another session at nine, and I can have a look around the back. I had never seen anyone, but then I always left through a different door, on a different street, ten minutes before they'd be let in. I could look for the photos. Or the file. Or my file? The thought of coffee tips the balance, and I decide to walk down and see what happens. Anything is better than waiting for the next shock.

On my way down Thomas Street, I have to pass about a hundred other coffee places so I can no longer fool myself into thinking this is about Starbucks. I catch my reflection in a store window and think about the baseball cap and sunglasses I could have worn if I had admitted to myself that I'm thinking of sneaking around the back of Roberts' office. Instead, here I am, clearly myself, being an idiot.

"Jonah?" I turn at my name, and there is Meredith, my would-be college nemesis, with a bus pulling away behind her. "What are you doing here?" She makes it sound like she is being stalked. By me.

"Hey Meredith." I try to keep my voice neutral. "I live around here, out for a coffee." She glances at her watch, in a hurry, so I chance it. "Do you want to join me? I'm walking down to Starbucks."

"No," she says, "I have an appointment, but thanks." We are walking the same direction, so I shorten my pace and she falls into step beside me.

"Seriously, Jonah, Starbucks?" She smiles at me, but still makes her point. "All these independent retailers, and you're supporting an international conglomerate?" I think she means multinational corporation, but I am not going to argue.

"Reminds me of home, I guess." I am thinking of where we are headed. Did Meredith say she had an appointment? She got the same list of therapists I did. Roberts.

"But isn't the point of foreign travel to try new things?" Her voice is a bit tight, nervous. I'm trying to think of what I may have said about her to Roberts. I can't remember a thing. It probably didn't seem important enough.

"I guess so." We are coming up on Roberts' building on our left, and Meredith walks past. I want to look at my watch, but don't. "See you later." I cross the road at a diagonal toward the café.

"Enjoy your coffee!" she says and continues straight across. In Starbucks, I immediately check through the window and see her doubling back, looking at her phone. I look at mine: eight fifty-nine. Un-fucking-believable. There is a chance I am not the worst client Roberts has. The guy behind the counter greets me like an old friend, and I have to buy something, even though I am here for other reasons.

A quick espresso at the front window, and I can tell for sure by the shape of the building there is a room behind the consultation room, an extra high window and then solid brick. The fireplace must have been built between two rooms, maybe serving to heat both when it was built. As I had remembered, there is a gated alley behind the building, probably for deliveries, and the gate is open. I can't remember if it is always open or if this is unusual.

It'd be good to have a reason to go in. Or at least, a cover story. Hanging next to the restroom in Starbucks is a clipboard, the bathroom cleaning schedule for the past week held tight in its jaw, and a pen on a string. I lift the clipboard and dart across the street, straight into the alley. Nobody looks suspicious if they are confidently carrying a clipboard. As I pass by the gate, I notice a lock, dangling by its open hook. Maybe delivery hours? Trash collection? I'm lucky.

About ten steps into the alley, there is a sleek black Jaguar F-TYPE two-seater coupé pulled to the side, gleaming as if it's been teleported from the showroom. This has to be Roberts' car, saying it all, without speaking. Not the type of car a man who wants children buys. Cut into the brick wall next to the car is a black steel door with a handle. I reach up to see if it's unlocked, still not really sure what I'm doing here.

"Hey, what's the story?" A man is halfway out of the next door down the row, wearing a high visibility vest over work clothes. I didn't hear it open and freeze in place at the sound of his voice.

I hold up the clipboard and try to look busy and serious. "Checking the security! That gate is supposed to be locked." I gesture impatiently at the gate, and then at the luxury car. The best defense is a good offense.

"Right," he says. "It'll only be a couple more minutes." There's a pause. "Are you American?"

"Yep." I can't believe we are starting a conversation.

"I have two brothers in New York. It's a great country!" He looks like he is getting friendly. I twist the handle and pull, and of course, it's locked. Was I expecting a guy like Roberts to leave his back door open? I step back to the Jaguar.

"Whereabouts are you from?" he continues, and I am starting to sweat.

"Virginia." I've said it from habit, and I'm annoyed at myself. This isn't turning out to be a great stealth operation.

"*The Virginian*. I used to love that program." I have never heard of it, but I nod anyway, acknowledging his comment.

"It's a lovely car." He walks toward me, and I pull the clipboard closer to my chest, hiding the bathroom cleaning rota.

"It is." I cross in back as he approaches the front.

"Real space age." He cups his hands to cut the glare and bends to look through the driver's side window. "Look at that."

I'm not sure how to avoid it, so I do the same on the passenger side and there, on the seat, is a DO NOT BEND envelope with my name on it, and the address "Department of Psychology, Trinity College." Next to it is another envelope, with Anna's name and the Castleknock center address. They're stamped, ready to go, and I'd bet the house they have our photos in them. I'm tempted to try the door on the car, but I'm pretty sure that will set off an alarm. Not to mention freak out my chatty companion. This answers one of Anna's questions—he did have them.

"Must be nice," he continues. I glance at the dash and there is the typical interior, and then above, tight against the rearview mirror, a dual purpose dashcam. One camera pointing out at the street, one camera pointing into the car. My companion straightens up and a little light blinks. No doubt the camera is motion-sensored. Filming us, pressed up against the windows.

"Anyway." I stand up quickly and move away from the car. "Be sure to lock that gate when you're leaving." I'm alert to cameras now, and immediately notice another one, high on the wall above the back door I was just testing. Perfect. I imagine Roberts, trapped in his analyst chair, discreetly watching me on the feed from two cameras while Meredith complains about what an asshole I am.

"Will do, will do," he says, and gives me a friendly wave as he heads next door. I watch him go in, and although I want to run away, something holds me in place.

I stand there, clearly in Roberts' vision, whether he's watching live or watching some recording, later. I can so easily picture him in there, trying to work, his wife dead and buried only days ago. Shame washes over me again, and I am disgusted at myself. Was I really trying to convince the police that Roberts killed Teresa? Why? Because he listened to the bullshit rantings I came out with to avoid talking about my mother? Or maybe *because* I told him about what really happened to Amy and my mom? Or at least, what I thought happened. Am I really that much of a child—immature and vindictive? Looking into that camera on the wall, I wonder if that is how Roberts sees me. A child. A confused child? A lost child? Maybe he's right.

I dash back into Starbucks and hang the clipboard on the wall. No one pays any attention.

On the way to Castleknock, I try to focus on what is happening in the here and now. It goes without saying I'm a complete idiot in terms of investigative operations, but I did learn that Roberts has the photos, and also that he is sending them back to us. I can imagine he is happy to get rid of the one of Teresa and Anna. Maybe he didn't take them from Teresa's office on the day of the murder, or accident, or whatever. Maybe he took them the next day. Or maybe the police took them, and then returned them to him. Either way, it doesn't fit with a murderous plan. I wish I could ask someone, but nobody involved would speak to me about it.

It's quiet at the clinic. All of the appointments are cancelled, but many of the staff are in doing paperwork or rescheduling and there is something comforting about seeing them. The formidable speech and language manager has brought in fresh flowers for the kitchen table and homemade scones.

Anna takes out the little workbooks and we begin calling the parents, sitting this time in her office, rather than Teresa's. There is a desk set aside for Patrick, but no sign of him, so I take over the space. In addition to the workbooks, Teresa had a file in the cabinet that summarized what happened in the first parent meetings, including consent forms, and how the kid did in session one of the group, with a separate page for each child. This is open in front of me and I brief Anna on what's there, and also on what I remember about each kid.

She looks better today, but the atmosphere of grief surrounds her like a dense cloud. There is a sense she is operating on autopilot and I'm on edge; one false move and she could crash. I want to talk to her about the photos, but I don't want to crack the thin layer of coping. We start with one of the girls and she listens to me carefully, then dials.

"Hi," she begins, "this is Anna, a psychologist from the primary care center." The mother on the end of the phone is clearly up to speed on the news, and Anna has to manage the outpouring of sympathy before bringing up the separated parents group. It is a strange experience for me because if I close my eyes, she sounds completely normal—like she is calling about a dentist's appointment. Her voice is clear and calm, even soothing in its tone and pace. With my eyes open, though, I can see her struggle, her elbows on the desk, her head held by her fingertips, and her eyes focused on the grain of the wood in front of her. Grief at work.

We get through the first five and, so far, all the children are coming back on Monday. Next on the list is Seán, so we take a quick breather.

Going down for coffee, I take a good look at Anna. The thought of her and Teresa together rises to the surface. Probably because of her grief, my first impression of her was of fragility, but physically she is solid and muscular. She's wearing a dark sweater, and black, straight-leg pants, with low-heeled ankle boots. She is graceful without looking like she's trying, and her long fingers on the banister look strong, like a pianist's. She has good hair, red and wavy, and she doesn't seem to be wearing makeup today. Having said that, she looks well put-together, so perhaps the makeup is subtle. I wonder how they got together—who made the first move.

"Eventually, Jonah, we are going to have to talk about it." She has caught me a little by surprise. This could be Seán. This could be Teresa. This could be Roberts.

"Okay," I say, and reach for a mug. I am trying to look casual, but I don't think I can manage what's coming. I'm not sure if I should tell her about my little amateur foray into Roberts' territory this morning. I can't go any further with this sleuthing plan she is working on. He knows too much about me, and now he has a recording of me trying to break into his building.

"Changing supervisors is awkward, even without the trauma going on here." She takes a breath. "Normally, I would talk to the supervisor who's finishing, go over what's needed in the placement, that kind of thing. But this time, I can't."

I look down at her standing there next to the coffee maker and it strikes me that in all her grief and outrage and loneliness, she is worrying about meeting her responsibilities to me. I have a nearly overwhelming urge to physically comfort her, to put my hand on her shoulder or something, but I don't. "Anna," I say, "Teresa and I were keeping the secret that I'm a jerk on a goof-off year abroad who doesn't really care about psychology or other people. Do you think we could keep that up?"

For the first time I hear Anna laugh properly, and it feels good.

56

After all the buildup, the call to Seán's house is just as straightforward as the others. Tríona answers and confirms he would like to come back, and when we go through the rest of the list, we have eight confirmed and one mother who is still considering. It is strange to think this is simply a service to them, that the loss of Teresa isn't an endpoint, for any of us. At work, anyway. Things go on.

Anna releases me but I have nowhere to go, so I work downstairs in the kitchen and eat a couple of the speech and language scones. At four o'clock, it is starting to get dark, and I still haven't heard from Sailí. Even though it is against my normal practice, I send her another text. I'm trying to tell myself that a sad face emoji isn't pathetic when I get an emoji back from her. Angry red face with horns. I'm smiling to myself when the phone rings. Hallelujah.

"What do you want?" Sailí starts with what I think is a pretend angry voice.

"I'm in crisis." I step into the waiting room for privacy, and stare out the window at the parking lot.

"Again? Jesus, what is it this time?" I'm relieved that her exasperation sounds warm.

"Moira has left me with a completely stocked fridge and firm orders to make room for more groceries on Sunday night. I'm not sure I can do it. I'm alone in the apartment all weekend."

She doesn't reply, but her silence lets me know I'm making progress.

"Hey, thanks for the art, by the way. It is so beautiful. The twins will never believe I'm an artist." It occurs to me they must have talked to her when she dropped it off. I wonder what was said. They probably told her about my father.

"You aren't," says Sailí.

"I'm not." She has me backpedaling now. "I mean it, though. Thank you. That was the day Teresa died."

"I know," she says, and her hard heart softens. "I'm aware that you played the dead lady card in a sad attempt to manipulate me, but I'll come over anyway. To help you with your crisis. But not tonight. I'm busy tonight. I'll come by in the morning. We'll still have a full twenty-four hours of consumption." I'm tempted to ask her what she's doing tonight but I'm afraid to rock the boat. I am so delighted she has agreed to come over, it makes me wonder just how casual this relationship is.

On my way past reception, I hear a hushed voice. "Jonah, did you see this?" The receptionist reaches out with her phone, and there is a headline: "Man Charged with Psychologist's Death." Below is a photo of a grim-looking Gary headed into the police station. "He could have killed you too," she says, "easily." I honestly can't tell if she is trying to get a reaction, so I don't give her one.

"Terrible," I say, and keep walking, buzzing myself out the door. Outside, I pull the story up on my own phone and read it, but there is nothing new. Gary is in custody on charges under the Offenses Against the Person Act, and there are several photos of his rage-filled face. I imagine that leaves Seán home alone with Tríona. Twenty-seven Park Manor—their address—springs to mind, unbidden. I put the address into Google Maps and it's only a half-hour walk from the clinic. With Gary in custody, I could walk by? I've spent my entire life waiting to be caught for something, and now I have nothing to lose because everything is a mess anyway. Maybe I'll run into Seán? Or maybe the police are there, searching? If they've charged Gary, I'm not likely to be a suspect anymore, but I wouldn't like to push my luck. For the second time today, I wish I had a ball cap with me as I turn left toward Park Manor instead of right toward the bus. But at least it's getting dark.

The Gary homestead is so big it looks like it was meant to be high on a hill, overlooking the sea, rather than squashed in next to a bunch of other large homes in a tight subdivision. Because it is at the end of a row of houses, however, they have some extra land, and one side faces a dense thicket of trees and bushes that represent the divider between neighborhoods. When I casually walk to the termination of the paved road and turn around, I get a good view of the interior of the ground floor. The house has a single-story extension to the side, and almost the entire end wall is made of glass, presumably to give the best view of the mature trees. It's dark outside, and the lights are on inside, so it is easy to spot Tríona sitting on a couch in the kitchen, watching television on a huge flatscreen. Behind me are more trees, and directly across the road from Gary's house the property is "sale agreed," or under contract, and clearly empty.

I take a quick look around and then step over the low wall at the edge of Gary's property, blending in, I hope, with the dark shadows of the trees. I back up a little, to where the wall rises to shoulder height, and I nearly run into a very fancy doghouse but, luckily, no dog. Scanning the yard for any more surprises, I see an extensive set of playground equipment and I'm reminded of someone in my class calling Gary a "good father." In the small gap between the doghouse and the perimeter wall I am hard to see, but it is also difficult for me to see much.

There is what looks like an office behind the room Tríona is in, and it has another low couch, this one pointed at the yard, and a large desk with its back to the road. Anyone sitting at the desk would have an unobstructed view of the play area, and the trees beyond. Not a bad aspect. The two rooms are divided by a hallway with a door that leads directly into the yard. While I'm watching, Tríona pours herself a large glass of wine, and lifts her feet onto the low table in front of the couch. Settling in.

Looking at the office wall of glass, I wonder about the file from the clinic. Did Gary take it away from Teresa while she was working on it that Friday night? Surely the police have already searched. But then again, it was only late yesterday afternoon Risk and Legal discovered it was missing, and Tríona looks pretty comfortable sitting there, not like a woman who had the *Gardaí* here all day. How long does it take to get a search warrant in Ireland, I wonder?

I'm pretty sure it is dark enough for me to get closer to the house and have a look in the office window, so I glance around and take a few steps toward the house.

"Jonah?"

The sound of my name nearly makes my head explode. I

completely freeze because I simply cannot figure out what is going on.

"Jonah, is that you?" The voice is young and nervous, coming from low and behind me. I turn slowly and look down. The doghouse. It is dark enough now that I can't see a thing through the little doorway, so I crouch down to get a better look.

"It's me," I say, my voice low. As my eyes adjust, I can see a small face peeking out of a heavy blanket at the back of the structure. His eyes are huge, and between that and the little house I am reminded of children in fairy tales, when the witch is coming. "Sorry if I scared you." I scan the other corners more carefully, still riding the wave of my adrenalin. No dog.

"What are you doing here?" he asks, his voice still a bit ragged. "Is it about my da? He's in jail, Jonah. The guards took him. I *told* you this would happen. I *told* you to tell Teresa." I realize now that he's crying.

"Oh, Seán, I'm so sorry." He's blaming me, and why not? The poor kid. "I think your dad'll be okay, Seán, I really do. He's a smart guy and the *Gardaí* will figure out he didn't do anything wrong, wait and see." As I'm saying it to Seán, I believe it myself. Why would Gary take things into his own hands when he was already moving forward with a legal case? He had a plan, and he isn't the kind who would panic.

"But he's in jail. And Teresa died. And it's all my fault."

This has caught me off guard. "What?" He isn't blaming me, he's blaming himself. I know what that's like.

"Teresa asked me about what my mam said, there in her office, with you, and I didn't say anything. I cried, like a baby, and didn't tell her my mam was lying." Now he is crying in earnest, his hands over his face, and I get the weight of it, the guilt and shame. My old companions. I reach into the doghouse toward Seán but my fingers touch only dirt, he is so far back. I sit down cross-legged in front of the arched doorway, digging in for this.

"Seán, listen to me." His hands drop from his face and he looks a little surprised. It's probably the first time he's heard me use an adult voice. "I want you to listen very carefully." He nods and I continue. "You are a little kid. Everyone else in this situation is a grown up. It is impossible for it to be your fault."

He whispers now, and I get a real sense of what he thinks he did. "I told Da. I told Da that my mam had talked to Teresa, and it was bad, I knew it was bad what she said. And he said he was going to talk to Teresa, and he was raging. And my ma, she didn't even want it anymore. She didn't want him to get in trouble, but she said it was too late. Too late, because it was in the file."

Now I get it. He's not entirely sure his father is innocent, and he thinks he set him off. So that's how Gary found out so fast. Tusla hadn't contacted him. I glance behind me and Tríona is still in her spot on the couch. Where does she think Seán is?

"Oh, Seán," I say, and decide truth is the best option. Screw confidentiality, this kid needs some facts. I think of the brakes on my mom's car, and push the thought away. "I was there when your dad talked to Teresa. He *was* angry, but he had a good plan. He was going to take us to court because he wanted to be with you. He knew it didn't matter in the long run what your mother said. He was really mad, but he wasn't going to do anything stupid. It was good you told him, so he could get himself organized. I was there, Seán. He left and I stayed with Teresa." As I explain, I am trying to see Seán's reaction, to see if he accepts my explanation of what happened. I'm so focused on staring into the dark doghouse, I only notice the car headlights behind me when they light up his face in the glare coming over my shoulder.

"What the *fuck?*" Gary's booming voice hits me and I turn and try to stand quickly, my legs in a tangle. I'm not sure the car is fully stopped when he comes bounding into his own yard and shoves me hard in the chest, his weight and muscle pushing me backward so I stumble and fall hard on my back, landing inches from some metal equipment. My head hits the ground, hard. He stops and stares into the doghouse, and Seán comes bounding out, like a puppy.

"Da! You're home! I thought you were in jail!" He grabs on to Gary and slows him down. Gary folds his arms around Seán and I stand up slowly, dazed. Am I about to get in a fight with this guy?

"That's right I'm home, Seány-boy, me and the guards had a grand old chat, and they've sent me home, good as new! Run in there, now, and put the kettle on for me, would you?" he says, his voice warm but his eyes are cold, on me. The headlights are illuminating the whole scene. A strange man, a boy who was trapped in a doghouse, a rescuing father. My mouth is dry.

Seán scampers off toward the wall of windows without even

a glance back at me, and a few feet in, he and the yard are lit up with motion sensor floodlights from the roof. That would have happened to me if Seán hadn't called me back earlier. He slams in through the door and I am alone with Gary. I notice Tríona hasn't moved.

"Gary, I was just checking on Seán. I apologize. I shouldn't have come here. It's been a crazy week." I have both palms out in front of me, like I'm trying to talk down a wild animal.

"Wait a minute." Gary's head cocks to the side. "You're the skinny fucker from the clinic, aren't you? Jesus Christ, have you lot not done enough?"

You lot? Does that include Teresa? Who is now dead? My hands drop to my sides.

"What? This is our fault, this mess?" I'm pissed off now. "Everything was going great before, was it? A real heaven on Earth?" Gary steps toward me, and I think he expects me to back down, but I step toward him until there are inches between us. "Go ahead, Gary. Beat me up if it'll make you feel more in charge of this shit storm, you asshole." It feels so good to say it. I brace myself for a beating.

"Hey!" Another voice. "Can somebody pay me so I can get home to my dinner?" Gary turns to look, and over his shoulder I see a man half in and half out of a taxi. The car that Gary came in.

"For fuck's sake." Gary strides over to the taxi, reaching into his back pocket for his wallet. I follow and when we get to the car, Gary opens the back door, grabs me by the arm, and shoves me in so quickly I bang my head on the frame, probably his intention. He slams the door and hands the driver a couple of bills. "Take this chancer back where he came from. Or as close as you can get." As the driver does a three-point turn, I see Gary shake himself, square his shoulders, and head inside.

"You're welcome," the driver says, looking at me in the rearview mirror. "I saved your life back there, for sure. What do you have, a death wish?" I can see his grin too. I'm not ready for chitchat, so I give him my address and stare out the window of the cab, silent. Gary must have been released on bail. Or bond. Or remand, or whatever it's called. I'm actually glad. I'm glad for Seán that his father is home. I think about our conversation as the dark city passes by. Even though I nearly got a beating for defending the clinic, I kind of agree with Gary. I wish Teresa had decided to wait on the damn mandatory reporting.

When the taxi pulls up to the apartment, I attempt a smile of thanks into the driver's reflection, but I see by his expression he has interpreted my silence as petulance. I try again. "Anyway," I say, as I step out of the cab, "what's a *chancer?*"

He turns in his seat and takes a good look at me, up and down. "You are."

57

Early in the morning, I gratefully answer the door to Sailí, and we dive into our twenty-four hours of creature comforts. After food, television, and some time practicing the carnal arts, I discover, however, that I am not out of the woods entirely.

"Jonah," she says, her head propped up on her hand, her lithe body stretched out next to me on the couch. "I'm a little worried about you."

"What are you talking about?" I ask. "I think I'm in a pretty good position here."

She skates over my attempt at humor. "What happened with your dad?" Clearly, she was talking to the twins. I don't want to go there. "What was he doing here?"

I let my hand wander from her hip down into the valley of her waist, and then up again. "He was checking on me." I keep my voice light. "He wanted me to come home, but I wasn't ready."

"Was he angry?" She is not distracted. "When you didn't go?"

I lean back and stare at the ceiling. I picture him turning away from me. What was on his face? Anger? Disgust? "I don't know what he was feeling, Sailí." I can hear the little warning creep into my voice.

"Jesus, Jonah," she says, and I'm amused at the expression. "You really do try hard with this I-am-an-island shite." I stop being amused. "It's not that big a deal, you know, to open up a little, have a chat. These aren't very hard questions." I have probably had a version of this conversation with every woman I have ever slept with, apart from Georgia. But I am still blindsided.

I lie there, breathing, until I can trust my voice. "What do you want from me, Sailí?"

"Jonah," she says, her tone gentle, "I don't want anything. I want you to be okay. To not be walking around all the time like you are expecting the worst." Is this how I come across? Recent events suggest that perhaps I am right to expect disaster.

I roll back onto my side, facing her, and let my hand wander again, putting a bit more effort into distracting her. Eventually, it works.

58

The time with Sailí passes too quickly and I am back in Castleknock on Monday, worried about what is going to happen with the group. After her initial attempt, Sailí and I didn't talk about anything, much, and colluded to navigate around sensitive topics when we did. I kept the phone on silent, but when I checked it, no one was looking for me anyway. The twins arrived back, laden down with food and clean laundry, as usual.

Anna comes in late but appears to be doing okay. We work separately until after lunch and then I head up to her office. Patrick is leaning over his desk typing into a laptop.

"Hey," I say, and he looks up.

"Hey. Anna is next door in Teresa's office, if you are looking for her." He sits back in the chair and stretches. "Are you doing okay? She'll be a good supervisor, but it is still so unreal." Sunlight floods into the room from the big windows and in the parking lot, cars pull in, like any normal day.

I'm conscious that Anna is right next door and probably listening. I don't know what Patrick knows. "I'm okay, thanks for asking. Are you okay?"

"I'm good. I'll have to get external supervision, though, and that's a pain. Anna's great but I need a senior to supervise at my level. The academic team at Trinity are trying to find somebody, but it's short notice. I can't wait until I qualify and I can do my own thing." Such a normal conversation; so inconvenient that Teresa is dead. For some reason it makes me want to shake him. Instead, Patrick goes back to his laptop, and I go next door.

Anna sits at one of the little tables. She is looking through the stack of workbooks.

"All set for the snack later?" She looks up and there is crushing sadness in her face, behind the practical veneer.

"Yep, I'm good. Juice and extremely boring cookies ready to go. I'll wait for your signal to go down and bring it up."

"Sounds good, although we call them digestives here." Anna looks like she is ready to move on from our interaction but pauses, her face serious. "Jonah, I don't want to freak you out right before the group, but I do want to talk about that other thing, soon." She looks at the open door, so I know she is aware of being overheard. I step in and close the door behind me. There is no doubt in my mind this time that she is talking about Roberts.

"About Roberts?" I whisper.

"Who?" Anna looks confused. "Oh, William, yes. Teresa's husband. I feel . . . I feel like I don't want too much time to pass before I start thinking about that in a more serious way. I'm not hysterical anymore, or in shock, or whatever that was, I'm sad. Sad and angry. I can't help but think. You know?" The way she is sitting, looking up at me standing by the door, makes her look so young. "I've spent so much time trying to figure out how to get Teresa out of that relationship it's like I can't stop now, even though she's dead."

I don't know what to say. I want to tell her about the photos in Roberts' car, and my crazy meeting with Seán and Gary on Friday night, but I'm not sure that's smart. She is trying to pull herself together for the group, and I don't really come out in a great light with either story.

She looks at me and then looks away. "I don't know, Jonah. I don't know what the truth is."

"Okay." I whisper, and I really want to be okay, but I'm not.

"Are you freaking out?" she whispers back, and I get that she is teasing me.

"'Yes." I smile at her, and the knot in my shoulders loosens a little.

She smiles too. "Sorry. Bad timing."

Back to the task at hand, Anna asks me to wait downstairs for the kids to come in and flag it for each of them that she is in the room instead of Teresa. That way, she says, they have a sense of familiarity when they see me and are ready to transition to her being there. I head down to reception, and as I clear the last step, one of our little participants is buzzed through the door.

"Hi!" I say, and the sweet rosy face of Miss Curly Hair looks up at me. Not a prayer I will remember her name.

"Hi, Jonah!" She puts me to shame.

The mom is talking to the receptionist, so I talk directly to Curly. "You can go on up! Today there is a different woman up there, her name is Anna, and she is so nice. She has red hair."

"Grand!" She heads up, her hand firmly on the banister. It's that easy.

As she goes up, Patrick comes down.

"Hey, Jonah, do you want me to wait down here?" He sits down on the bottom step to fix his shoelaces. "I can man the door and send them up to meet with you and Anna. It might be easier for them if both of you are there in the room—some sense of familiarity along with the new."

"Anna said the same thing." I lean against the receptionist's desk now that the mother is gone. "But she wanted me down here. Helping them with the transition, I guess?" Some psychology thing, I stop myself from saying.

"Interesting." Patrick doesn't look convinced. "I would have thought it would be better upstairs. Where you are more known to them." This exchange is confusing to me. Why does he care? I retreat to the familiar position of the military brat: following orders.

"Whatever. She's the boss." I turn to the next kid coming in and Patrick stays where he is, sitting on the bottom step, messing with his shoes.

One by one the participants arrive in their school uniforms, dropped off by harassed but sympathetic mothers. None of the kids mentions Teresa or hesitates to go upstairs, easily scooting past Patrick. It is like they have lived here all their lives. A couple of mothers say, "I'm so sorry," or the ubiquitous "Sorry for your loss," and I accept their kindness. What else is there to say?

Last in is little Seán, one hand held firmly by his mother, the other holding an old-fashioned schoolbag, the kind with the buckles in front.

"Hello, Seán!" This is one name I know for sure. I am praying that neither he nor his mother mentions my uninvited presence outside their house. It occurs to me that she may not even know.

"Hiya," he says, and although I give him the same little speech

I gave the others, he moves to stand next to me instead of going up the stairs. "Are you coming?" he says, looking up.

"I am," I say, and turn back to Tríona, who tells me in a tight voice not to let Seán go home with Gary if he turns up, she will be back to collect him herself. It's an awkward moment, and I look to Patrick for how I should respond, but he is looking at Seán. Seán keeps his eyes on me, carefully watching my reaction. "I'll pass that on to Anna," I say. "She is the boss." That's twice I've said it.

Tríona seems reassured and turns to leave. Seán's fingers grab my hand and although I have no idea what is appropriate here, I shift my palm to the outside to close my own fingers around his. Together we turn, holding hands, toward the stairs where Patrick has to move to let us pass. Jesus Christ, I'm holding hands now. I'm sure I'll hear about this in the pub, later.

59

By the time I'm up the steps with Seán, Anna and the other children are waiting in the circle for the cushion game. I get a chance to catch up on the names, and they all settle in well. Turns out the name "Anna" is a favorite with the girls. Thank you, Disney.

Anna reviews the "Everything changes" topic from the first day of the group and then we are into "Getting Married or Getting Together." Curly Head mentions the wedding photo of Teresa as a princess, and we all spend a moment or two remembering how beautiful she was.

"Ma said she died. It was in the paper." The spaghetti poo boy from week one. He's whispering. Every face turns to Anna, including mine. We all know she is the only adult in the room.

"It is so sad. Another change, like you talked about last time. But a very sad one, for me." Anna looks sad and calm at the same time. Her eyes are dry, but I don't know how. All of the children are nodding and somber. There is a pause.

"Like my granny," pipes up one of them.

"Or my granddad," says another. There is a chorus of deaths then: family, friends, pets, even characters in books or on television shows. There is so much loss in these little lives.

"Would you like to make a picture for Teresa?" Anna asks, and glances at me in apology for the surprise change of plan. "We could decorate a heart and then put it up here in this room? Her office?" The children are all for it, and Anna takes out a huge piece of red paper from behind one of the bookshelves. When she folds it in half to cut out the heart shape, I have a flash of Amy and my mom at the kitchen table, and the thousands of pink and red hearts cut out in our house over the years. Loss.

Anna unfolds the heart, puts it on the floor, and takes down markers, glue, glitter, and stickers, as well as more colored paper. "We will do this until snack time, but then we have to get to work on the other stuff, yeah?"

All in agreement, the industry of grief starts. Each child is caught up in the activity, some stretched out on the floor drawing directly onto the heart shape, others working on little side projects to eventually paste on the heart, I presume. Anna has the glue out, and glitter is already coating her fingers. I unscrew a plastic jar of pompoms she can't get a grip on and there is a dash for the ones with shiny strands in them. In the midst of all this, I notice Seán with his back to the group, looking into his bag.

I walk over, assuming it's that same little toy he and spaghetti poo boy were playing with last time, but he takes a brown folder out of his bag. He sets it on the bookshelf and then glances over, catching me watching. The color drains from his face and his expression tells me something serious is happening; he thinks he is in trouble.

"What's this?" I say in a friendly way, picking up and opening the folder. There is my handwriting, small and precise, describing my conversation with Seán in the waiting room. And Teresa's handwriting, more confident and expressive, notes from her meeting with Tríona. My stomach drops before I have words for what I'm holding. The missing file. Seán waits for my reaction, and I try to keep my expression neutral. "Hey buddy, thanks," I say. "We were looking for this. Thank goodness you brought it back." Seán releases his breath, and then I realize I'm holding my own.

"My ma had it. She borrowed it from Teresa, I think to have a look. That day my da was raging. After I told him about, you know." The children are working around us, and I look up to see Anna glance over. I hold her gaze, and she understands that something is up.

"What a relief, we really need this file," I say, and Anna arrives, glitter now covering fingertips to elbows. I step closer to her and say quickly, but cheerfully, "Hey, Anna. Seán is so helpful. He brought back this file that his mom borrowed from Teresa the other day. The day his dad was so frustrated, he says. On Friday? I remember he was a bit frustrated that morning." Anna gets it right away—the day Teresa died. There is an immediate intensity to her expression, and she turns to Seán with gentle eyes.

"Hey, that's really good," she says. "When did your mam come in? Was it when your da was here? I should thank them for the file." She's gathering information like a pro, but you'd never guess it.

"No, no," says Seán. "It was just me and her. Me and Ma came back after tea, and she only popped in to tell Teresa it was all okay. That she didn't need to report my da because it was all made up. Remember what I said to you?"

I nod. "Yep, I remember." I'm thinking, tea, that can mean dinner here. In the late afternoon. In the evening? When Teresa was here on her own?

"She wanted to tell Teresa it wasn't true. I was in the car. Your man knows, he was here, you can ask him. He saw me in the car. Then she borrowed the file, she said, to check it, to make sure Teresa took the part out about Da. I thought you'd need it back, so I brought it back for you." He's happy, smiling. There are a few beats of silence.

"What man knows, Seán? Who saw you?" Anna's tone stays light. I'm confused but I don't say anything. All of my energy is going into looking relaxed.

"That fellow from the stairs, downstairs?" He's looking at me like I know what he's talking about.

Then it hits me. "Patrick?"

Seán says, "The fat fella?"

I am looking at Anna but talking to Seán. "Yeah, that's him. He was here? When your mother borrowed the file?"

"Sure he was," says Seán, his attention being pulled back to the art project. Teresa's heart. "He let my ma in the door, when he was going out, and he waved at me. Ask him." Through the security door. So she caught Teresa by surprise. And he never said a word.

"That's super, Seán." Anna shows him her hands. "I'll let Jonah put it high up on the shelf there. Otherwise, it'll be covered in glitter." Seán nods cheerfully and sits down at the sparkling little table. Anna and I stand there, breathing. I want to open the file again but it's not the right time. I set it up on the shelf, high, like she said.

"Get Róisín to help us. We need to figure out how to get Tusla and the *Gardaí* here without the children knowing. We can't send Seán home with Tríona. And Patrick, we have to think about him," says Anna, in a low voice.

"Not Róisín," I whisper. "Róisín and Patrick are together."

"Reception?"

I think of Patrick on the stairs in his weird stakeout. Now it makes sense—he wanted to deal with Seán. Confuse him? Scare him? For all I know he's still there. Or right next door in her office. "Nope." There's another beat while we think. "Speech and language?" I suggest. Anna tilts her head. It's a possibility.

"Okay." We are both conscious that Patrick and Tríona know Seán is a witness. Tríona might also have noticed by now he took the file. Which means she knows we know.

"Okay, I'm getting ready to get the snack!" I say, my voice cheerful and loud, and Anna follows up.

"Nearly time to finish our artwork and get down to the real business." She herds the kids around the big red heart and starts gluing.

I open the door quietly and slip out. Instead of heading downstairs, I go up.

60

At the top of the stairs, the doors are all closed. The last door is the one with the coveted little tables in it, and I'm pretty sure that is the treatment room. The first room is an office, I think. I listen at the door and hear nothing. A light tap, and I gently open the door. The ceiling light is off, but there is enough light through the windows to see the big-haired and tight-dressed tyrant sitting in her chair looking sheepish. It is possible she was asleep.

"I need your help," I whisper. "Me and Anna are in a fix. It's about Teresa."

Clearly, she likes intrigue. "Is that right?" She is already whispering. "What is it?" I come up next to her chair and kneel down. As quickly and as quietly as I can, I tell her the story, and as I describe the bare bones of it more things fall into place. Patrick working late. He would have seen me and Teresa outside on the Thursday night, and he could have told the *Gardaí*, trying to set me up. Patrick talking to everyone after the accident, not to give comfort, but to find out what they knew. Patrick trying to get control of the group, where he could keep an eye on Seán. Patrick under pressure, at the end of his training, barely passing, and terrified to admit his part.

She doesn't interrupt or react, but I sense her shift into action mode, and I know from experience it's impressive when that happens. "Leave it with me," she says. "I'll sort it out before the group is over." Thank God. I slip out of the room and down the stairs to the psychology floor. From there, I make plenty of noise going down for the snack. In the kitchen are Patrick and Róisín.

"How's the group going?" says Róisín. "Are they okay?" Her

concern for the kids comes through as I pick up the tray of juice and treats. I think it is sincere. She is probably clueless.

"They are fine," I say, and despite the fact I want to rip off Patrick's head, in this moment I am totally focused on the kids. "They talked it out and now they're making an art thing for Teresa we can hang on the wall. Jesus, Anna is amazing."

"Pint after work?" says Patrick. "I'll text the twins?"

"Sounds great." I head up. In the hallway upstairs, I set the tray down on Róisín's desk for a second.

Fuck Patrick, I text the twins. *More later.* Immediate response: thumbs up.

61

I don't know how she does it, but Anna gets through the rest of the group like nothing has happened, while the big red heart dries on Teresa's desk. She leads the children into talking about couples—about getting together or getting married. Lists, pictures, sharing. The kids are totally on board, even hyped up on the sugar from snack time. I'm surprised at how open they are as they move quickly past the "getting together" stories to describe the fights, the storming out, the two-houses scenarios, and the getting-back-together moments. Mostly, they act relieved that everyone has a similar story. I get it, now, the point of the group. Their experiences are so important to each other, that they are not trapped in their own silences. As we start winding up, though, I'm getting more anxious about what is going on downstairs. I can imagine Anna is the same, but I can't see it. Normal, normal, normal.

Before we end, Anna asks me to take the snack tray downstairs as part of the "tidy up." I figure this is code for checking out the plan, and I'm relieved to do it. I pick up the tray in one hand and open the door with the other, slipping through. There is the speech and language woman, waiting. She makes a face at the room behind me, Patrick and Anna's office, and leads me down the stairs.

"Okay," she says, at the bottom. "Tríona turned up for Seán, and she is now talking to the *Gardaí* in the meeting room. The doors are closed. I called Gary, and he is upstairs in my office, talking to Tusla. Róisín is in the kitchen with more *Gardaí*, and Patrick is in Anna's office, alone. We didn't want to go in to get him with the group going on. The other parents here for pick-up are in the waiting room. They don't know a thing." She rolls her eyes.

"You are amazing," I say, and I mean it.

"I know Teresa thought I was crazy and difficult, but we all loved her. I loved her." I see the tears rush to her eyes and then her Trojan effort to push them down. "And I know Anna loved her." A little twinkle takes the place of her tears, and I can't help but grin. God bless this woman.

"What about Seán?" I whisper.

"Keep him in there till last, and then we'll take him up to his father." We both look down at the tray in my hands. "Not a chance," she says. "That's where I draw the line." She turns and heads back upstairs. I am loath to go into the kitchen but I'm running out of time, so I crash through the door and drop the tray next to the sink, intending to leave as quickly as possible.

"Jonah!" I look over at Róisín, who is tearfully talking to a female *Garda*. "I didn't know about Patrick, about any of it, I swear." I don't know what to say back to her.

I dash back out and up the stairs, in time to see Patrick coming out of his and Anna's office, looking furtive in the hallway.

"Oh, Jonah, hi," he says, casually leaning against Róisín's desk in the hallway. "I thought you were still in with the group." I give him a look and open the door to Teresa's office, sticking my head in awkwardly while I try to bar Patrick's escape with my body in the hall.

"All clear!" I cheerfully report to Anna, and Patrick tries to move past me toward the stairs. I catch him by surprise, pushing hard against his chest with my right hand, so he stumbles backward toward his office, and I can step fully into the hallway to impede his progress. Anna shepherds the children toward the stairs behind me and I say over my shoulder, "Can you just hang onto Seán in the room for a minute, Anna? Maybe he can help clean up?"

"Sure thing, Jonah!" she responds as the other kids troop down the stairs.

I step toward Patrick, who is rubbing his chest. "Were you looking out the window again, Patrick? Did you see a few unusual cars pull in?" My voice is low, and I try to make it sound friendly in case the kids hear me, but he can see my face. I'm sure he saw the *Gardaí* arrive through those big windows. "Watching from Anna's window, like when I was out there with Teresa that night?" I want him to know I know.

His face twists with his own anger. “She blew you off pretty well, didn’t she? Not as big a hit with the ladies as you believe. You think awfully well of yourself, don’t you, Jonah? You think you know a few things, but Teresa saw through you. And she’s not the only one.” I can hear the kids have moved into the waiting room, and the stairs are clear. Anna has closed the door to Teresa’s room, her cheerful tone with Seán barely audible.

I step a little closer and he doesn’t back down. If anything, his anger is building.

“I do know a few things, you asshole,” I hiss at him. “I know you opened the door to that crazy woman and let her through security and never warned Teresa. I know you talked to anyone and everyone trying to find out what they knew, while all the time you knew what had happened to her, and you never said a fucking word.” I’m warming to my theme. “I know you were waiting for that little boy today. It’s no wonder you wanted to manage the kids coming in for the group—that kid was the only witness. What were you going to do?”

The blood leaves his face, but he is not ready to admit anything. “You don’t know what you’re fucking talking about.” Patrick tries to push past me again, and we struggle. The *Gardaí* are downstairs somewhere, but I don’t know if they are between the stairs and the door, and I don’t want the kids to witness anything. Patrick plants his feet and puts his full weight into pushing me backward, and I take a few steps back but swivel, pulling him off balance and toward the stairs. For a moment he teeters at the top, his eyes wide and panicked, just where Teresa must have lost her footing, and then I reach out and grab his shirt to steady him.

“Are we all right?” One of the Guards starts up the stairs as Patrick turns to run down, and I am pleased to see he has broken out in a sweat.

“This is Patrick,” I say. “I think you are waiting for him.”

62

When I open the door to Teresa's office, Anna and Seán are trying to get Sticky Tack onto the back of the big red heart. Anna leaves when I come in, and I show Seán how to warm up the tack first, so it sticks better.

"I didn't know that," he says.

"I'm an engineer," I say, forgetting my cover story. "Engineers know that kind of thing."

"I thought you were a psychologist," he says, kneading the Sticky Tack in his little fingers. Totally concentrating on doing it right.

"Hm, I don't know about that," I say.

"Well, Seány-boy!" We both turn at Gary's booming voice. "How was your little meeting?"

"Da!" says Seán. "I didn't know you were coming!" He hugs his father and points at the heart, which I am now holding against the wall. "It's for Teresa, Da. We made it in the group because she died." There's a silence and Gary avoids looking at me.

"It's lovely, Seán. A lovely heart. Well, time to go! Turns out it's me and you tonight. Let's get pizza. Don't tell your mother." He gives Seán a conspiratorial wink and they head out of the room without a glance back, the warmed tack set absentmindedly on the desk. I don't know how it is possible to hate Gary and feel sorry for him at the same time.

I grab the file from the high shelf and leave the room, turning left instead of right. I have a hunch Anna has fled to her office, and there she is. Sitting with her eyes closed.

"Anna?" She opens her eyes and looks at me, unfocused and

exhausted, glitter still clinging to her fingers. "That was something else in there. You were so great with the kids."

"What a fucking waste," she says, taking the file and dropping it onto the desk, her glittery fingerprints giving it a cheerfulness it doesn't deserve. "As if there isn't a copy of the report already at Tusla." Anna leans back in her chair with her hands over her face. I glance down and next to the file is the envelope I saw yesterday in Roberts' car, and a scattering of photos, mostly Anna and Teresa, but also the one of Teresa at the church door with her father. Roberts must have sent it to her. He must have known somehow that she treasured it.

Anna lowers her hands and catches me looking at it. "He has a copy of this one on the wall in their house. I saw it the day before the funeral, and he must have seen me looking at it. God, I loved her. He must have known."

I realize my mistake. I am giddy with relief that I am not to blame, that I haven't caused this. That something happened Friday night between Teresa and Tríona that had nothing to do with me or Roberts. Teresa's death is not on my shoulders. But that's no relief for Anna. This was a meaningless death. There is nothing but grief here. I think of Roberts' eulogy, when he thanked everyone who made Teresa feel loved. He knew.

63

On the way out of the center, hours later, I try to call my dad. For the first time in a long time, I'm sent to voicemail, and I leave a long message explaining what's happened. I'm not sure how long his voice mail program allows, but it goes long enough for me to say "I'm sorry" about fifteen times at the end of the message. I want him to understand I'm not responsible this time. And I want him to understand more than that. But I can't make him. I catch the bus toward the twins' place but get off in the city center, near Trinity, and text the twins instead. I'm at least two drinks in by the time they arrive in Bowe's. They get pints before they come over. Priorities.

"Monday night? You're turning into quite the party animal," says Peter, sliding in next to me on the bench seating. He's right, the bar is nearly empty, and I clearly have a problem. That or my day was completely fucked up. Michael sits on a stool across the table. He's wearing a hoodie and looks like a gangster. As if.

"You are not going to believe what happened today." I have been sitting here alone, going over it in my head.

"I don't really care," says Peter. "I seriously can't take any more of the Jonah drama. I swear to Christ, it's one damn thing after another with you." The twins clink their glasses and I laugh, despite myself. "What's the story with Patrick?"

"Fuck Patrick," I say, and I really, really mean it.

"Okay," says Michael, making a production out of deleting Patrick's contact details off his phone. "I never really liked that smarmy bastard anyway. Him or his uptight girlfriend."

"Yeah," says Peter. "Asshole." He deletes him as well, showing me the phone. There is something so reassuringly straightforward about the twins.

"I don't understand why you guys don't have more friends," I say. "Seriously." I mean it, but it sounds like sarcasm.

Michael holds up his phone, the contacts list open. "More of this carry on from you, fella, and you're next. We have plenty of friends. Legions of friends. Nice art, by the way. Are you thinking of taking up interior design?"

"Psychologist artists," says Peter. "Trouble, every one of them. You're lucky to be friends with us, Jonah. We don't mind that you do art and talk about your feelings all the time, do we, Michael?" They lift their glasses again in solidarity. I am so grateful I nearly tell them how glad I am to have them. Luckily, I catch myself.

64

Eventually, I tell everyone the story, everyone who'll listen. I repeat it to Annemarie, to Georgia, to Sailí, to Mick and Margaret, to the twins, to Risk and Legal, to Ciara the lawyer, to the *Gardaí* over and over, and several times to Moira before she understands. With Moira, I eventually have to use little props for the characters spread out on the counter in the twins' apartment, moving them from place to place as the narrative develops. There's confidentiality, for sure, but it's all in the paper within twenty-four hours and nobody knows who the leak is, although we all have theories.

In Castleknock on Wednesday, we have a debrief session and the Risk and Legal team come in to give us all another heart-warming lecture, complete with PowerPoint slides and the under-worked stenographer. No one is to talk to the press. We get it, but really there is nothing to add, anyway. They have it all. Anna moves around like a zombie in the clinic, but she's there.

Sailí listens carefully when I go through it again, for the hundredth time, sitting next to me on the sofa in her apartment with her feet on my lap. I say it all again, it's like I can't stop talking about it. Around us canvasses lean against everything. She has finally finished the commission and I am glad. I crave her attention.

"But what was wrong with Patrick?" Sailí says. "I mean, what happened? Why did he let Tríona in?"

"He was still there, working late on overdue reports, when Vera the caretaker left. The door automatically locks, you have to be buzzed in for security. He was leaving when Tríona came, and he held the door open for her. That's when Seán saw him from the car." I think of that moment, Teresa up in her office, working on the file. I am long gone. Patrick keeps on moving, Friday night. Teresa has no idea Tríona is coming up the stairs, trying to cover up her lies.

"I guess when Patrick heard she'd been found dead, he realized what he'd done, that he was implicated. He's so close to the end of his training, I imagine he freaked out. I mean, he didn't kill her, but he didn't take care of her, that's for sure. And then after, he didn't say a thing to anybody. He would have happily let the dad take the blame." Or me, I think, since it came out that it was Patrick who told Tommy and Mairéad about the parking lot fiasco, and planted the idea that I was obsessed with her. But I don't have to go into that with Sailí.

"Jesus," she says, "what a mess. So did Tríona mean to kill her?"

"I don't know." Nobody does. Probably not even Tríona. The papers are saying she claims it was an accident, that all she wanted was the file, and Teresa wouldn't give it to her. She said she grabbed it off the desk and Teresa was trying to stop her from leaving with it when they struggled and Teresa fell down the stairs. She was too frightened or out of her mind to call for an ambulance and she just left, pretended everything was normal. A *dissociative state* her lawyers are claiming, that she didn't even know what she was doing. Using psychology to defend the woman who killed Teresa.

I push away the thought of Teresa there at the bottom of the stairs, alone, the lost shoe. It's horrific and heartbreaking. "It's a mess, like you said. She went in for the paperwork, thinking that taking it out of the center would make a difference, would be like taking back her statement." Who knows what was going on in that mind? "I guess the report to Tusla was going to backfire on Tríona, or she thought it would. Gary was going to take her to court, and it was all going to come out—the constant lies about Seán, the false allegations against Gary. Turns out, Seán was way better in general than she said. All fine at school, good friends, everything. Just trying to deal with a screwed-up mother." I immediately think of my own mother.

"So, no need for Tusla? That was all a big mistake? A bunch of lies?" Sailí has the comfort of moral outrage. I don't. I know what unintended consequences are like.

"Teresa didn't have a choice. She had to respond to what Tríona said in case there really was a risk to Seán, and she had to report it. What if it had been true about Gary? That's why it's *mandatory* reporting. They don't want people trying to figure it out for themselves. People make mistakes." I think of how I argued against the report. What a waste. Poor Teresa. "But, in a way, she was right. We just had the wrong parent. She knew that kid needed help." It's the first time I've thought of it that way. Seán *did* need help, and Teresa got it for him. And paid with her life.

"Jesus," she says again. There's a pause. "Did you tell your dad?" She knows this is a painful topic for me but that doesn't seem to stop her. She's brave.

"I tried, Sailí," I tell her. "I tried to call but he didn't pick up. I left him a voicemail. He hasn't responded."

Her face softens but she is not letting me off the hook. "Jonah, a voicemail? Seriously?"

When she says it that way, I get how pathetic it sounds.

"Okay, Sailí, okay. I'll tell him. I'll write him a long letter and send it in the mail."

"Oh, for God's sake, Jonah." She laughs. "You don't have to make such a meal out of it. Send the man an email."

"I will," I say. It sounds so easy when she says it. So normal. At least I'll know for sure he got it. And I'll be able to explain that Teresa's death was nothing to do with me. Then he can choose to respond. Or not.

Sailí has gotten serious, her blue eyes squared up to mine. "Are you going home?" She means home, home. For good.

This is the question everyone is asking. The course is ready to let me go with a pass, to get over the disastrous placement, and let's face it, get rid of me. Georgia wants me to move in with her in New York and spend Christmas in Martha's Vineyard with Maggie. I'm sure if I pushed it, Professor Crehan would take me on in January, a second-semester start. No doubt I've learned enough about unpredictable humans. Everyone has asked me this question, except my dad.

"I don't know," I say. She is looking at me with concern, but there is a layer of something else as well.

"Well, don't let me hold you back," she says, shifting her feet onto the floor.

"It's not you holding me back," I say, "it's that I haven't gone to speak at all those Irish Rotary Club dinners I'm supposed to go to for the scholarship. I owe Mick that for all the legal help, at least."

She looks at me sharply and I try to look innocent. "You are the worst, Jonah. The worst."

"I know." I lean toward her.

"I can't even say you are the worst boyfriend," she goes on, but the fight is out of her, "because technically, you aren't even *my* boyfriend! You're just visiting my field!" I slide one hand around her back and nuzzle her neck with my five o'clock shadow. Her arms go around me like they belong there and I feel her pull me closer on the couch. The heat rises from her skin and it is getting warmer—I'm not going anywhere yet.

65

I wake early on Wednesday morning. Too early to get up, but my mind is racing and I can't relax. Sailí is asleep next to me, her regular breathing like an island of safety I'm tethered to in the dark. It's hard not to think too much when there is so much to think about.

My phone is on the table beside me and I take a quick look. Nothing new. I checked it only a few hours ago and any sensible person in Ireland is fast asleep. But it's only midnight at home—another evening has passed with nothing from my dad.

I open my email in the darkness and start a message to him with the sequence of events that lead to Teresa's death, and the end of the story at the clinic. For confidentiality's sake I just call Gary and Tríona and Seán by their roles—dad, mom, son—and it gives me some distance. I can think about it as a series of happenings. Actors on a stage. A tragedy.

Once I start writing, though, it is hard to stop, and now it's about us. About our conversation on the Liffey's bank, in the dark, telling our secrets. I ask him why he never told me about the brakes, and I apologize for never telling him my part, for holding back, for lying by omission. I don't stop there. I tell him how hard it was with Mom when I was growing up, before and after the accident, and how much I miss Amy. How lost I feel. How I wish things were different. It pours out of me, all these unsaid things, and then I stop. Read it over. I picture my dad, asleep, preparing himself for another day without his daughter, without his son. Where would he read this? On the phone in bed next to his brain-damaged wife? Alone, in his home office on the laptop while he tries to squeeze in work between care duties? I'm not doing that. I pull up the discard email button. But I want him to know I had nothing to do with Teresa's death. I need him to know that. My finger shifts to the backspace and I watch the words disappear. All the way back to the Castleknock clinic, where I'm describing the difficulties of a different mother, father, and son, and I send that.

Eventually, I give up on sleep and slide out of bed. I dress quietly and leave Sailí, still warm and dreaming, and head for the twins' place. My place. The air outside is surprisingly wintry, and the city is waking up as I pass through.

My hands are chilled in my pockets and my face is numb when I get to the apartment building, but I walk past anyway and end up down the road, outside Roberts' office at seven fifty-eight. I don't know what I'm doing, but there is a familiar ache across my shoulders. I don't know why I'm here at his office, or why I am staying in Ireland. I don't know if I want to stay in psychology or go home where I know who I am as an engineer. I don't know about my dad, my mother, or Sailí, or Georgia, or even what I am doing for Christmas.

My watch hits eight o'clock and I push the buzzer. Nothing happens. I push it again, and still there is no response. I'm shocked when my eyes start to water—I so want that door to open. Roberts might be an asshole, but he didn't kill his wife, and he didn't tell the *Gardaí* that I came on to her, and he didn't even react when I tried to break into his office. And he is the only person who really knows what I am. I take out my phone and look up his contact details, from that very first call. I press the phone icon, and it starts to ring.

"Hello?" I hear his voice and I freeze. He lets the silence happen, and I don't know if he knows it is me, or thinks some nut is calling him. Some other nut. Eventually, I find my voice.

"Dr. Roberts? It's me, Jonah."

"Hello, Jonah." Nothing special, and I am straining to hear it. I am there in the doorway, on the phone to him, trying to picture his reaction. As if he ever has any.

"I'd like to come in for an appointment. I am outside your door."

"Outside the practice door?" he says, and it occurs to me he might not be inside. Of course, it's not like he sleeps on that couch every night. Waiting for me. Jesus Christ, what am I expecting?

"Yeah. The practice door. Can I make an appointment? Can we go back to my times?" I don't care how pathetic I sound. Luckily, Peter isn't recording me this time.

There is a long pause. I don't know if he is thinking or checking his schedule. Finally, he replies, "How about once a week to start? The Wednesday early morning time is still free, if you'd like it. This day, next week, to start."

I want to ask him about the Friday time. Why can't I have that too? Then I remember that what happened to me on Monday about Teresa, and Tríona, and Anna, and Patrick, also happened to him. He already knows the story; I don't have to explain it to him.

"I'm so sorry about Teresa," I say, and this time he responds.

"Thank you, Jonah. Thank you." There is a pause and I think that maybe he will say something to me, something about her, or about what happened, or about me and what I said. "See you Wednesday?" he asks.

"Thank you," I say. "Yes."

We hang up, and I stand there in the cold Dublin morning, alone.

ACKNOWLEDGEMENTS

My mother would like me to thank, first and foremost, my husband. And though I am very grateful to him for his endless support, my first acknowledgement of gratitude must be to my parents, Mary and Harry Wilson, for teaching me that reading is never a waste of time.

Thank you to the Irish Writers Centre, for their structured support of writing, and the wonderful experience of the Novel Fair, which got the first draft written.

Thank you to early readers Mary Wilson, Cassandra Rosado, Sarah Wilson Powell, Mary Hinderer (and her book club), Diane Gillen, and Méabh O'Raghallaigh, and to sensitivity readers Paula Grace and Mark Mulrooney. My gratitude to Stephanie Hughes, who accessed Tipperary slang through her two helpful brothers and to my dear friend Abbie Bowker, for technical assistance on printmaking.

Thanks to my friends and my husband's friends, who let me use their beautiful Irish names, and to the Bredviks, who let me use their beautiful Colorado cabin.

Thank you to Dan Mayer, who commissioned the manuscript, and to all at Seventh Street Books/Start Publishing including Ashley Calvano, Jennifer Do, and Natalie Lukatsky. Special thanks to editor Rene Sears and copy editor Meghan Kilduff, who accepted both my professional emails and my personal cries for reassurance with grace. If anyone who is reading this book is not directly related to me, it is probably due to my publicist Wiley Saichek, and I am very grateful to him for his work.

In my darkest moments of self-doubt, I could always remind

myself that Sharon Bowers, my agent, would never have agreed to represent me just because she likes me as a person. Thank you, Sharon, for giving me a chance.

Thank you to the incredibly talented Irish artist Chris McMorrow, who enthusiastically allowed me to use his work on the cover, and to my friend Michael Lavelle, for the author photo. Michael, Carol, and Ulrike, my writing group, thank you for your encouragement and honesty.

I am very grateful to writer Gráinne Murphy, for her texts of support and guidance, and to writer Michelle Gallen for talking me through some tight spots. Also, both Michelle Gallen and writer Seraphina Nova Glass read the text and kindly provided early quotes for publication. Thank you.

My children Eoghan Óg, Marcas, and Méibhín; the Wilsons and their many hangers-on; the O'Raghallaigh family and its many extensions; my colleagues and my treasured friends (including you, Heidi Keusenkothen) provide me with essential support and I am so grateful and glad I have all of you.

And finally, thank you to my husband, Eoghan, for the fifty-euro gift certificate that got me writing again, and for everything else.

Printed in the United States
by Baker & Taylor Publisher Services